After the Party

After the Party

CRESSIDA CONNOLLY

VIKING
an imprint of
PENGUIN BOOKS

VIKING

UK | USA | Canada | Ireland | Australia
India | New Zealand | South Africa

Viking is part of the Penguin Random House group of companies
whose addresses can be found at global.penguinrandomhouse.com.

First published 2018
001

Copyright © Cressida Connolly, 2018

The moral right of the author has been asserted

Extract from *A Word Child* by Iris Murdoch, published by Vintage Classics.
Reprinted by permission of the Random House Group Limited, copyright © 2002

Set in 12/14.75 pt Bembo Book MT Std
Typeset by Jouve (UK), Milton Keynes
Printed in Great Britain by Clays Ltd, St Ives plc

A CIP catalogue record for this book is available from the British Library

HARDBACK ISBN: 978–0–241–32724–1
TRADE PAPERBACK ISBN: 978–0–241–32772–2

www.greenpenguin.co.uk

To my lifelong friend
Danny Moynihan
and
Katrine, Tallulah and
my godson, Kit

Yet such things happen . . . lives are thus ruined, thus tainted and darkened and irrevocably spoilt, wrong turnings are taken and persisted in, and those who make one mistake wreck all the rest . . .

Iris Murdoch, *A Word Child*

Phyllis, 1979

When I came out of prison my hair was white. I think it was a shock for them all, but for the children especially.

I'd had brown hair before but now it was yellowing white, like the mane of an old wooden rocking-horse. They hadn't set eyes on me for such a time: it must have seemed to them that there had been a horrible substitution, like in Little Red Riding Hood *when the wolf is in the lacy bed, where the grandmother should have been. Here was this haggish-looking old person instead of their mother. My clothes must have seemed very drab, too. And then of course prisons smell awful. The lack of fresh air makes everything musty and stale, and the tar-tang of regulation soap sticks to your skin and of course your clothes aren't laundered. Heaven knows what I must have smelled of, when they came forward to be embraced. It was the first time they'd touched me for I don't know how long. They were pretty reluctant about it, shuffling when their aunt prodded them to come towards me, not that I really blame them.*

They all thought it was the awfulness of prison that had made me old, like those old wives' tales where someone sees a ghost and goes white overnight from the shock, but the truth was simply that one couldn't get one's hair dyed. Hair dye was not provided, and why should it have been? It was meant to be a punishment, not a hairdressing salon. Some of the women combed shoe-polish into their hair, close to the head around the parting, but since we were only allowed black shoes there was just the regulation black shoe-polish, so that wouldn't have worked for me.

Of course I had never been the beauty of the family, but my hair was the one thing people had admired; it was long and abundant, not quite the colour of a conker, although that is how people did describe it. Someone said to me once, when I was young, that my hair was as glossy as the flank of a well-stabled horse, and it is true that it did have a great deal of shine. I don't think I am being vain in saying so. When we were children our nurse used the tall tin jug which lived in the nursery bathroom to rinse our hair and she would add a few drops of malt vinegar to the water, for extra shine. She had a habit of pressing then sliding her wet palms close against our heads, to be certain all the soap had come out. Our hair squeaked beneath the firmness of her touch. I liked the feeling of her hands pressing against my skull, but the others would complain terribly. I don't suppose people use a jug to rinse their hair any longer, do they? Now people have those rubber tubes you fit over the bath taps, with nozzles on the end like a watering can. They have the same slightly scorched smell as hot water bottles. I rather like it.

My mother had gone grey in her late thirties and I was the same. I'd been having my hair dyed for some years before prison. Both my sisters knew this perfectly well, but somehow Patricia allowed the children's fright to affect her, so that she began to believe herself that it was something that had happened in an instant. I know that is what she used to tell people, as if it was some sort of fable or story. 'My sister was sent to jail and her hair turned white.' It was one of those things that snowballed, rather, until everyone in the family believed it had happened from the upset of it all.

But I wasn't upset. I did not mind being imprisoned. Well, that is not really true; I did mind very much, of course. Being separated from the children, taken out of one's home and set down among hostile strangers, kept under lock and key; and the catalogue of daily smells, urine and carbolic and a sticky, fishy smell like wallpaper paste . . . But the thing was, I thought I deserved it. What I did was terrible. Terrible. The shame of it will never leave me until my dying day. Such a stupid, sordid thing and yet I believed it to have had a terrible consequence.

Had it not been for my weakness, someone who is now dead could still be alive. That is what I believed and consequently lived with every day in prison.

1. Sussex, June 1938

Both her sisters had offered to put them up while they found a house. In some ways Phyllis would have preferred to stay with Nina, even though things would have been more cramped. As it was, Hugh favoured staying with Patricia, whose house would be so much more comfortable; and as ever Hugh prevailed. But what rankled was that Hugh hoped to have business in town over the coming weeks and probably wouldn't be with them for more than two or three days a week. It was his wife who would be spending all her time with one sister or another, and not himself. When Phyllis ventured this point, he looked blank.

'I can't see what that has to do with it,' he said.

'Well, what I meant was, it's me who'll have to be beholden. And I don't like to feel indebted to Patricia.'

'You should be indebted to Nina, if we were her guests. It doesn't make any difference, surely,' said Hugh. 'It won't be for long, so you need not concern yourself. Patricia will enjoy having you.'

And there the subject was closed.

On the train down to Sussex the children had irritated their father by kicking their legs against the heating grille beneath the seats, until he had remonstrated with Phyllis to stop them. Unaccustomed to matters of discipline where the children were concerned – overseas she had always had a girl of some sort, to look after the children – she hesitated before murmuring in their direction. The two girls desisted, but their younger brother did not.

'Couldn't you tell Edwin a story or something?' Phyllis asked Julia, conscious of a note of pleading in her voice. The eldest of the three, Julia had her nose in one of her mother's old detective stories, but something in the bored droop of her shoulders suggested she was not lost in her book.

'What about?' asked Julia.

'I don't know, darling. Anything.'

But the younger girl, Frances, had stepped in with an impromptu tale of elves, talking sparrows and magical shoes. Heaven only knew where she dreamed up such things. Hugh read the newspaper while his wife looked out of the window. She had not been back to England for three years and then only very briefly, for Nina's wedding. Now the fields seemed almost absurdly green, the colour of new peas still bright in the pod. It made her happy, to see such vividness: from the boat the cliffs at Dover had looked so dingy, like the cut side of a stale loaf of bread, and the earth above the dull chalk had seemed as scant as a smear of Bovril. It was hard to believe that such thin soil could support the growth even of grass, let alone flowers, or vegetables; still less trees. Looking homeward with eagerness from the deck of the ferry it had felt disappointing, suddenly, to see that sturdy England was built on such thin earth. To the right, towards Broadstairs, the land was like a line drawn with a soft grey pencil, between a sky and sea likewise grey. This was not as Phyllis wanted England to be, not as England was in her memory. Their few days in London afterwards had presented no less dreary a picture, a constant drizzling rain smudging the streets, blurring the outlines of the buildings. But today the sun was shining and the world was bright and full of colour.

It was early June. Phyllis and Hugh could have stayed on to spend the summer in Belgium, but it had seemed prudent to arrive home in plenty of time to find a house, before Edwin started prep school in the autumn. Julia, who was fourteen, had already been boarding at Coombe Park for a year; her twelve-year-old sister Frances would now join her there. And there would be things for the children to do here in England, to keep them occupied over the summer. In one or two of her letters, Nina had mentioned summer camps which she and Eric were somehow involved in putting on, along the coast at nearby Pagham or Selsey. They were tremendous fun, she said, and the children could join in, making camp-fires and playing games and sea-bathing, or doing handicrafts and PE.

Phyllis felt rather let down that Patricia did not meet them at the station herself, but sent a driver, a rather elderly man called Hitchens who did the garden and various other outdoor jobs at Rose Green, as well as what Greville called 'ferrying us about'. Greville was never specific when he could be vague; whether this signalled inability to grasp a point, or only unwillingness, was a question his wife's sisters had often returned to. He tended to move his arms about a lot when he spoke, as if attempting to fill in the details which were missing in the sketched picture of his conversation.

The car turned right on to a gravel drive which ran between a dark hedge of holly and hornbeam. Presently one side opened on to pasture enclosed within rails of park fencing, while to the other was a small beechwood. Green light filtered through the trees. As the drive curved leftwards, the front came into view: two storeys faced in pale Portland stone with eight generous windows, four above and four below, and a sturdy two-pillared portico. It was a pretty house, more distinguished than architecturally interesting. Patricia stood waiting for them by the main door, her fair hair waved, a double string of heavy pearls at her throat, a creamy silk blouse tucked into a narrow, belted skirt. At first glance she was beautiful, with perfectly round grey-green eyes like marbles and a small nose with just a little dent in it. But the very symmetry of her features created a sort of blankness in her expression which became either maddening or mesmerizing to people as they grew to know her.

'You've cut off your hair!' said Phyllis. Patricia raised an automatic hand to her neck.

'Have I? I must have done it ages ago. Hello, Julia, Edwin. Frances! You've grown!'

The children hung back, blushed. Hugh leant forward to kiss Patricia's cheek, although neither spoke any words of greeting. Phyllis, taller than her sister, embraced Patricia, inhaling the particular scent of her which in contrast to her appearance was oddly masculine; a smell like bracken, or moorland.

'Would you like to go up straight away, or come through for some tea?' Patricia asked, leading them in.

'Go up, just for a minute or two, if you don't mind,' said Phyllis.

Hugh stood with a hand on the round hall table, while the women chattered up the stairs, the three children behind them.

'Antonia is out on her pony,' Patricia was explaining, 'but she's simply longing to see you all. She'll be back very soon.'

'Where's Greville?' asked Phyllis.

'Oh, he's somewhere,' said Patricia. 'You know what he's like.'

Patricia led the way. Phyllis was shown into a high-ceilinged room facing the garden, with a duck-egg blue Chinese paper of birds, while the children's rooms – lower, with high mahogany beds – were along the nursery corridor, near the top of the back stairs.

'Come down to the drawing room, when you're ready,' said Patricia.

Alone for the first time that day, Phyllis sat down at the dressing table which stood between the two windows. She looked not at herself, but out at the garden. Flower beds lined with low box hedges were flanked by gravel paths which lay to either side of an expanse of lawn, with shallow steps down to a stone pond at the far end, where a deep ha-ha gave on to an orchard. The walled kitchen garden, with its fruit nets and long glasshouse, was to the left. To the right was the fenced paddock beside the drive. The light was soft, buttery. Why was the light here so different from Belgium, Phyllis wondered, when the distance between the two places was not so very great? She thought that it must be because Belgium essentially faced north, whereas here in Sussex things inclined south, towards the sun. In Belgium everything seemed harder: shutters instead of curtains and so much spiky wrought-iron work and tall, slender windows glinting an evasive slate colour. Looking now across the summer lawn, her earlier misgivings about staying with Patricia melted away. It was lovely to be back. Phyllis felt, for the first time since their arrival on home shores, a sense of grateful belonging.

A tea-table had been set up by the drawing-room window, with a cloth of drawn-thread work and a covered muffin dish and a fat silver tea-pot, like a sultan's headdress, on a silver trivet.

'Tea is always the best thing, in England,' said Hugh, taking a little sandwich. 'Tea and breakfast, actually. It's the luncheons and dinners that let the side down. On the Continent it's the other way around. Filthy food last night, wasn't it?'

'We had dinner at the hotel,' Phyllis explained. 'Lord knows what it was. Something brown.'

'It was mutton, wasn't it?' said Frances.

'Kedgeree! Now there's a thing,' said Hugh. 'One doesn't see kedgeree, abroad.'

'Should you like it?' asked Patricia. 'It's too late, I think, to arrange it for tomorrow morning; but the day after, I'm sure we could have it, if you'd like. Do say, if there are things you long for.'

Just then there were footsteps in the hall, and Greville and Antonia appeared, both smiling broadly as if they had very recently shared a joke. Greville's frame appeared slightly too small to support his features, like an ex-jockey. His daughter, at thirteen, had spread in all directions, her wide knees and general ampleness very evident in her jodhpurs. The tea-cups rattled on their delicate saucers at her approach. Phyllis felt a pang of fellow-feeling for her niece. She had always been called a heffa-lump as a girl, while both her sisters were svelte. Phyllis had hardly eaten for weeks before her wedding, but with limited success. It was living in South America that had finally seen the end of her chubbiness. To meet her now, no one would have guessed that she had once been otherwise: she was tall and slen-der and there was a slight forward tilt to her frame; like someone in a play stepping eagerly out of French windows, racket in hand, towards an imaginary game of tennis.

'Ah good, you've got everything,' said Greville, as if he had seen Phyllis and Hugh only minutes, and not years, before.

'Say hello to your cousins, Antonia,' said her mother.

The girl went red. 'Hello,' she said, not quite looking in their direction.

'Good ride?' asked Phyllis.

'Not too bad. It was more of a lesson, really,' said Antonia.

'Would help if she knew one end of the beast from the other, wouldn't it, Tiddly-wink?' said Greville.

'Can I see your pony, after tea?' asked Edwin.

'What a good idea!' said Patricia. 'You can take them all out, to see Dingle. They're probably not used to ponies.'

Antonia blushed deeper.

'Actually, I had a pony of my own, in Argentina,' said Julia.

'Journey go all right?' Greville asked.

'Absolutely,' said Hugh.

'So nice that you could come,' said Greville. 'We've got

people in to dine tomorrow, but it's us four, tonight; give you time to settle in. Is that right, darling?'

'Yes,' said Patricia. 'We've got the Templetons, and Johnny Thredham – who's just got back, you know – and Pammy and John Nightingale. Oh, and Anita Orde-Windham. She's coming on her own, because Richard's still in Kenya. And Pea-Brain will probably look in, after dinner.'

Phyllis had never heard of any of these people before, but noticed what pleasure the reciting of their names had given her sister. Greville knew a tremendous amount of people – it was one of the things that had made Patricia plump for him.

'What about Nina and Eric?' asked Phyllis.

There was silence, for the barest moment.

'We thought it would be more fun for you to go over to them, when you're settled,' said Patricia brightly. 'Perhaps the day after tomorrow? See their new house.'

'Peculiar sort of place,' said Greville.

'You must show me round the garden,' said Hugh.

'Oh yes,' said Greville vaguely.

'The garden's more my department,' said Patricia.

'Oh yes, of course,' said Hugh. 'Well, I'm sure Phyllis would adore to see it all. I should certainly enjoy a tour.'

It was not until after dinner that night that the sisters found themselves alone together. Leaving the men at the table to their port, the women went into Patricia's little sitting room, which gave off the hall. It was a pretty room, with a chintz of climbing roses and a walnut desk with a tortoiseshell and silver inkwell and matching letter-opener and stamp-box. Here she wrote her letters and household lists in the mornings, on cards as smooth and stiff as a starched collar, printed with her name and address. Patricia had never looked prettier, her sister thought. Her shorter hair made a golden frame to the picture of her face.

'So, darling, tell all. How has it been, really?' said Patricia.

'Well, it was dreadfully cold in the winter, foggy; especially after Argentina. But I had a nice local woman for the children, so they're all fluent now. I feel languages are so useful.'

'Do you?' said Patricia.

'Well, aren't they? Hugh always says so. Of course I missed all of you awfully,' Phyllis said. 'One minds the lack of female company the most.'

'I can't imagine there was anyone very interesting for you to talk to.'

'No.'

'And Hugh?'

'Well, you know. He can be difficult. But he made great friends with some very nice people, so that helped. They had us shooting, backgammon parties, bridge, that sort of thing. But one never liked to get too fond of anyone, knowing we wouldn't be there for ever. And he's always best when he has a scheme to be working on and the rubber people kept him pretty continuously occupied. So he was busy.'

'But what now?'

'I know,' sighed Phyllis.

'Is he still . . .?' Patricia grinned at her sister.

'Demanding, do you mean? I fear so, yes. I mean, I wouldn't mind sometimes, but not every day.'

'I think you're jolly lucky, actually. Greville has to be coaxed like anything.'

'Funny how different they all are, men. It's a pity one can't tell, just by looking at them.'

'Quite,' said Patricia.

Hugh Forrester had worked for British Rubber ever since leaving the navy after the war, but in the spring the company had made it known that there would not be another posting for him. Nor was he to be offered the London directorship he had expected. For the time being, instead, Hugh would go into the head office once or twice a week, to advise. He had invested soundly over the years, so income was not the trouble. But he was a man who disliked idleness, who enjoyed having people to oversee, things to do. He had been a Commander during the war and put in charge of various important things, all very hush-hush. It was said among the family that he had been instrumental in the setting up of naval intelligence, although it was not something he himself ever mentioned. He was efficient and good at detail; he could be pedantic. He would be ill-suited to retirement, his wife thought.

Hugh was getting on for sixty, although he looked much younger. He was still a handsome man. At the time of their marriage, people had said that Phyllis was lucky to have got such a good-looking husband, even if he was twenty-four years her senior. Hugh's posture was very distinct, very fine. People meeting him for the first time were always struck by this and often ventured, on the strength of it, that he would be a highly competent horseman. In fact, he disliked horses – a dog was one thing, he always said, while a horse was very much another – and did not ride.

'I'm sure Hugh will find plenty of things to do,' Patricia said. 'He's very clever, after all.'

'Oh yes,' said Phyllis. 'I'm sure.'

'I long to know what you'll make of Nina's place,' Patricia went on.

'Is it awful?' asked Phyllis.

'Fairly.'

They both laughed.

'I liked Eric, at the wedding,' said Phyllis. 'And from her letters she seems very contented, I must say. They seem always to be doing things, these camps and so on.'

'I don't know when Nina turned into such a busy little person.'

'What do you mean? She's always been like it.'

'I suppose. In any event, they're always at it. Party business, I mean; these summer camps. No sign of any little mechanics, though.'

'Eric's not a mechanic! You are naughty.'

'A garagist, then.'

'I do hope she will have a baby before too long. She is getting on. I mean, she's thirty-six. One wouldn't want her to've left it too late.'

'I'm sure they're doing their best,' said Patricia, deadpan. They laughed again.

'I don't know that I've got anything very suitable for your party tomorrow night,' it occurred to Phyllis. 'I didn't put anything smart in with the things we were bringing. I think my good evening clothes are still with the carriers.'

'It's hardly a party. Just a few friends for dinner. You can borrow something of mine,' said her sister.

Phyllis remembered trying on both her older sisters' clothes as a girl, when she had been too bulky to fit into them; how coolly Patricia, the eldest, had looked on as hooks and buttons refused to meet their partnering eyes and buttonholes; how Nina had tried to cover up Phyllis's shame by draping their mother's ostrich-feather stole theatrically over the girl's shoulders and telling her she looked wonderful. Now Phyllis would be able to do up Patricia's dresses with ease, although they would always be too short for her.

In their room later Hugh sat upright against the padded bedhead while Phyllis was at the dressing table, putting on her cold cream.

'Greville's less of a fool than he seems,' he announced.

'Really? I thought you always found him rather maddening.'

'Once you get him talking about anything serious he's actually pretty sound, I'd say. Once one gets through the waffle.'

'Oh good,' said Phyllis, absently. 'He absolutely dotes on Antonia, have you noticed? He beams every time she opens her mouth.'

'Knows some interesting types, too. I'm going to dine with him at his club next week, meet one or two of them.'

'Patricia will keep rattling off all these names. I can't take half of it in.'

Hugh always fell asleep first, lapsing into a light but regular snore which punctuated the night like a metronome. Phyllis lay on her back in the dark, conscious of the silence outside. The sights of the day unspooled in her mind's eye: the brick backs of London houses seen from the train, with their rows of washing pegged out in the early summer sun; the hedges and the fields and the tussocky pasture; the Sussex lanes shaded by elms which reached far overhead, their branches meeting like gothic arches. Outside in the velvety darkness all around lay England. In the still air and in meadows and marshes and country towns; in smooth rivers and deep woods; at the edges of pastures where cattle dozed. Near to them now in the sleeping house was the sea, quietly lapping in sheltered inlets where little boats bobbed on the black water, safe in the shallow harbours of home. Home. Even thinking the word made her chest catch with a little jolt of happiness.

2. Sussex, June 1938

There were only three weeks to go until the first campers arrived for the summer season and Nina's pencil had already been sharpened and resharpened so that just a stub barely three inches long remained. It was all the lists she'd had to draw up. Extraordinary, how much there was to do. There was shin of beef for a hundred and twenty to get in for stew on the first night, as well as the sausages for breakfast the following morning. If they had sausages every morning it would cost God knows what and with a long season ahead it was important to stick to budget from the start. But you couldn't not give people meat for breakfast, so the plan was to have bacon and egg one day, sausage and tomato the next; with black pudding once a week on Saturdays. Ninety-eight were booked in for the first week, but it was as well to over-cater, in case more turned up. If the weather was fine you always had to count on stragglers. Nina had already ordered in the vegetables and eggs for the first two or three days, along with quantities of milk and tea and sugar. Her predecessor had warned her that they always ran out of sugar, since some people took as many as three spoonfuls in their tea. She had taken the precaution of ordering in what seemed an unfeasible amount, but at least it could find other uses, in custard and pies and crumbles for pudding and so forth. She just prayed it wouldn't be damp before the cooks found somewhere sensible to store the stuff, or it would form a rock. She was pleased with herself at having secured bread and buns for the camp at no charge, for the duration. This was thanks to Mr Pugh, who owned three bakeries in the area. He was a keen member himself, and would be attending during week three, with his family.

Normally the camp kitchen was overseen by Big Jim, who came from Worthing, and Little Jim, from Hornsea: they generally took charge of ordering and arranging delivery of comestibles. Nina couldn't remember what had been done, in previous years, before such duties fell to herself. Had Big Jim – who knew what he was doing, having been in charge of an army field kitchen – come a day or two early, to sort out the orders? She rather thought he had. This time neither of the Jims were arriving until the first day, a mistake in the planning which exasperated her all the more for being her own fault. There were a significant number of children and young people this year: should they be allocated the same quantities as the grown-ups, or did children eat less? Someone had said, rather alarmingly, that the young – the teenaged contingent – ate much more than adults, their appetites stimulated by the sea air and activities. The butcher would know, perhaps. She added 'ask butcher to advise' to the catering list. All the lists were already too long. She'd received the 30/- subscription from most of the people who'd booked in advance, but there were always latecomers it was difficult to budget in advance for. She would have to set tasks, that's what Eric was always telling her. It was no good offering people a choice; nothing ever got done if folk were at liberty to pick and choose for themselves. Everyone went for the easy jobs, then. There was a meeting of the Women's Committee the following evening, which gave her time to decide which jobs to hand out to which people. It paid to be decisive.

Jennifer Talbot Smith was a nuisance. Meddlesome. She had been in charge of the Women's Committee when Nina first joined the local group and had been among those who had been asked to stand down from official posts, a few months back, when changes were being made from the top down. Noses were out of joint. While it was true that the woman had plenty of experience, innovation had never been her strong suit. Whenever Nina proposed something new – however small, it could be something as minor as arranging a children's entertainer to come to camp for an afternoon – she always looked affronted, as if each idea was somehow an insult to the glorious memory of her captaincy. Nina had to tread on eggshells, with Jennifer and her clique. Now that her sister Phyllis was back, Nina hoped she'd be able to get her to come and help. It would be useful to have an extra pair of hands, especially now, in camp season. And Phyllis had a natural mildness; people were never riled by her. She would be a useful adjunct.

It irked, slightly, that Patricia couldn't be persuaded to do more. The trouble with Patricia – one of the troubles with Patricia – was she had too much time on her hands. She never really committed herself to anything, never rolled up her sleeves or got her hands dirty, literally or otherwise. She drifted. Same thing with Greville. They gave the odd donation and came to an occasional meeting and provided dinner and a bed to some of the most senior speakers who came down from London, usually people Greville had some connection with. But you couldn't rely on them when it came to actual nuts and bolts.

Phyllis came to visit after lunch on her third day. Patricia had suggested she leave Julia and Frances and Edwin at Rose Green, where Antonia could entertain them for the afternoon. Phyllis thought it more likely that it would be her three who would be required to keep their cousin amused: Antonia seemed rather a listless sort of girl.

'Won't you come, too?' asked Phyllis.

'No, darling, you go alone. Nina will like having you to herself. And anyway, I've got no end of things to catch up with, letters to write and so on. I've done nothing but yak since you got here.'

Nina's house stood a little way along from the garage, set back from the road politely, like someone waiting to be introduced. It was constructed of the local brick, with flint detail above each window, like pale eyebrows. Before the road was made it had been a small farmhouse and there was still a duck pond to one side, which Nina referred to as 'our puddle'. The ceilings were low; there was an inglenook fireplace and beams and doors with latches instead of porcelain knobs.

'How's Greville?' asked Nina straight away. 'Is he driving you potty?'

'No, he's actually being very kind. He's taking Hugh to his club today to introduce him to some people.'

Nina raised her eyebrows and smirked. Hers was the most expressive of the three sisters' faces, a page on which everything was written in clear ink. She was attractive rather than pretty, the neatness of her nose and mouth shown off to especial advantage in profile. It was a face whose animation suggested humour, although she was not in truth much of a wit. When she smiled too widely the line of her gums became visible above and below her rather small teeth.

They took a turn around the house and the garden before sitting down. Phyllis told her sister about Belgium and their house there, how the children had got on abroad and her concerns for Frances and Edwin, starting at new schools. She fretted about Edwin in particular. He was still very young to be going away from home. Although, as she said ruefully, they had no home just yet. Nina was always easier to talk to than Patricia, who seemed to have caught from her husband a habit of permanent distraction, as if she were always expecting an important telephone call and had only half an ear on what was being said.

'Hugh talks of building a house. It's something he's always

dreamed of. You know how he has such a lot of opinions about everything.'

'So he's threatening to put some of them into practice?' said Nina, grinning.

'He has strong views about which direction windows should face to encourage a house to air properly, that sort of thing.' Phyllis sighed.

'Will you stay with Patricia, then, for the duration?'

'Oh no, I'm sure not. Heaven knows how long it might take, finding somewhere to build and then doing the drawings and all that: we'd be there for ever. No. We'll find somewhere to rent, I'm sure.'

'I'll ask about, if you like. What with my committees and Eric's, and the garage, we know a fair number of people around here. That is, if you're planning to settle around here?'

'Oh, we are. I'd want to be near you both, of course. You can't imagine how much I've missed you. But I've been gabbling and I haven't heard nearly enough about you. You must tell me about it all, your work.'

'It's very exciting. I do want you to get involved, it'd give you such a lot to keep yourself busy with, once the children have gone back to school; and I really think one has a duty to help out. I'm just a local beaver, of course, but we get some tremendous speakers: big-wigs very often come down from London and give talks, you know. There's so much to do, what with meetings and committees and the newsletter and various other pamphlets and what-not. Eric's very big on all that side of things. Editing, dealing with the printers and suchlike. You know me, I like to be useful. I like the practical day-to-day stuff.'

'I remember it was always you who groomed the ponies, at home. All Patricia and I wanted was the riding out. It was always you who cleaned the tack for all three of us. Daddy was livid when he found out, after he'd made such a point of us each having to learn how to do the mucky things. D'you remember that?'

'He didn't believe you should ever expect someone to do a thing for you that you couldn't do yourself.'

'No,' said Phyllis. Privately it occurred to her that if that were the case, no one would ever ask anyone to do anything. The whole point of jobs, surely, was to get other people to do things you didn't want to do.

'I liked the smell of the saddle soap, anyway,' said Nina.

'So, what about these camping parties?' asked Phyllis.

'They're not parties! Camp is for education and practical work.'

Phyllis looked rather crestfallen. 'Oh. I thought you said they were such tremendous fun.'

'Well, learning is fun, in itself. And there is a fair amount of larking about, obviously. There are socials in the evenings and activities for the youngsters. And sea-bathing, of course. It is fun. There's such a spirit of co-operation; so many bods sharing a common feeling and purpose, coming together. You'll enjoy it, honestly.'

A silence fell between them.

'And quite honestly, Phyllis, this peace work is vitally important. I do think one has a duty to do whatever one can.'

'I wish you wouldn't make it sound so grave and threatening. England feels so reassuring and safe to me. I couldn't stand the thought of another war.'

'None of us can – that's a very real part of what we're trying to address. England's not the nursery, you know. You can't simply pretend that everything will turn out for the best. We face a very real peril.'

'That's what Hugh says, too. He gets rather exasperated with me. I always have this feeling that we're a doughty island kingdom, and that everything will be all right, somehow.'

'Quite frankly, you're being bloody naïve. It's not a fairy tale, with knights and princesses. If people like us don't get control of things we are at real risk of being taken into war.'

Phyllis felt her eyes prick with tears.

'Well, do at least come along to the next meeting,' Nina said, more kindly. 'That'll help you understand things better. You don't need to say anything yourself. But do come along and listen.'

'I will. I promise I will. And what about Eric? How are things?'

'The garage is going pretty well. We're lucky, in this part of the world, there seems to be the demand. Then he's getting some great ideas as to the future of the industry, exciting ideas for anyone in motors. One of the more senior people in the Union – well, he was until recently – has become rather a chum of Eric's: Alexander Raven Thomson, fascinating man. He has all these notions about roads, which is right up Eric's street, to coin a phrase. They both detest Hore-Belisha – all the meddling – as you can imagine.'

'Who on earth is whore Baleesha?' said Phyllis.

'Ex transport minister. He brought in a test that people have to pass before they're permitted to get behind the wheel of a car! Can you imagine anything more stupid? And he made it illegal to drive more than thirty miles an hour in the towns; it's denying people the freedom of the road. Our lot are hell-bent on defying any further restrictions on the freedoms of the motorist. Anyway. Raven Thomson's plan for the future is to build a "ring-way", a road with several carriageways, all the way around London, which would radiate out into other connecting roads, like the spokes of a bicycle wheel. Then there'd be a Southern Way spanning the south coast, from Dover to Plymouth. Including Chichester, you see. It'd be near us, very good for business. These huge roads would join up all the towns and cities in

England and they'd be able to transport all sorts of things from one place to another at top speed, so they'd prosper like anything. It's rather wonderful. Eric's got very interested, they spend hours going over it all. They're thinking of writing something, the two of them, to get their theories across to a wider audience.'

'Heavens,' said Phyllis, whose mind had been wandering as her sister went on. 'D'you really think cars will catch on, to that extent?'

'Oh yes,' said Nina. 'It's just a matter of time. Not only cars, all sorts of things. You can't imagine what you've been missing, while you were away. It's remarkable, the number of ideas one hears of at meetings and socials. There's a view on almost everything. You'll find it all most intriguing.'

'Does Greville do much?'

'Not really. He knows a lot of people, though. He doesn't get very involved with committees and so on; the everyday, organizing type of stuff. But he does bring like-minded people together, informally. They have people to the house. Dinners, that sort of thing. And of course some of them are what you might call top brass, not that I'm naming any names. His sister practically grew up with Cimmie Curzon, though. The wife who died. They went to school together in Eastbourne. Terrible shame. Don't think she's so keen on the current incumbent – the sister doesn't much like Diana I mean – although Greville seems to get on with her. She's more of a man's woman, apparently.'

'Loelia, was that the sister's name?'

'Loelia, yes, I think you're right. I daresay you'll run into her, if you're staying with Patricia for any length of time. She and her husband are regulars. He's a bit of a bore, but you'll like her.'

'Any children?'

'I believe there's a boy. I think he's off at school somewhere. Speaking of children, how's Antonia?'

'She seems fine. Rather quiet.'

Nina raised her eyebrows once again, inviting further comment. Phyllis pretended she hadn't noticed.

Back at Rose Green, Patricia inquired about the visit. 'What did you make of the house?' she asked.

'I thought it was very nice,' said Phyllis.

'You must admit, though, it is like a public house, with those low ceilings. Poky sort of place. And being right on the road. One half expects someone to step forward with a schooner of sweet sherry on a tray. I mean, they've stopped short of actual horse-brasses, but only just.'

'It's a very nice house,' Phyllis said again.

'Did she try and get you to go to a meeting with her?'

Phyllis coloured. 'I said I would, yes.'

'I loathe meetings. They're so terribly dull and they go on for so long. One always has to pretend to listen, whoever is talking: pretend one person's view is as worthwhile as another's. Some piffling little man, I mean a draper or a taxi-man: as if one cares what they think! Quite frankly, if anyone cared about the opinions of people of that sort, one wouldn't need leaders. And then where should we be? It's not so bad when there's a good speaker down from London. It's the local branch stuff that's so tiresome.'

'Nina seems to think I could learn a lot, if I went with her.'

'Yes, well, she would. She would think that. She and Eric eat and drink committees. Don't forget that's how she met him in the first place, at some meeting or talk she'd signed herself up for, near the Grange. He was driving the visiting speaker, did you know? She always keeps that detail rather quiet.'

'But do you agree with them, broadly speaking?' asked Phyllis.

'Oh yes. Lord yes. It's our best hope, for the future of the country. And for peace. There's no doubt about that. Greville thinks so too.'

At Patricia's dinner party the evening before, Phyllis had taken a liking to one of the wives, Sarita Templeton. There wasn't anyone else present that Phyllis would have wanted to make friends with. The other women had all seemed to be minutely differing versions of a type: confident, rather brittle, fair-haired women with good figures, all wearing big rings of diamonds and sapphires. They agreed with everybody else about everything and laughed appreciatively at things the men said, none of which struck Phyllis as funny at all. She had forgotten that this was how women flirted in England, by laughing prettily at their neighbour's every utterance. Continental women tended to cup their chins in their graceful hands so that their bracelets slid seductively down their arms, then stare intently without laughter. Phyllis had lived abroad for so long that she had forgotten, too, that social form demanded general agreement. In Argentina, even in dreary old Belgium, people at parties quite happily disagreed with one another about all sorts of things. Argument was a sport overseas, but here in England it was considered bad manners.

The man they all called Pea-Brain seemed no dimmer than anyone else. Nevertheless he was treated with a teasing cherishment, as if he were a sort of pet or mascot. He had straight hair which he kept scooping back and thick lips which somehow made him embarrassing to look at, as if there was something shameful in the exposure of such fullness. He teased his friends' wives in a practised way which was attentive enough to amuse, but not to offend.

'Are you going to introduce me to this heavenly creature, or do I have to stand here like a lemon all night, in a swoon of anticipation?' he asked Patricia, smiling in the direction of Phyllis.

'You fool! You've barely taken off your coat! Of course I was going to introduce you, as soon as you'd got a drink,' she said, batting him on the upper arm.

'Thank heavens, I think I'm in love already,' said Pea-Brain.

'She's my sister, you dafty! She's a respectable married woman.'

'The next sleeper for Paris is still at the station,' said Pea-Brain. 'Let's elope to Constantinople, straight away.'

Phyllis reddened. She was not used to this sort of joshing.

'Maybe you can murder him on the Orient Express,' Sarita whispered.

Phyllis laughed. 'Don't say you read Agatha Christie as well?'

'I adore these books,' said Sarita. 'I always get them sent, from Truslove and Hanson, whenever a new one comes out. Have you had *Death on the Nile*? I think it's one of her best.'

'No, I haven't. I haven't had a chance to go to Boots, since we got back.'

'There's no need to use a library! I can lend them all to you. I will invite you.'

After pudding the women left the men at the table and followed their hostess upstairs to brush their hair and re-do their faces before repairing to the drawing room for coffee. Sarita was more exotic-looking than the rest, more reserved and yet somehow less forbidding. A pair of tortoiseshell combs held up her hair at either side of her head, framing a face slightly too long to be called oval; she had a long brown neck and slender hands: she looked almost Indian, although she actually came from Brazil. Patricia had told Phyllis about all the guests, beforehand. Fergus Templeton was Sarita's second husband, apparently; she had a divine-looking little girl from the first husband, who was some sort of millionaire. There was a whiff of scandal, Patricia couldn't quite recall the details: it was to do with the first husband trying to get custody of the child. There had been some

sort of scene at a grand London party, voices raised, people star-
ing. Fergus played polo.

'Why are you saying that with such emphasis?' Phyllis had
laughed. 'Is playing polo code for something else? Do you mean
he's queer or something?'

'Oh Lord, no, nothing like that. It's only that it costs a lot to
keep polo ponies.'

'I don't follow,' said Phyllis.

'Well, I mean it helps to marry someone rich, if you want to
play polo. That's all.'

But when Phyllis saw his wife, she didn't believe for a second that
Templeton would have married her for money. Anyone would
have fallen in love with someone so unusual and glamorous.

While Patricia was pouring out coffee, Phyllis went to sit
next to Sarita. It turned out that the daughter was the same age
as Frances, Phyllis's younger daughter: would she like to bring
her, one day, to swim in the Templetons' pool?

'People think we're crazy, having a pool when we live so close
by the sea. But since I like to swim every day, it's more conveni-
ent. The beaches here, it's not really sand, there's nowhere to sit
down where you can get comfortable. And we had the little
pool house designed by such an interesting mosaicist: you must
see it, you'll love it! The floor is made of pennies. Is very
amusing.'

She said her 'esses' softly, so that 'crazy' sounded like 'craissy'
and 'is' like 'iss'.

'I'd like to very much,' said Phyllis.

She told Sarita a little about her time in Argentina and how
much she missed South America, missed the lovely bright birds
that had flitted into their courtyard in the mornings. There had
been cobbles, sunlight, bells. They had always intended to go up
to visit Brazil, but somehow they never had: the only trip they'd
made had been to Uruguay once, for a few days in Montevideo.

Now there probably wouldn't be another chance; it was a pity. Sarita had never been to the Low Countries and asked about it all, the landscape and the weather and the food. She seemed really keen to hear everything Phyllis had to say. Having been the youngest of three, this didn't happen to her very often and Phyllis felt suddenly rather interesting. As a rule she felt that she was slightly outside of things, that she had always come into every room a fraction too late, after the decisive thing had been talked about, the necessary arrangements made. Phyllis wasn't someone whom people consulted.

The following morning, to Patricia's evident chagrin, Sarita had already telephoned for Phyllis, while she was out for her morning walk. Her older daughter, Julia, was annoyed that the invitation from Mrs Templeton did not include herself, but was only extended to the younger and in her mind less deserving Frances.

'I always get Antonia. She's such a lump,' said Julia.

'Don't be unkind! Antonia is a lovely girl,' said her mother.

Patricia, too, was put out not to have been asked. 'I've never been in that house by day,' she said. 'Ravishing sort of a place. Whenever we've been it's for an evening party, with lots of other people. You must report. I long to know what they do with themselves over there.'

The Templetons' place was twice the size of any of the houses Phyllis knew, L-shaped and Jacobean, with tall grey walls into which windows seemed to have been cut at random. It nestled against the shoulder of the Downs, at the end of a long drive flanked for at least a mile by chestnut trees with low branches which swooped down to the grass. A footman opened the door into a panelled hall flagged with pale stone, where a single huge log smoked desultorily in the grate, despite the summer month. Ragged pennants hung from poles high above their heads.

Chairs with ornate legs like bishop's thrones stood at intervals at the sides of the room. The little girl appeared almost at once. She had dark ringlets and deep blue eyes. The young footman had vanished.

'I don't know where Mummy is,' she said. 'She told me you were coming, but then she disappeared.'

Phyllis didn't know what to say. 'I expect she's been called to the telephone. She hasn't actually left the house, has she?'

'I don't think so,' said the girl.

'Where is your . . . where is Mr Templeton?'

'Out. He's at the yard, with the ponies.'

'Oh. Well, shall we go and wait for her somewhere? Do people wait in the drawing room, usually?' said Phyllis, trying to be helpful.

'What about the man who let us in? Shall we ask him to look for the Mummy?' suggested Frances.

'Or we could go and look for her ourselves, if you like?' said the child.

'Yes!' said Frances. 'Then I can see around your house, too.'

'Darling, that's not very polite,' said Phyllis, although she too would have liked a look.

The child smiled for the first time. 'There's a room through there with a secret door. A library. The door looks like a bookcase, but if you press it you can get into the morning room,' she said.

'Why don't you sit in there on a sofa,' said Frances, taking charge. 'While we search.'

Phyllis rather enjoyed waiting in the strange house. One of the drawbacks of being a guest was that she seldom had any time alone. She always felt as if she was on duty somehow, even though Patricia was her own sister. In Belgium, she had had people to give lessons to Edwin and his sisters and take them on outings: here, the children were always underfoot waiting to be told what they were doing, like gun-dogs moping outside the shooting season. When at length Sarita appeared with the girls, now chattering animatedly together, Phyllis was almost sorry. Sarita was very welcoming, but there was something different about her today. She didn't seem quite all there; there was a sort of haziness that Phyllis could not identify. She had forgotten all about the pool and their proposed swim, only suggesting that they take tea outside, so the girls could go and explore in the grounds. If she noticed the basket Phyllis was carrying, with their rolled-up towels and bathing things, she gave no sign of it. The children ran off almost at once, leaving the two women together. Sarita sat with a sort of half-smile, barely talking, her tea untouched in its cup. The hour passed awkwardly, but when it was time to go, she clasped Phyllis with what seemed like real affection.

'Please come again, won't you? Emilia is not in school, it becomes lonely for her here. And I would like to hear more about your travels.'

Yet Sarita had not addressed a question to Phyllis all afternoon and appeared to have quite forgotten about lending her books. Perhaps she had other things on her mind. Perhaps the child's father was being difficult: something private. Templeton had not put in an appearance. As the car pulled away, Phyllis looked back. There stood Sarita on the shallow steps to the front of the house, not waving, her arms hanging limply at her sides. There was something forlorn about the way she made no gesture, as if she was a child being left at school for the first time, as if she was sad to be left behind.

Phyllis, 1979

They covered the whole thing up, of course. People wouldn't remember him now, but Fergus Templeton, the husband, was great friends with the fellow who was the Queen Mother's trainer at the time. No one would have countenanced any bad publicity about someone with those sorts of ties. Things were pretty tight in those days; it was considered very low to speak to journalists. People just didn't. You wouldn't believe the kind of things that went on among people of that sort, and the newspapers never heard a word of it. Scandals, shenanigans, goodness knows what. People were good at keeping their mouths shut, then. Or at least that's what we all thought.

Templeton was a bit of an oaf, really. Maybe you don't need to know this, it isn't entirely relevant to your area of interest, but it'll give you a sense of what things were like in those days. How people like that went on.

The Templetons had a dance — this was before we came back to England, before we knew them — and by the small hours several of the men were more than half-cut and in high spirits. The dancing had stopped some time before; the band had packed up and gone. I'm not sure who the others were, but my sister's friend Pea-Brain was one of them. Well. Fergus had the idea of going down to the farm — which was a fair way off, it was beyond the modern yard where he kept his ponies, not by the original stable-yard to the house — he got it into his head that it would be a caper to go down to the farm and get themselves a pig. History doesn't relate what they intended to do with a live pig, once they'd got it. They just thought it would be the best possible fun to fetch one up from the farm and bring it into the house. So they got into someone's car, five or six of them crammed in, and off they bumped down the track. You get frightful ruts in those farm tracks down in Sussex, it's the chalk.

Not that that would have stopped them. They left the car down at the farm with all its doors open.

It was more sheep country than pigs, but they kept half a dozen sows or so at the farm and apparently there were some porkers down there which were fattened and about ready to be sold on. When Fergus told the story later he said they'd had a devil of a job trying to round one up. Turns out pigs can get up quite a speed and of course they're as clever as a dog, so they're not about to let you capture them, unless there's something in it for them. Then someone remembered how greedy they are – well, they're famous for it – so they found some feed pellets and a bucket; and of course as soon as the pigs caught sight of the bucket they followed the men towards the gate. Somehow or another they managed to separate one of them and coax this creature all the way back up to the house, using the pellets as a sort of trail.

I don't know why the walk back up from the farm didn't sober them up enough to make them see how ridiculous the whole thing was. By then it was getting light. They got the pig into the big hall, the entrance to the house, and there was a certain amount of standing about: I gather they didn't quite know what to do with themselves or the wretched animal, now they'd got it this far. They'd sort of run out of steam at this point. In due course one of them went for another bottle: they were on the brandy by then, I believe. That got them going again.

They'd run out of pellets for the pig by this time, so the animal was losing interest and snuffling about the place and making a frightful mess everywhere, until Fergus went down to the kitchen and brought up a bin he'd found under the scullery sink, full of peelings and scraps. I don't know when they decided it would be good sport to get the animal up the stairs, or whether they had any idea, beforehand, of what they might do with it once they got it up there.

At the top of the house, on the south side, there was a low parapet. It was possible to get out there, up a narrow staircase which ran from the end of the top landing. There was a little door on to this staircase and then once you got up to the top there was a wide shallow gutter, lined with lead, which ran behind the parapet all along the front of the house. Sarita took me up once, to see the view. From the ground you would never have known it was there. It was a sort of shelf, not meant to be walked along. Emilia was strictly forbidden ever to go out there, or to take visiting children, and the door was kept securely fastened. But five or six very drunk men with determination on their side aren't going to let a couple of bolts get in the way of their fun.

I've never seen a pig go up a rather tight staircase, but evidently it is quite possible, although the animal was making a fair bit of noise by then. It tried to bite – actually did get its jaw around someone's calf, agony apparently – and scrabbled about. At various points someone had the bright idea of picking up its back legs to make it easier to manoeuvre, like a living wheelbarrow. But of course the pig didn't like that and made a dreadful commotion. They'd finished off another bottle of brandy, between them. It was the end of a long night; it was a miracle they were still standing. One or other of them must have suggested it, but they all joined in. They'd have had to work as a team: pigs are heavy. Imagine a side of bacon. A porker like that would have weighed as much as a heavy man, maybe more. Pigs are big, much bigger than people imagine them to be.

Apparently the animal squealed like mad as soon as they started trying to pick it up. This made them all double up with laughter, so that one or other of them kept letting go and the pig, half-lifted, would fall down again. At this point one of them noticed that its hooves were surprisingly dainty in relation to its bulk and this made them laugh all the more, as if the animal was a plump old lady with absurdly tiny little feet. The hooves kept skittering against the lead and the animal kept squealing and butting into them all, trying to escape. The noise it made gave them all a fright as well as making them laugh, like getting the giggles at a funeral. It was so loud and shrill, as loud as a terrified child. Apparently it had a sort of other-worldly quality, like a banshee or a harpy or one of those creatures; as if it was a bad omen. Even later when Fergus told the story – and the telling was much punctuated by laughter; he still thought it was tremendously funny – he did admit that the noise was awful, an awful thing, and

31

that it had given them all pause. Especially at that time of the early morning when it was so very quiet, only the first birds making any sound.

The pig screamed non-stop as it fell. I don't know if it woke everyone in the house or if they were too blotto from the party. Anyway, Fergus and the rest of them didn't hear it actually hit the ground because the noise of its shrieking drowned out the sound of the impact. They were almost surprised when they leaned over and saw the entrails coiling out from where the skin had split and no sound coming from it any more. The noise just stopped. The head had broken right open, like a coconut at a funfair. They stood on the narrow parapet, swaying slightly from the exertion and the long night of drink, the sudden quiet after the pig's shrieking adding to the sense of giddiness. No one quite knew what to do next.

'Christ, what a racket,' someone said.

'Gives one a new respect for sausages, I must say,' said Pea-Brain.

After that it became rather a catch-phrase among them all. If there were sausages at breakfast, someone or other, lifting the cover off one of those silver serving dishes on the sideboard, would inevitably say: 'Gives one a new respect for sausages.' It always got a laugh.

Lord knows how they got the carcass cleared up, whether they got people in from the farm to do it, I never asked. They must have had to keep the dogs inside.

Poor Sarita, it was such a ghastly business. Not the pig. I mean what happened later, after the other party. At the time everyone said there was nothing anyone could have done to help, that it couldn't have been avoided. But I knew that was not true. I should have helped her, but I did nothing. No one helped Sarita.

3. Sussex, July 1938

True to her word, Nina asked around and found a house for Phyllis and Hugh to rent. It was at Bosham, set back from the harbour wall behind a deep apron of springy lawn which was shaded by two tall blue cedars. The drawing room had a pale green sofa and two chairs upholstered in a floral chintz of brown and green which matched the material on the upholstered C-shaped seat of the bay window. This looked out across the water towards the church on the far side of the horseshoe bay.

Phyllis loved the house. She was entranced by the view and the situation, close to both her sisters; so conveniently near to Chichester for trains and provisions and yet so tucked away. The owner, who lived in London, had only used the house for Fridays to Sundays. A woman from Pagham was already employed as a twice-weekly char and now she would come in every morning. Nina thought she knew of someone else who would be able to cook.

It was such a sweet relief to be out from under Patricia's feet. Not that her sister had ever shown any sign of impatience, but Greville had begun to inquire how the house-hunting was coming along, never with any temper, but with increasing frequency. And the children were sick of always having to entertain their cousin Antonia, poor lamb. Phyllis had spent a large part of her time abroad wishing she was back at home, close to her sisters, and was surprised to discover how much she liked being alone in a house after all. Not that she was alone, really, what with the children and Hugh not having enough to do. But one didn't have to be on duty, under one's own roof. One didn't have to smile and pretend to be interested in the garden; one didn't have to

33

wait until everyone else had looked at the paper or taken a biscuit or had their baths. Throughout the weeks at Rose Green, Phyllis had never once had a hot-enough bath. She had sat at the edge of every chair she had occupied – quite literally the edge – ready to spring up at a moment's notice, either to do her sister's bidding or to get out of the way. It was wonderful now to be able to go into the drawing room and sit uninterrupted, reading. Patricia didn't approve of detective novels – she always said they were the sort of thing housemaids read – and teased Phyllis about them.

On their first Sunday in the new house, Nina and Eric and Patricia and Greville and Antonia came to lunch. Phyllis had noticed that her two sisters so arranged things as to barely be together; still less so when their husbands were at home. There was no hostility between them that Phyllis could detect, but they seemed not to include one another in their plans. She wanted to bring the family back together again, all three of them. Now that she had her own household she would be able to do so.

'Nina did well for you, didn't she?' said Eric proudly, of his wife. 'Found you a nice place here.'

'Very. She did brilliantly. We're so grateful,' said Phyllis.

'Dining room's rather small,' said Greville.

'I do think the view's heavenly, I must say,' said Patricia.

'Isn't it,' said Hugh.

'Such a pity about those trees,' said Patricia.

'Oh no, we like the trees. It's nice to have a bit of shade,' said Phyllis.

'Well, of course. I meant it's a pity they're the wrong sort of cedar,' said Patricia.

Phyllis laughed. 'What do you mean? How can there be a right sort and a wrong sort?'

But Patricia was serious. 'Well, the right sort are from the Lebanon and these are from the Atlantic. It's well known. These are blue, you see. They're just not what one would have chosen.'

34

'You can't mind, even about a tree! You are the limit, Patricia,' said Nina.

Patricia smiled. 'It's the sort of house one would expect to belong to a London surgeon. The kind with grand rooms in Harley Street, you know the sort of thing, with a huge polished brass sign and railings and those black and white tiles on the step.'

'I think Nina said the man is a doctor of some kind!' Phyllis laughed. 'He had a yacht down here, but now it's gone over to the Isle of Wight. Isn't that what you told me, Nina?'

'She, not it,' said Hugh automatically. 'Yachts are vessels: vessels are always referred to as "she".'

'Be nice to put in some aubretia along that wall at the end,' said Eric. 'Aubretia puts on a lovely show.'

'Plants are really more Patricia's side of things,' said Greville, as if his brother-in-law's gardening advice had been directed at him.

'Flowers from the beginning of spring right up until the first frost, does aubretia,' said Eric.

'It's more of a picnic than a real lunch,' said Phyllis.

'D'you hear that, Tiddler?' Greville asked his daughter. 'A picnic!'

Antonia grinned.

'How lovely,' said Patricia.

'I thought a walk, after lunch,' said Hugh.

After they had eaten at a table out on the flagged terrace, they all set off around the harbour. The children scampered ahead with their cousin, chattering: having complained of Antonia's company over the preceding weeks, they now seemed filled with delight at being reunited. Eric had brought a kite and wanted to show them how to launch it; he walked quickly, ahead of the rest, trying to catch up with the children so as to give them their lesson. There didn't seem to be enough wind for flying a kite. The tide was out and little boats lolled on their sides in the sandy mud, like the tongues of overheated dogs. The bottoms of the exposed hulls were dark from the water. Phyllis fell into step with Nina and Greville. Hugh and Patricia lagged behind, bending over to identify the wild flowers which emerged in tiny clusters between the stones closest to the tide's edge.

It had been Patricia whom Hugh had liked, to begin with. The sisters all knew this, but it was only when she glanced back at their stooping figures, their heads almost touching, that it came to Phyllis to wonder for the first time whether Greville, too, was aware that Hugh had once pursued his wife. It was something she had never thought to ask Patricia. She wondered whether the picture they presented would seem to Greville, as it did to her, one of close unity and shared absorption, of two people with much common ground between them. But Greville was listening to Nina talking, and didn't pause to look back.

When Hugh had first appeared at the Grange Phyllis had still been in the schoolroom, her hair in plaits. He had been far older than them, a friend of the girls' uncle, their mother's younger brother: it was he who had brought Hugh over one bright afternoon, to play tennis. Then Hugh had been brought to a croquet party, then a luncheon. Their father had liked him, with his rather formal manners and neat hair. And he had a distinguished war record. He was already Commander Forrester, then.

Patricia had been barely eighteen, her fair hair still long, like the hair of a princess in a fairy story: long and rippling, with the dark shine of high-carat gold. There had been a touch of the imperious about her, even then, despite being so much younger than Hugh. She had neither said nor done anything to discourage him, but received his attention as if it was nothing less than her due. This was not so much because she wished to give him hope as because she felt it correct to acknowledge his advances rather than shun them. If she also got some practice in the ways of wooing, so much the better; it was no bad thing to be prepared for what she was confident would be several such courtships. But afterwards, when she had turned him down, there had been recrimination. Her father felt she had led him on. He had suggested a week or two of reflection, before she came to a final decision. Patricia's cheeks had flushed to a high colour and she had run up the stairs after shouting at her mild and bewildered parents: 'I don't want to and I shan't let you make me!'

She did find Hugh handsome and ever so slightly perplexing, and she was not unmoved when he produced a ring: a square emerald with gently stooping shoulders of diamonds, like a piece of angelica against the butter-icing coloured velvet lining of the little leather box. And although she had let him kiss her more than once – no one knew, not even Nina – and had felt as a result a melting low in her abdomen which took her entirely off-guard; despite all this, she knew that he lacked a certain stature. He was nice, even attractive, enough; but he would not be able to give her what she wanted. She wanted someone younger and more dashing, who could produce for her a world of dances and banter and fun; of long curving banisters and silver grape scissors and lovely clothes; of rooms scented with cigar smoke and hot-house gardenias and expensive scent; an enclosed world, reflected in old and darkly spotted mirrors hung low on broad half-landings or above side tables of gleaming rosewood. She had grown up with all this, or a slightly less sophisticated version of it. Her family was not worldly, but it was established, comfortable. They were county people, with well-stocked stables and a cellar full of port and silver pheasants adorning the dining-room table. What could be more natural than to wish to replicate, or actually improve upon, the milieu of her own childhood, so happy and secure?

Because the trouble with Hugh was that he had no family. There was nothing to fall back on. His father had died young, overseas, leaving a widow who promptly returned to England

and moved in with a married sister so as to be able to have her young son, her only child, with her during the holidays from his prep school. Hugh had gone up to naval college straight away after leaving school, as his father had before him: there was a well-off godfather who had helped educate the boy. At the time of his introduction to Patricia he had left the navy and was still establishing a civilian career for himself. After she rebuffed him, the girls heard that Hugh had gone abroad; somewhere in South America, it was thought. By the time he came back, six years later, Patricia had married Greville and Phyllis had grown up. Nina too, although Nina was too definite, too opinionated for Hugh. Phyllis no longer had plaits but wore her hair pinned low on the back of her head; she was gentle, something of a book-worm. Phyllis Forrester: it sounded nice. And after all, she was used to wearing Patricia's old clothes, or such of them that she could fit into. She still accepted hand-me-down presents of cast-off blouses, gloves, even an occasional hat. It was not unnatural to her, having things her eldest sister had tired of or grown out of. She was used to not choosing for herself.

Phyllis was so grateful to Nina for finding them the house. The one drawback was that it made her feel obliged to look willing and go to one of the meetings. While she poured the tea, and Patricia sliced the Dundee cake, Nina enthused about the forth-coming talk. There was to be a guest speaker from London, who Nina assured them was a very interesting sort of chap, full of ideas. There would be sherry and sausage rolls afterwards for the organizers, among whom – thanks to her sister and brother-in-law – Phyllis would be lucky enough to count herself. She didn't seem to be bothering to try and lure Patricia.

'It's a mixed crowd, you'll see. But there's always someone nice and you'll certainly find it stimulating. Give you something to think about,' said Nina.

'Does she want something to think about?' asked Greville.

'Of course she does! Otherwise she just sits about with her penny dreadfuls.'

'I've got plenty to think about already,' Phyllis protested. 'You don't imagine Hugh troubles himself with coming up with things for the children to do, day in day out, do you? It all falls to me. Half our things are still in packing cases and no one but me knows what's what. I've got a great many things to be getting on with.'

'Do you good to get out and mix a bit,' said Nina firmly.

The meeting took place in a function room at the back of the White Hart Inn in Chichester. There was a not unpleasant smell in the room, like the mildew odour in a seldom-used village hall. A rickety-looking wooden platform stood before rows of chairs and benches, enough to seat about sixty. Arriving early to greet the guest of honour with her sister, Phyllis wondered if the room would be filled; she rather thought not. Were so many people interested in politics, ideas? She didn't remember that they had been, when she was growing up: it was a given that everyone was a Tory, but she couldn't recollect anyone being moved to discuss it. Now Nina bustled about, putting out cups and saucers on a side table for people's tea afterwards and distributing leaflets, two on the seat of each chair. It was no surprise, really, that Nina should attach herself to this sort of thing. She'd always been inventing clubs, when they were children. She had constructed endless bossy lists and written them out in little rule books she made by hand, as well as making special badges to connote membership. Then too Phyllis had been the more biddable sister. Nina had the old familiar air of contented purpose about her this evening.

Eric arrived, his hair freshly brilliantined, a thin, rather asthmatic-looking man by his side. This was Peter Heyward, tonight's speaker. Eric seemed very animated. He called Phyllis over to be introduced. Gradually the room filled. Phyllis had expected that most of the audience would be working men and was surprised to find that this was not the case, for none of the audience appeared to conform to any particular type. There was a group of young women who arrived all at once, chattering like starlings: clerks, perhaps, or shop-girls. Three rather distinguished-looking women came in, two of them wearing fox tippets despite the summery weather. With pronounced hauteur they made their way straight to the front row of seats and installed themselves, each with one ankle tucked politely behind the other, just as Phyllis and her sisters had been taught a lady must always sit.

Hugh came. Several people looked as if they might be farmers. A small group of them conversed with a handful of patrician-looking men, two or three of whom had narrow moustaches. This group, too, had gone straight to the front of the room and now seated themselves alongside the fur-tippeted women; evidently seeing themselves as people of distinction, they did not stand up to greet their interlocutors, although they smiled genially. The last to arrive were a large group of men, all over sixty by the look of them. Nina had told her that there were a lot of ex army and navy men in the Movement and Phyllis guessed they were former servicemen, from the tidiness of their dress. Far from the hall being half-empty, as she had envisaged, they had to send into the pub for more chairs in order to accommodate the numbers. Everyone seemed to know each other. Only the nine or ten grandees in the front row seemed slightly set apart from the rest.

The guest speaker was welcomed and introduced by Eric, and duly applauded. 'He's a terrific talker, you'll see,' whispered Nina.

'I am not ashamed, Comrades, to acknowledge that our Island is indeed a nation of shopkeepers,' he began. 'Indeed, I would surmise that there are representatives of such businesses with us here this evening.'

There was a murmur of assent from several individuals among

the crowd. 'What I say is this: Shopkeepers of Britain, awake! Shopkeepers of Britain, your duty is clear! The time for action is here. For our small shops – lively going concerns run by local people for the benefit of their local citizenry – are threatened. Commercial travellers are threatened. Yes, threatened. That is not too strong a word. The distributive trades and all who work in them face a mighty menace! That menace is the menace of the chain stores, with their monopoly of manufacturing, and of wholesalers. Unless we act, and act promptly, this monopoly will take over the distributive trades and our small shops will close their blinds for the last time. Many of these shops are family concerns, passed down with pride from father to son over generations. Some of you may represent such concerns, indeed I would ask any such traders to raise their hands.'

At this, two dozen or so among the audience put their hands up and one or two stood.

'You are blameless,' the speaker went on. 'You have done no wrong. You have served your customers loyally and well and brought up your families among them. But the time approaches when here in our streets we shall see enacted the battle of David versus Goliath. For these behemoths the giant chain stores have no use for you, the shop-owners; nor you, the trained assistants of the kind now employed here in Chichester, and in their hundreds of thousands in towns and villages along this coast and up and down the length and across the backbone of our land. No skill will be needed to put sixpence in the till: no training will be necessary to simply put a purchase in a bag. You trained and skilled assistants will be a thing of the past if the chain stores are allowed their sway. And so will your employers, the owners of the small local shops who have served their customers so loyally and so well.'

The speaker carried on, listing the big stores that were the culprits in this battle: Universal Stores, Debenhams, Marks & Spencer, Montague Burton, Lyons.

'There is no such thing as a cut price! A cut price is a cut job!' Heyward had gathered momentum and was shouting. 'And, Comrades, I remind you that cut prices and sweated labour always march side by side. Since our paramount aim is to raise the standard of living in these isles for our own workers and their families, we will ruthlessly suppress these emporia of low prices, whose flourishing can only lead to a lowering of that standard. Under our rule, for the first time in history shopkeepers will have direct representation in Parliament. Tonight, Comrades, I call to you to join our Union: unite for Britain, and for British retailers' jobs!'

The speaker sat down and was loudly applauded. Many got to their feet, still clapping. Those who were still seated felt outdone by their standing companions, and duly rose. A palpable warmth filled the crowd. It was the warmth of a shared belief passionately felt and a set of shared values in immediate peril: a mixture of piety and indignation that even Phyllis found heady.

'Very sound. Very sound indeed,' said Hugh, as the commotion died down and people began to make their way out of the room.

'Isn't he?' said Nina. 'I'll have to greet a few people, make sure they've got everything they need. Why don't you go ahead with Eric and the others, into the lounge bar?'

Hugh and Phyllis went out, along with three or four of the local organizers. One of the distinguished-looking men – Phyllis didn't catch his name – fetched her a glass of sherry from the bar. Hugh was impatient to meet the speaker, Peter Heyward, but he did not appear straight away. The younger of the two women with the fox furs – her two female companions seemed to have left – sat beside Phyllis, bringing with her a corona of scent. It was a rich smell, as of flowers cultivated under glass: a hot-house smell of jasmine or stephanotis, but with something troublingly animal beneath it, as if there were a dead mouse somewhere under the flowerpots. The fellow who'd bought their drinks seemed to be her husband. The woman struck up a conversation. She announced herself as Venetia Gordon-Canning.

'I don't believe we've met before, have we? Are you a member, or did you just come tonight as a friend of Peter's?'

'Well, neither, really. I'm sort of here because of my sister. What about you? What brings you here?'

'Oh, me. I'm not anything, really. We come sometimes when there's a speaker. Show willing. My husband Andrew's uncle – they're very close, closer than he ever was to his own father – is a great advocate of it all. He's rather a big-wig in the Movement, as a matter of fact. Is that your husband?' she asked, gesturing in Hugh's direction.

'Yes. That's Hugh. We've just come back from abroad.'

'Lucky you. He's frightfully good-looking.'

They both laughed. It turned out that Venetia too was facing the prospect of the long summer holidays ahead, with an eleven- and a thirteen-year-old: before the evening was out she had extended an invitation to Phyllis and the children, to lunch.

'Nothing formal, we'll eat with the children,' she said. 'This sherry's rather gruesome, isn't it? Sticky. Wish I'd asked for gin.'

At length, Eric and Nina brought the speaker into the bar and introduced him to everyone. Hugh spent a good twenty minutes talking closely with him. In the car on the way home, he was buoyant. 'I've heard more sense spoken tonight than in any other quarter since we got back,' he said.

'I didn't really follow all of it, but it certainly sounded as if he had a case,' said Phyllis.

'Heyward suggested I go along to Great Smith Street when I'm in town, meet a few of the more senior people. I'd like to help.'

'Oh good,' said Phyllis. 'Well, I'm sure they'd be glad to have you on board.' She did not quite see why this should be so, since

Hugh had been a company man and not a politician, but the willed kindness of saying it made her feel for a moment almost noble.

'I should've thought they would, yes,' said Hugh. His sense of his own worth was something he had always borne gravely. He was not a man to be teased.

It was the first evening they had spent out of the new house and Phyllis found it delightful to return there. The drive was to the back of the property, and as they came to a stop at the end of its shallow curve their headlamps caught a glint of water, the deep colour of gunmetal in the softness of the summer night. The tide was in. Phyllis loved the changing tides, how the surging water altered the prospect beyond the windows from hour to hour. You could look out of the bedroom window and see little pools set into the rippled mud below, as still and flat as the artificial pond in the table-top gardens the children sometimes made, using the lipstick-mirror taken from its suede side pocket in their mother's handbag. Then the morning could go by and the next time you glanced out it would all have changed: there would be water almost as high as the lawn, as if you could step straight from the end of the garden into a mysteriously waiting coracle and be carried far away, to distant lands. There would be tiny waves fringed with white, rising like the icing on the top of a cake, and the water would no longer be still but would swell and fall, gulls with folded wings bobbing on its surface. Living in this delightful place made Phyllis feel that luck was on her side.

4. Sussex, July 1938

At the camp-site Little Jim had with him a son of perhaps nineteen or twenty as well as a grandson of about ten, the first
strikingly handsome and both of them surprisingly tall, given
Jim's stature. There seemed to be no women in their party. The
son, who was the little boy's uncle, was called Freddy; the grandson was named Frank. The child had a quick, slightly goofy smile
which held the promise of mischief. Little Jim introduced him to
Phyllis and Edwin, who had been persuaded to join in for the first
day of the summer camp. The girls had been awkward and refused
to come. They were sewing dolls' clothes at home, sulking.

'You like a laugh, don't you, Frank?' Little Jim looked very
proud at this, his arm around the boy's shoulders. He stood
barely as high as his grandson. 'He likes a good laugh.'

Edwin, slightly younger, took a great shine to the boy, gig-
gling at his jokes and following him about the site. At lunch and
tea Frank came to the cookhouse to help his grandfather and the
catering volunteers spoon food on to people's plates. Afterwards, while Jim enjoyed a quiet smoke, Frank collected up
crockery and stray knives and forks. He called them irons.
Edwin, who had never shown any inclination to help the cook
at home, imitated his new companion. Freddy was to be in
charge of blowing the bugle to summon campers to the cookhouse at mealtimes. Other than this he didn't seem to be doing
much to help, but stood about like a film star waiting to be called
for his scene, smoking and narrowing his eyes, attracting glances
from arriving females.

This year's camp-site was on the saltings at Selsey, right by the beach. There were views across the Solent towards the Isle of Wight on one side and to the distant South Downs to the other; an old windmill marked the entrance and there was a row of coastguards' cottages a couple of fields away. Neat lines of bell tents were at the front of the site, with latrines and showers to their left. In the middle was an open area with a flagpole roughly at its centre, where someone had already raised the Movement's standard and arranged straw bales in a circle on the rough grass. The larger communal marquees, where everyone took meals or listened to talks, were towards the back of the site, along with a couple of smaller tents which would house a makeshift book-shop and a first-aid station. Beyond these at the north end were one or two wooden huts, which were reserved for the top offi-cials and the Leader's use.

Nina's principal task was to check provisions three times a day, after meals. It wasn't only a matter of food supplies: there had to be adequate stores of lavatory paper and soap, as well as wood and kindling for camp-fires, enough blankets to go round, and paraffin for the storm-lamps. Quantities of calamine lotion would be required in case of sunburn or stings. The first-aid tent must be equipped with iodine, aspirin and liniment, as well as bandages. It also fell to her to make sure that the laundry van came on time and that the latrines were emptied every day. Transport had to be arranged for those campers who arrived by train at Chichester. She carried a small lined notebook and sev-eral pencils with her wherever she went.

Showing Phyllis around, Nina paused and pointed towards some tall elms to one side of the camp-site. 'Do you know whose house is over there? You'll never guess,' she asked her sister.

'Umm . . . Laurence Olivier.'

'No, you chump! Whatever made you think of him?'

'I must have been reading something about him in the paper. I think it said he lives in Sussex, somewhere.'

46

'Have another guess,' said Nina.

'I can't. You tell me, I know I won't get it, otherwise.'

'The First Lord of the Admiralty, that's who. Duff Cooper.'

'Goodness. Is he there now?'

'Shouldn't think so. I don't believe he comes down much, which is probably just as well. Wouldn't be best pleased to wander to the bottom of his field and see us, camped next door. Our flag raised, within sight of his garden. So near, and yet so far, as they say.'

Phyllis laughed, to please her sister.

Away from Nina and Patricia, she was glad to be making friends of her own. Venetia Gordon-Canning had had Phyllis and the children to lunch and she in turn had invited them back to Bosham, one day when Hugh was in London. Venetia was cheery and outspoken, an amusing companion.

She smoked non-stop, the ends of her cigarettes stained the colour of cherries by her lipstick. Phyllis enjoyed her company, although she preferred Sarita, who was softer and didn't make such bold personal remarks, as Venetia was in the habit of doing.

'I hate it when one's got the curse, don't you? Such a bore having to skip games,' announced Venetia one afternoon.

'I don't find it makes much difference, really,' said Phyllis, who seldom played anything more strenuous than an occasional game of croquet on Patricia's lawn, despite having been rather sporty at school.

'Doesn't it? Your Hugh must be jolly adventurous!'

'What's it got to do with him?'

'Well, darling, the men don't generally care for getting bloodied, not unless they're out hunting. Andrew won't come anywhere near me.' Seeing Phyllis's shocked expression, she laughed. 'Oh Lord, you thought I meant actual games, as in netball. You really are a goose.'

★

Sarita never made Phyllis feel ridiculous. She was never glib, indeed Phyllis detected a trace of melancholy in her nature, for all that they often laughed together. Her first husband had been half-French on his mother's side, and during that marriage she had lived for most of the time in Paris, which she now found she missed very much. Phyllis was surprised that Sarita had no nostalgia, though, for her childhood home. She said that Brazil felt like another world to her now, as remote as a place she'd read about in a book. She confided that she had always known she would come to Europe as soon as she was old enough to travel without her mother and father. She and her sister had been taught French and English from an early age and had had German lessons with their brother too, from when she was about twelve. There had been an atlas in their schoolroom which they had looked and looked at, touching the names of the great European cities with their fingers.

'We used to lie in the garden at home and imagine what Europe would be like, how we would swing down boulevards under tall lime trees buying all sorts of things, the things we had read about in books. We imagined soft leather gloves with buttons made from pearl; and beautiful nightclothes made of silk and Brussels lace; and little books of the great European poets bound in calfskin with gilt edges. And then we would dream of cold afternoons, coming in from snow to dark cafés selling *chocolat chaud* and all kinds of strange cakes. Our German teacher used to tell us about Sachertorte and Hanoverian butter cake and the wonderful smell in the cafés of almonds and cinnamon; and at home the cook used to make sometimes rhum baba, so we thought there must be hundreds of things like this, different ones in each country, things that we had never tasted. Did you know there is a little cake in France called a financier? We saw that name in a book and wondered what it could be. We imagined everything we would try, once we got away. We never thought of other kinds of food, only pastries . . . And we imagined our-selves standing on ancient stone bridges arching across the Seine, the Thames, the Tiber . . . these names had a magic for us.'

'There was a place in Belgium that did the most wonderful little cakes and things made of choux pastry, all in doll's house sizes: we used to get them once a week for the children, as a treat. Eclairs the size of a baby's finger. But was it all as you'd imagined, once you arrived?'

'Oh yes. I was never disappointed. Paris is such a beautiful city, so much to see. The house, my husband's house, was very comfortable, very elegant. We would go to the opera some-times, the ballet. Yes.' She looked wistful. Phyllis wondered if she should ask what had been wrong with the first marriage, but she didn't like to pry.

'And did your sister come with you? Did she stay in Paris with you, after you were married?'

'No. My sister stayed behind. Rosanna . . .' she broke off. 'Every-thing was as I had hoped it would be, once I came to Europe. The one thing I didn't imagine was the grass. The grass is much better here than it is at home. There the grass is different: thicker and coarse, it scratches your legs, your feet. Here the grass is soft, like fur. I never used to walk on grass without shoes at home.'

'I love having bare feet. On grass, or sand; even wet sand. At Bosham when the tide's just gone out I sometimes go down to the steps at the bottom of the garden where the water meets the sea-wall and take off my shoes, so's to feel the squishing between my toes. It feels cold, from being covered with water. It gets warmer after the sun's been on it, before the tide turns. It's not exactly mud, but it's not quite sand either.'

Sarita smiled. 'You are the nicest woman in England.'

'I don't think I really can be,' said Phyllis.

'Everybody else wants something,' said Sarita.

★

Julia and Frances had not had a successful day of dolls' dress-making while their mother and brother were away. Both of them preferred cutting out to sewing, but they had been able to find only one pair of scissors and had squabbled as to who would have the use of them. The old nightdress their mother had provided as fabric refused to lie still on the table, but kept ruching; the scissors weren't sharp enough. Then after their difficult morning they had been given luncheon meat and beetroot. Beetroot, imagine, with no salad cream! No one could be expected to eat beetroot without salad cream on it. For afters the custard on the rhubarb crumble had had huge lumps and they didn't anyway like rhubarb, but preferred apple or better yet blackberry and apple. They had been made to rest after lunch when anyone could see that they were far too old to have a rest and then the afternoon had dragged on with nothing to do. They rather thought they would come to the camp-site with their mother tomorrow: it couldn't be any worse than staying at home.

'Don't say for afters, darling. Say pudding,' said Phyllis. 'And it's not blackberry time, yet. There'll be plenty of blackberry and apple, in due course.' She felt tired from trailing around after Nina all day. Had she and her sisters been as hopeless as Julia and Frances were at keeping themselves entertained, when they were girls? She was sure not. But they had had the ponies to keep them occupied, and the woods to play in. Perhaps it wasn't fair not to let her children ride; perhaps she could look into renting a paddock from some local farmer. But since they were going off to school in September, it would hardly be worth the bother. There was always Antonia, but her pony was sluggish and prone to kick. Could they ride with Venetia's children from time to time instead, or with Sarita's daughter Emilia? She resolved to find out.

★

At the camp-site the following morning Little Jim was waiting for them, ready to assign a task to Edwin.

'Tell you what: you and Frank are going to be on milk duty today. Soon as you hear the horn you come up here and start ladling milk from that churn into them white jugs, by the tea-pots. See? We want it all lined up, ready, so folk can take their cup of tea with them to table, same time as they get their meal. We don't want them milling around looking for their tea after they've eaten, or they'll stop here all day and we'll never get cleared up. Oh yes, and if you're going to be official, you'd better wear one of these.'

Jim handed him a silvery badge engraved with the circle and flash. Edwin could not have looked more pleased if he had been given a pound note.

Julia and Frances stood about, fidgeting and looking awkward.

'You girls go and join that table of Cadets, why don't you? Then you can introduce yourselves during breakfast, in time for some games later,' said Nina.

'Those boys at the far end look rather rough,' said Julia doubtfully.

'They may well be,' said Nina. 'Not everyone here is fortunate enough to come from your background, you know. You'll find they're good hearted fellows, once you get to know them. Everyone gets treated the same here.'

The girls trudged off.

'Do them no end of good to meet some of our Cadets. Put some spirit into them,' Nina told Phyllis. 'Where else are they going to get the chance to mix with lads from Stepney, or New-castle, or Manchester?'

'We never had to play with children of that kind,' said Phyllis. She felt indignant. 'Didn't do us any harm. And I don't notice Antonia being forced to come away from Rose Green to mix with the hoi polloi.'

'Quite,' said Nina. 'And look where it's got her. Tubby and friendless.'

'That's a bit mean,' said Phyllis. 'She can't help it.'

'You've been complaining that the children are under your feet – you should be relieved they've got something useful to do here. Look how Edwin's taken to it, already. The girls will be happy as sandlarks soon enough,' said Nina.

And it was true. There was quoits in the morning and a tug-of-war after lunch, after which a great gaggle of the young rushed down to the shingly-sandy beach to swim. Phyllis didn't set eyes on any of the children until after tea. It was the first day that she hadn't heard so much as a ghost of a whine from them since they'd come back to England. For all Nina's mutterings about the camp being an education, Phyllis was rather relieved to find that the morning study groups were optional. She had to admit that she was rather enjoying herself, too. Her sister seemed to know all sorts of people – it was fun going about the camp-site with her, stopping to talk and banter with various characters and checking things as they went: whether there were enough blankets and pillows, or whether they'd got in sufficient potatoes to last until Monday, or finding out how many had signed up for the talent contest scheduled for Saturday night and how many for the boxing competition.

'Never a dull moment, is there?' she said.

'I thought you'd like it here, I'm so pleased,' said Nina.

'I didn't say I liked it,' said Phyllis. Sometimes it didn't do to let Nina think she was getting her own way.

But Nina just grinned.

In London, Hugh too had been getting involved, having spent three days at what he now referred to rather proprietorially as HQ. Eric had asked Peter Heyward, whose Chichester speech Hugh had so much admired, to take him in and introduce him.

'I think the best thing I can do is get my speaker's licence, so I can be of active use as soon as possible. I'd have done an extra day if I could, but I had to go in to the company on the Thursday, to advise about association with northern European firms. Still, shouldn't take many more days, the speakers' training. The Leader is launching a peace campaign as a matter of the greatest urgency and naturally I want to help with that as much as I can. There are plenty of drivers and leaflet distributors and suchlike already: be a waste for me to do that sort of thing, quite honestly,' he told Phyllis.

'Do you have to have a licence, then, to speak? Surely you know how to speak already,' said Phyllis.

'To address meetings, yes. It's procedure. Everyone does, however naturally able.'

'We've all had rather fun with the campers while you were in town. We had a bonfire last night, and singing. Someone had a ukulele and it was priceless, because . . .'

'Oh good.' Hugh cut her off. 'You've most likely heard that the Leader will come down to camp himself one day the week after next. The Sunday, probably. He's really a man with the most tremendous magnetism. Never uses notes when he gives speeches, did you know? It's all from memory, or off the cuff. Remarkable man. I don't see how the hell else this country can remain at peace and come to any good. He's all for putting our national and imperial interests first, unlike most of the current lot.'

'He certainly seems to inspire immense loyalty. Nina says it's always packed out, the day he comes. A lot of trippers, apparently, from London.'

'Greville's asked us to dine this Saturday, by the way,' Hugh added. 'I must say, he goes up in my estimation.'

'Oh good,' said Phyllis.

Phyllis, 1979

Quite honestly it was a blessed relief that my father was dead before I went to prison. I don't think he'd ever have got over it. It's what other people would have thought, you see, that's what he couldn't have borne. He had been something of a county big-wig, a JP, Master of the local hunt in his time, when Mummy still rode, all that. There'd been some talk of him standing as a Member of Parliament, at one time. Of course he was high Tory, through and through. He would have minded terribly about me. He was a bit of a stickler for form.

People were, then. One of my father's cousins — a cousin he'd always particularly liked, they'd played tennis together, mixed doubles, when they were growing up — had an illegitimate child and he refused ever to have her through the door again. Wouldn't even send her a Christmas card. That was absolutely typical of people's attitudes at the time, even nice, gentle people like Daddy was.

My mother was still alive when I went in, but she was pretty gaga by then from the fall. Old Mrs Manville, who'd been with us since time began, looked after her in her final years. I don't know if my mother ever really took it in, I certainly hope she didn't. After I got out I never brought it up with her. What would have been the point? I hardly even saw her in the last year or two. It wasn't really worth it, going to visit: she couldn't seem to grasp who one was. Mrs Manville did all the talking for her, Mummy just sat there. And to be candid I didn't much relish having to be in the same room with Mrs Manville. Relations with Mrs Manville weren't of the best, not after the dressing-down she gave me. Not that it was any of her business, frankly.

You can't imagine what it was like at Holloway. There were maggots in the food — it was crawling, quite literally — and cockroaches everywhere, and the stench was unbelievable. They put the lights out at five in the afternoon and that was it; we were in total darkness for the next fourteen hours or so, at least we were in wintertime. It's funny, because it was actually the end of May when I went in and there was a hot summer that year, but in memory it was always winter. In fact, the thing I remember most vividly about the time in Holloway was the cold. We had a grimy-looking pair of sheets and two blankets each, but there was no heat in them, they were thin and stiff, like worn felt. You simply could not shake off the cold at night, irrespective of the season. It always felt like the worst bit of the winter, like February; that sort of chill you can't get rid of, the sort that feels as if it's coming from the inside of you. We'd get terrible chilblains. And of course you couldn't even have a bath, to get warm; there was never enough hot water. We only had a bath a week each, and that was if we were lucky and they hadn't rounded up a lot of tarts. Mind you, it was fun when those girls came in, generally at weekends: they kept us entertained with their stories. They were in good spirits, usually, because they knew they'd soon be out, that they were there for the one night, two at the most. We did like them, but it was maddening the way they used up resources, all the tea and the sugar and the bathwater.

On Sundays we got a small jam ration to have with our bread. I don't know why the bread always had to be stale. Perhaps they hung on to it, deliberately, until it was almost rock-solid; perhaps that was part of the punishment. The tea was just brown liquid, it tasted of metal and not tea at all. But at least it was hot. On Wednesdays there was sea pie — that was the one dish that was remotely edible. I forgot what butter tasted like, while I was there. We only had lumps of hard white margarine, like axle grease, once or twice a week. It may even have been lard. There weren't enough knives and forks for all of us — Lord knows why not — so we had to take it in turns. The last food was given out at four o'clock: what would have been tea-time, in one's old life. When we lived abroad I used to miss toasted tea-cakes and Garibaldi biscuits. You couldn't call the prison food any kind of supper — greasy cocoa and bread with cheese, or what they called cheese. A lot of us got tummy troubles. There was a particularly nasty bout of gastric flu that left a lot of us very weak. It was difficult to sleep, one was so empty.

At first we weren't allowed to get parcels. After a time they relented and people got cigarettes, and of course people smoked like mad because they were hungry. I hadn't been a smoker, but I became one. Still am, as you see. It kept the pangs at bay and gave one something to do. There were nearly seventy of us, on the wing: a wonderful group of women. I shall never forget the courage of those women. If it hadn't been for them I think I would not have retained my sanity. They were resourceful and always humorous. A tremendous bond of loyalty grew up among us. They were plucky. I think it would be fair to say that in their modest sort of way they were magnificent.

We kept in touch afterwards, after we got out. Letters, Christmas cards. And then in later years we would meet at the annual reunion in November. That dwindled too, of course, over time, although I always went. After we were released there were numbers of them I never heard from again, they didn't want to be reminded. You can't blame anyone for that.

5. Sussex and Buckinghamshire, July 1938

Phyllis took the three children to the camp-site every day. They had all made friends there: Edwin and little Frank were inseparable and Julia and Frances never now complained of boredom. Somewhat to her own surprise, Phyllis found that she, too, enjoyed the outdoor life with its routine and simple pastimes. It was so easy, not having to dream up things for the children to do every day, knowing they would be happily occupied. For her own part it was interesting meeting people from all over the country, sometimes joining study groups in the mornings, then spending the afternoons doing things she mostly hadn't done since schooldays, playing rounders or badminton or sea-bathing. Helping Nina with the endless lists and supplies was oddly pleasurable; it was nice to be of use, part of a community. It had never occurred to her before how isolated she had been living abroad, although in her heart of hearts she had considered that marrying a man so many years her senior had sometimes made her lonely. Or perhaps it was less to do with his age than his temperament. Hugh had always been very much preoccupied with his own concerns, the company and his place within the company and the people he encountered on behalf of the company: she had simply followed the drum. They had never stayed long enough in one place for her to have established a real life of her own. At the summer camp she felt a lightness of spirit and a sense of easy camaraderie she had not known since she was a girl, running half-wild out of doors with her sisters, playing in the woods and fields around the Grange, where they'd grown up.

Sometimes Edwin begged to be allowed to stay at the camp-site and Little Jim said the boy was welcome to bunk with his grandson Frank, any time. Young Frank's father kept a pub in Essex and could not get away, although he would be coming to join them for a couple of days towards the end of August. By the end of the second week Edwin was spending half his nights under canvas, while his mother and sisters generally went home before high tea was served, at five o'clock. On two or three occasions they had been persuaded to stay on for camp-fire singing or other entertainments, on evenings when Hugh was in London. Julia and Frances protested at the unfairness of their younger brother being allowed to sleep in a tent when they had to go home to a stupid bricks and mortar house every day, until Nina suggested that they could become proper campers for the special Cadet week. At twelve, Frances really belonged in the Greyshirt Youth group, but Nina was confident of being able to smuggle her in with the teenaged Cadets, provided fourteen-year-old Julia kept a bit of an eye on her and she didn't do anything silly. Julia and Frances were billeted in a tent with two older Cadets, both girls of seventeen. It had been fine to visit the camp in their home clothes for the odd day, here or there, but now they would need uniforms so as to fit in with the other youngsters. The girls were especially delighted with the silver belt buckle with its dramatic insignia, which made them both look very grown-up. Frances liked the secret society aspect of the buckle, the fact that outsiders wouldn't know what the symbol stood for. Julia tightened the wide elastic on hers, cinching the uniform in at her waist.

The Cadets holiday was to take place during the third week of camp. Phyllis decided that this would be a suitable time for her to make the much deferred visit to see her parents. Until now there never seemed to have been a spare day. She asked Hugh.

'Can't you get one of your sisters to go?' he said. 'I'm really rather caught up with things in London at present. Anyway, you'll have the children to keep you company. Julia can help with the cases, if you can't find a porter.'

'I wasn't thinking I'd take the children,' said Phyllis.

'Oh?' said Hugh. 'Surely the whole exercise is so that the children can see their grandparents. And vice-versa.'

Hugh's own mother had died when Julia was a baby, before the other two were born. 'I didn't think there was much point,' said Phyllis.

Nina would clearly be far too busy for the foreseeable future, so she approached Patricia.

'Yes, of course, darling,' said her sister at once. 'We can get Hitchens to take us up. It's such a bore otherwise, one has to change trains twice.'

'Really? It isn't too much trouble?' asked Phyllis. She felt a rush of gratitude and affection for Patricia.

'We won't have to stay the night if we go by car,' said Patricia. They both laughed.

As a girl Phyllis had been taken to her aunt and uncle's house in Northumberland, a long journey undertaken in order for her father to offer some little succour to his brother, who had just received bad news. Everything in that house of grief had seemed motionless, as if under a spell. The only things that seemed to move were the flies which buffeted the glass of the bedroom windows and then lay dead, sprinkled like black confetti, on the windowsills. Her uncle was her father's older brother. His only son, Timothy, had been killed at Arras. The boy's mother was said to be inconsolable, a word which had made Phyllis half expect to hear her shrieking and sobbing and stomping about in the attics, like the first wife in *Jane Eyre*. Instead she found her aunt had been effaced, the somewhat hearty woman who had gardened in all weathers replaced by a wraith who seldom emerged from her room and barely spoke. There was a quiet in the house which was denser than ordinary silence, as if it had been thickened with sorrow. On her way up to bed, Phyllis had tiptoed along the landing and stood in front of the door to Timothy's room, daring herself to look in. But she had not been brave enough. She was frightened she might see his uniform, that there might be bloodstains on it, although when she told her sisters about this later they said she was being silly, and that his uniform would have been buried with him, in France.

Phyllis had not seen her cousin for some time – he was six years older and had been away at school on an earlier visit – but he had been a figure of interest and affection among the three sisters, the only male relative of their generation. When he'd last come with his parents to the Grange he had been kind to her, the pudgy youngest, asking her to be his croquet partner against her sisters. He was a dear boy. Patricia, closer to him in age, had taken it especially hard and was red-eyed for many days after they heard the news. It was a tragedy, everyone said so. Phyllis remembered her father saying that the name had died with Timothy and now there would be nobody to take it into the future. Hating to see her father sad, she had volunteered: 'But I'm young, Daddy. I've got the same name, I'll look after it.' But her father had said she would marry and take her husband's name, as would her sisters: it wasn't possible for them to keep the name alive.

Now, as she crossed the familiar threshold of the Grange, Phyllis was taken aback by how unaltered the place was. Here, too, time appeared to have stopped. She felt almost as if she was no longer a married woman with three children of her own, but a girl; a young girl with tangled hair, still breathless with schemes and ideas for games, about to run into the house leaving the door open and call up the stairs to her sisters. She had heard people say that childhood places seemed diminished after a long absence, but it did not seem so to her. The Grange felt as capacious as ever, with its high ceilings and long flight of shallow stairs. The house had its own particular smell, waxy but with a slightly sour note, like the oil that their father used to clean his guns after shooting, mixed with the distinctive tang of old mackintoshes: a boot-room smell. The long-case clock continued to tick in the hall where old copies of *Horse & Hound* and *The Field* were still stacked on a round table. The passage of time was further concealed by each liver and white spaniel giving way to an almost identical successor, all with the same matted ears and doleful expression, as if the same dog had lived for many decades. The only changes were outside the house. The walled kitchen garden – once their father's favourite part of the garden – produced more nettles and fewer vegetables with each passing year: buddleia took root in stony corners. They kept no horses of their own any more. After their mother's fall their father had stopped riding and the stables were now occupied by a handful of mothy-looking ponies belonging to the huntsman's daughter.

'You must pick the redcurrants, while you're here,' said their father after he'd kissed them hello. 'It'd be a shame to let them go to waste.'

'After lunch, shall we?' said Patricia.

He led the way into the morning room, where their mother was sitting. She looked vaguely at her daughters. Her feet, in grubby tartan slippers, poked out from the old green rug on her knees. It was possible to see her ankles, which were swollen and a mottled, purplish colour.

'Look, darling, here are the girls to see you,' said their father.

'Have they brought the post?' said their mother.

Patricia laughed. 'No, are you waiting for an important letter?'

Their mother smiled ruefully.

'It's a pity Penelope couldn't have come with you,' said their father.

By Penelope he meant Nina. She had stopped using her given name in her schooldays. Only their father called her Penelope now. Their mother didn't call anyone anything.

'Yes, isn't it?' said Patricia. 'She's frantically busy with her summer camps.'

'She's a very capable young woman,' said their father. His middle daughter had always been his favourite.

'She's certainly a bossy-boots,' said Patricia. 'If that's what you mean by capable. She practically goes about with a whistle on a string around her neck, these days.'

Before her fall their mother might have murmured some light remonstration, but now she said nothing.

'Penelope likes to get things done,' said her father.

'Has she brought the post, then?' asked their mother.

Phyllis had not spoken since entering the house.

She knelt beside her mother's chair. 'How are you, Mummy?' she said. Her voice sounded much louder than she'd meant it to, as if she was talking to a foreigner.

'Well, you see, this wretched door won't open,' her mother said sadly. Phyllis looked over her mother's head at Patricia for a clue.

'Which door is that, Mummy?' said Patricia.

'It's . . . I don't know,' said their mother. She shrugged.

'Never mind. We'll get it sorted out later,' said Patricia.

'What door does she mean?' Phyllis asked her father.

'I'll just go through and see what Mrs Manville has arranged about something to drink for you after your journey,' he said.

Phyllis stood. She and Patricia loomed on either side of their mother's chair. 'Has the post been, do you know?' their mother asked.

'I don't know, Mummy. Shall I go and see?' said Patricia. She went out into the hall. Phyllis was left alone with her mother. She knelt beside the chair again.

'I've come back to live here, Mummy. We're not living abroad any more,' she said. She tried to bring brightness into her voice.

'Here? Are you living here now?' said her mother.

'Well, not actually here, not in this house. In a house of our own. Near Patricia and Penelope. In Sussex. Not too far away though.'

Her mother looked intently at her, like a robin watching a gardener. Phyllis felt two things at the same time. The first was that her mother was very present and could see clean through her, was perfectly aware of all the reluctance and false cheer in her. The second feeling, just as strong, was that she could grasp nothing whatsoever, as if she lived in another language, another territory. The place where these contradictory certainties met and could not be made to tally was forlorn. It was a relief when Mrs Manville came in with a tray, followed by her father and sister. If there were enough of them in the room at any one time they could muddle along, papering over the cracks.

They got through what remained of the morning. Before lunch they went out into the garden, their father leading their shuffling mother by the arm, still in her slippers. Her feet were too swollen to fit into her shoes. There was nothing very much to look at but the few remaining flowers of the stiff hybrid tea roses and the handful of plump bees hovering over the lavender bushes. The lavender had faded to the colour of ash. Phyllis pinched a papery flower between finger and thumb and sniffed, but only the faintest trace of its scent clung to her skin. There was a crack on the stone plinth of the sundial.

'Shall we go up to the kitchen garden now?' Phyllis asked her father.

'Rather far for your mother. You girls can go up after lunch-eon,' he said. 'Take a trug for the fruit.'

Mrs Manville had arranged a mostly cold lunch on the dining-room sideboard. There were lamb cutlets encased in brown jelly and a cucumber salad. Warm new potatoes had left dewdrops of steam on the lid of the serving dish.

'Tuck in,' said their father.

Their mother smiled broadly for the first time. 'Yes, tuck in,' she echoed.

'This aspic is like shoe-leather,' said Patricia. The spoon made a sucking noise, as she lifted it from the firm jelly. It sounded like a boot being pulled from mud.

'The Belgians are mad for aspic,' said Phyllis. 'They have it with everything, even eggs.'

'Heavens,' said their mother.

'Well, of course,' said Patricia. '*Oeufs en gelée.* Honestly dar-ling, you'd think Belgium was in deepest Zambezi-land, the way you talk about it. I mean, when it's slap-bang next door to France.'

'Don't they speak some queer sort of language, the Belgians, as well as French?' said their father. 'There were a group of them with us, during the war.'

Their father had been invalided out early on, when he had been hit in the shin by shrapnel. He still walked with a discern-ible limp.

'Flemish,' said Phyllis.

'No, that wasn't it,' said their father.

'I don't know, then,' said Phyllis.

'I thought I heard the post,' said their mother.

'That was Mrs Manville in the kitchen. I'm surprised you don't do something, to stop her crashing things about so. It would drive me mad,' said Patricia.

Neither of the older people responded.

'Haven't we been lucky, with the weather?' said Phyllis.

'Very good summer,' their father agreed.

'It's so nice where we are, at Bosham. We have the most lovely view across the bay and one can have picnics every day, it's such fun for the children because . . .'

'Walloon! That was it,' their father interrupted her. 'Nice fellows, actually, although they can be rather gruff at first. What were you saying, Phyllis?'

'Oh, nothing really,' said Phyllis.

It was a relief when lunch was over and they could get out of the dining room and go up to the kitchen garden, just the two sisters. They had taken a basket and each had been handed a pair of ancient secateurs, but only Patricia had any actual interest in garden matters. Phyllis snipped a few bunches of redcurrants, to please her father. Patricia picked gooseberries, complaining that most weren't ripe enough. There was a blackbird inside the fruit cage. It looked at them quite boldly with its clear yellow-rimmed eye. They saw that almost all the raspberries were gone. It was disappointing, since their father liked raspberries best, but so it seemed did the birds: there were several holes in the netting, which was intended to keep birds out. After a decent interval – they believed they had given it long enough for their father to feel they'd completed a proper tour of inspection – they strolled back down the mown path that sloped towards the house. Phyllis took a couple of gooseberries. She enjoyed the feel of them – so hairy – in her hand, but when she bit into one it left a streak of bitterness across the roof of her mouth.

As they came down the grass bank of lawn, a small box-like car came into the drive. There was something not entirely serious, even comic, about the little car. It was as if it were a home-made contraption heroically pretending to be a real, road-faring vehicle. The car came to a standstill by the front porch and a very tall, very thin man got out. It seemed barely possible that someone so long and lanky might emerge from such a small machine.

'Good Lord!' said Patricia. 'It's Jamie. Look, Phyllis.'

'I can see. I can see who it is,' said Phyllis.

Patricia called out to him and the man turned, shielding his eyes from the light with a hand. She almost skipped down the grass towards him while Phyllis held back a little. As she approached she saw that he was blushing deeply. She could feel her own cheeks burning, too. Patricia had already taken his arm and was prattling nineteen to the dozen.

'. . . so you can imagine!' she finished.

'Hello, Jamie,' said Phyllis now.

'Phyllis. How are you?' he said. She was surprised to see that his hair was long, growing over his ears to well below his collar. He was wearing a corduroy jacket the colour of sand and the top button of his shirt was undone. He looked as if he had been much in the sun. She had not remembered how very white the whites of his eyes were. They were the colour of porcelain, like the eyes of a child.

'I wasn't expecting to see you. We . . .' Phyllis said.

'We came up to spend the day with Mummy and Daddy,' Patricia interjected. 'That's our motor. Hitchens brought us. He's in the kitchen, I think.'

'We were picking fruit,' said Phyllis, holding up her basket. The redcurrants were translucent like glass beads, glowing against their pale green leaves.

'Yes,' said Jamie, grinning. 'Yes, I can see you have. I was just returning the cylinder of your Pa's mower. You're back, then?' he asked Phyllis.

'Come in, do. I'd offer you some tea, only we've not long had lunch and I fear Mrs Manville might cut up rough,' said Patricia.

'I mustn't stay,' he said.

'We came back a few weeks ago,' Phyllis answered. 'To Sussex, I mean: not here. The children's schools, you know.'

'Of course,' said Jamie.

'I'm sure Ma and Pa would love to see you,' said Patricia.

'They can see me any time, I wouldn't want to get in the way,' said Jamie.

'Oh, but you're not in the way,' said Phyllis. She was surprised to hear how indignant she sounded, as if someone had been scolding him, instead of asking him to come in.

'I've got to get back, I've got someone coming about buying some of the farm equipment I'm not going to be needing any more. Sheep gubbins.'

'Well, next time we're here we must telephone ahead so you can join us for luncheon. To tell you the truth I simply didn't think you'd be about. You were away for a time, weren't you?' said Patricia.

'I was. But there are things to see to now.' He smiled a little ruefully.

After their drive home that evening, Phyllis declined Patricia's offer of supper. It was unusual for her to have the house to herself, but tonight all the children were ensconced at the camp-site and Hugh was in London, staying at his club. Just for once, she didn't read. She walked through the empty rooms, not switching on the lights, enjoying the quiet, the almost-darkness. The outlines of the furniture were familiar and comforting. It was cloudy, and beyond the lawn it was impossible to tell where the sea ended and the sky began. She thought about Jamie. It had been he who had found their mother, after her accident. He had run back to the Grange to call for help and then returned to the field where their mother had fallen, to wait with her. It was he who had calmed her horse and led it back to the stables. Phyllis had gone out to thank him and found him in the stall on the hay, standing with his face buried against the animal's flank, weeping. She had never seen anyone except her sisters cry before. It felt as if she was witnessing something she was not meant to see, something intensely private, and yet she did not turn back to the house. She felt drawn towards him, as if gravity was pulling her, pulling her towards him. She stepped forward and reached out to feel the line of his shoulder blade under her outstretched hand. The heat of his skin through his shirt was startling and somehow surprising to her, as if crying should have made him cold to the touch. Jamie had not said anything, but had turned around and leaned down and in, so close that she could feel his breath against her face. He had cupped the back of her head with one hand and brought his face even nearer towards her. His lips had just found hers when they'd heard Nina calling from the yard. Phyllis had sprung back, alarmed to be feeling such an unexpected sense of deliciousness when she should have been wretched. Neither of them had said a word.

They had never mentioned what had happened: Phyllis wondered if he even remembered.

He would be alone at the farm now that his mother had died, after less than two years as a widow. She wondered if he got lonely. Probably not: he had always been self-sufficient, even when they were very young. He liked tinkering with things, clocks and woodwork and mysterious bits of machinery. It was they who had always sought him out as their playfellow, not the other way around, even though he was an only child. Without a brother, or any local cousin, Jamie had been the one boy they knew. Once they'd enlisted him as an unofficial fourth member of their childhood club of three, his natural sweetness of temperament had ensured that he never jibbed at any task they set him. He soon became the Robin Hood to their trio of Maid Marians, in the long involved games which took place in the beechwoods which separated the farm from the Grange. The girls poked pheasant's feathers into the bottom of their plaits and even smeared a little earth below their eyes sometimes, conflating Nottingham's heroine with the Red Indian girls they'd seen in their story-books. Jamie was their chief den-builder and principal boy. Later he became their somewhat reluctant practice dance partner. He had been an atrocious dancer: it was like trying to dance with someone made of Meccano.

'How was Daddy?' Nina asked Phyllis, at the camp-site the next morning.

'Same as ever,' said Phyllis.

'Oh good,' said Nina. She didn't ask after their mother.

Phyllis decided she wouldn't tell Nina about seeing Jamie. Her sisters meant well, of course, but they could be so interfering.

'Mrs Manville was pretty surly. I don't know why they keep her on, frankly. The lunch was awful.'

'Well, because she's devoted to Mummy. Who else would they find? They're used to her, anyway.'

In the half-empty canteen tent that lunchtime Phyllis noticed that Julia had taken advantage of her mother's absence to curl the ends of her hair and now wore it pinned up at either side of her head. The style made her look older.

'You look nice, darling,' said Phyllis.

Julia pulled rather a sheepish face. 'The girls lent me some Kirby grips. They do theirs every night. They put bits of paper round the pins,' she said.

'They being nice to you, then?'

'Oh yes. Very nice.'

'And not leaving Frances out?' There was no sign of her younger daughter.

'Well . . . she is quite a bit younger. But I think she's all right. She's found some boys to play with. I b'lieve they're playing cricket down by the gate.'

In fact Frances and one or two other girls, as well as a large gang of the boys, had gone across the lane from the camp-site on to the strip of grass which banked between the beach and the land, where marine flowers stuck up rigidly from the sand-sprinkled turf. They looked unreal, as if they were made of pipe-cleaners. Here the young campers had found an old beach truck on rails, standing at the top of the slope which gave down to the shingle of the beach. It hadn't taken them long to work out that if three or four of the stronger boys gave it a good shove, several others could pile in and be shimmied, squealing, in the direction of the sea. Once it was at a standstill they could hop out and quite easily push the empty truck back up the rails for another go. Soon a queue had formed, everyone wanting a turn. This they had been doing for most of the morning. One of the East End lads had already named the truck the *Shoreditch Express*. Phyllis knew that it would take someone with a more forceful nature than her own to make the young campers stop and come back to the dining tent in time for lunch. Let some-one else come and fetch them. She strolled off along the beach with her thoughts.

Half an hour later back at the camp-site all thought of whether the children had eaten their lunch had apparently been forgotten.

'Have you heard? There's terrific news!' Phyllis recognized the girl as one of the Cadets Julia had made friends with.

Phyllis gestured towards the sea. 'I was just . . .'

'The Leader is coming! He's coming to see us all!'

Phyllis went in search of Nina, whom she found in a state of high excitement. There had been rumours of a visit – always it was said to be imminent – and contingency plans had been made. The wooden huts which were reserved for such an occa-sion were to be aired and swept, stocked with clean linen and towels. Now the small tent used as a bookshop and library was to be cleared for the Leader's use, so that he would be able to talk with one or two key people without being overlooked. The whole site was to be neatened up, ship-shape and ready for inspection. The central area by the flagpole was to be mown. Not that the Leader was a stickler: in previous years he'd been more interested in sea-bathing and general fun than in any formality. It was a question of presence, Nina said. That was the great thing about the Old Man. It didn't matter whether he was addressing thousands in a city hall, or taking to the waves with a handful of campers: there was an authority, an ease, a natural air of command about him in all situations. Soon Phyllis would see for herself.

6. Sussex, August 1938

It was a minefield. Her new friend Venetia Gordon-Canning had invited Phyllis and Hugh to meet the great man at dinner on the Saturday evening when he was to be staying with them; and then Patricia had asked them to lunch on the Sunday, also for Phyllis to meet him. Neither of them had asked Nina, who was still hoping – along with everyone else at the camp-site – that the Leader would stay overnight in the pristine bunk of the wooden shed. Patricia had not invited the Gordon-Cannings to her luncheon party, nor had Venetia asked Patricia and Greville to her dinner the night before. Neither was sure whether he would be coming with his wife or alone, which played havoc with seating plans.

Nina and Patricia and even the usually irreverent Venetia spoke of the coming visit in awed tones. All three of them believed that Phyllis's first glimpse of the Leader was to be at their behest: they each talked as if they were bestowing a great gift upon her. Both hostesses had requested that Phyllis keep the details of their invitations to herself and this made her uneasy, since she was sure both her sisters would discover her deception. She felt especially awkward about Nina's exclusion from the rarefied world of cut glass and engraved cigarette cases and high gossip in which she found herself included. Matters were further complicated by the fact that everyone seemed to have different names for him. The rank and file at camp referred to him as either the Leader or Sir Oswald. Nina and Eric and the other more senior camp officials also referred to him as the Leader, but tended to prefer the slightly more familiar OM or its extrapolation, the Old Man. Patricia and Venetia and their husbands called him Tom: all his social circle did. So he was Tom when the Gordon-Cannings spoke of him as a guest or friend, but they both switched to the Leader when touching on Party business or politics; a habit which Hugh had adopted. Venetia let slip that his new wife always addressed him as Kit. Phyllis had no idea what to call him.

In the event, it hardly mattered. Phyllis did not get the chance to meet him during the day he spent at the camp, when he was constantly surrounded by enthusiastic campers and minor Party officials. Mobbed, really. An atmosphere of high gaiety marked the visit, an almost electrical charge, as if a brighter lightbulb had been inserted into the lamp of the day. He spoke of a Britain restored to greatness, yet encompassing all that was best about the industry and invention of the present day: 'From the ashes of the past shall rise a Merrie England of gay and serene manhood and adorned by the miracle of the modern age and the modern mind.' It was heady stuff.

Phyllis wasn't seated next to him at Venetia's dinner, of which she was glad, for what would she be able to find to talk about with such a powerful and important man? But she was pleased at least to have been introduced. He was the most well-known person she had ever met. Probably everyone in the country knew his name, recognized his face. As they shook hands, this thought made her too awed to take in more than the flash of an eye, a scrutiny which seemed to go on ever so slightly longer than it needed to. There was something tawny, a bird-of-prey glint. He carried his head in a very distinctive way, almost as if he were a military official surveying the troops. Imperious. She'd heard he was a champion fencer and wondered if this was why he made her think of Errol Flynn, a resemblance increased by his narrow moustache and pomaded hair. She had no opportunity to actually talk with him, but it was fascinating to watch him, up at the far end of the dinner table. He had such poise, such ease. She strained to catch something of his conversation. After dinner the men stayed a long time in the dining room, and when they emerged he took a seat by Venetia, on the sofa. Venetia laughed elaborately whenever he said anything.

Arriving at her sister's for lunch the following day, she could see that Patricia was nervous. She was flustered and snappish.

'Antonia, could you take the others outside before lunch? There's time for a game of croquet, if you don't dither,' she suggested.

'I don't really want to play croquet,' said her daughter.

'Well then, can't you run about on the lawn, play grandmother's footsteps or something. Honestly! What I mean is, I don't want the young taking up all the chairs in the drawing room.'

'Oh.' But still Antonia lingered.

'Go on then, please darling. Don't hover. It's a lovely day.'

Greville's sister Loelia was staying, with her husband Peter. She was a nice woman, with slightly protuberant eyes, like a pug. The drawing room was full of Patricia and Greville's friends: Pea-Brain, the Templetons, the Orde-Windhams, the Thredhams. Phyllis was glad to see Sarita, graceful in fawn silk, with a double strand of pearls fastened with a sapphire clasp the size of a Fox's Glacier mint. Everyone fell silent when the guest of honour arrived. Greville fetched him a drink while Patricia took him around, making introductions.

'We meet again,' he said to Phyllis.

'Why, have you met before?' said Patricia sharply.

'Only just in passing at the camp yesterday. We . . .' said Phyllis.

'Oh yes, well, the camp. And of course you know Johnny,' said Patricia, moving on.

As he shook Johnny Thredham's hand Mosley glanced back at Phyllis. There was a frankness and complicity in his look which made her feel terribly exposed. It was almost as if he were an X-ray camera and could perceive in her something wicked that she herself had not identified and could hardly welcome. Phyllis felt overwhelmed by his gaze – was this what people meant by star-struck? She lowered her eyes and stared into her sherry glass instead, waiting for him to look away. She was relieved that once again she had not been seated near him. As soon as he was introduced to Sarita he had eyes only for her: Patricia was clearly put out when he did not turn towards her after the first course had been removed, but carried on talking to Sarita until nearly the end of pudding. And Patricia had further cause to look pained when, towards the end of lunch, a disagreement between Hugh and Greville veered close to a quarrel. Hugh repeatedly asked whether his host was actually a Party member. At first Greville had attempted to deflect the question, but at last he could bat it off no longer.

'I'm sure Tom won't feel remotely slighted that I'm not. We've talked a great deal over the years and he knows my views. But quite frankly the only organizations I care to belong to are those my father was a member of.'

'The Party isn't an old school or a club. It's rather more important than that,' said Hugh. Phyllis noticed an obstinate set to his features which suggested he had had rather more to drink than was his custom.

'The zeal of the newly converted,' said Johnny Thredham in a lowered tone.

Fergus Templeton spoke up. 'Speaking of clubs, there's an old boy I sometimes get talking to at White's. I've never heard him say anything except "Splendid!" Don't think he can really hear one. It's remarkable how well it does as a response to almost everything. Except when someone says something gloomy, then it can go a bit wrong. Simon Lancaster was describing a funeral they'd been to and the old fellow kept saying, "Splendid. Splendid."'

Everyone smiled, relieved.

Pea-Brain spoke. 'Reminds me of a story I heard the other day. You all know Jimmy Jenkinson, I take it? Northants? Well, the local vicar wanted to see him about something or other, so JJ's wife had made him promise he'd behave himself from eleven thirty until midday and then she'd come in under some pretext so they could get rid of the fellow. So the vicar arrived promptly but he would keep boring on about this and that. You know what clerics are like, they get one foot in the door. Anyway, JJ got a bit twitchy as the hour approached and in the end he heard the clock chime. His wife came into the room as promised, so JJ stood up and said: "Ah vicar, you'll have to excuse me. It's twelve noon and I've got to fuck the nanny." And luckily the vicar was deaf as a post so he just rose and said: "Of course, of course."'

There was general laughter.

'How priceless!' said Patricia.

Phyllis looked at her. In other company she would have been shocked by such talk.

'Very colourful,' said Hugh.

'Mrs JJ was not best pleased,' added Pea-Brain.

'I should think not,' said Greville. 'But I daresay she soon got over it. Caroline Jenkinson's a good sort.'

'She's forgiven JJ far worse than that,' said Johnny Thredham.

'Quite,' said Pea-Brain.

The earlier awkwardness was forgotten among the lunch guests, but Phyllis knew that she had not heard the last of it. Her husband was sure to go on complaining about what he saw as weakness in his brother-in-law. It would spoil their journey home and possibly beyond, if she couldn't find a distraction.

76

In private Hugh often described Greville as 'lily-livered', and this question of Party membership was a sore point with him. It was all very well, entertaining the Party grandees, but real allegiance went rather deeper than the luncheon table. Hugh himself had joined up with enthusiasm and carried his membership card everywhere, tucked into his wallet as if it were a passe-partout.

A few days afterwards Venetia came for tea.

'Isn't he attractive?' she said. 'Everyone thinks so. All he has to do is look and one's horizontal. I know I was. Promise you won't breathe a word, though, won't you? Andrew's loyalty to the cause probably doesn't extend quite as far as allowing his wife a roll in the hay with Tom.'

Phyllis giggled. She was getting more used to Venetia. She chose to believe that her friend was endearingly mischievous, where once she might have thought her immoral. She felt lucky that someone so sophisticated should enjoy her company.

'Of course he was much more fun before he was married,' she went on.

'But I thought he'd always been married. Wasn't he married before?' said Phyllis.

'Oh, he was. I meant before he was married this time. When he was still married to poor Cim.'

'Oh,' said Phyllis. 'Are there children?'

'Three, with Cimmie. Her sister, his former sister-in-law, looks after them I believe. Not the sister he had the affair with, the other one: the horsey one. Obviously someone as busy as he is couldn't be expected to be in charge of a nursery. The talk now is that Diana's expecting a baby.'

'Crikey, that all sounds very muddling. Is he faithful to her, the new wife?'

'Heavens, no, I shouldn't think so. One rather hopes not,

anyway. The thing that's irresistible is that he always looks a teensy bit bored and yet a teensy bit amused at the same time. So one longs to win over the amused part of him and banish the bored part. I'd practically tap-dance if he asked me to. One would do almost anything to make him be pleased with one,' said Venetia.

Such loucheness was in sharp contrast to the jubilant talk at camp. Here it was agreed that the visit had been characterized by typical Leader weather: a brilliant day, hotter and clearer than those which preceded or followed. Old hands insisted that his sojourns – for he had been known to stay overnight, in previous years – were always marked by such a favourable climate. OM adored sea-bathing and could always be relied upon to be the first into the waves, so it was fortunate that he brought such weather with him. What was remarkable too was the feeling that everyone who met him came away with, the sense of an encounter that was unhurried, warm and entirely their own. And he was a true gentleman who saw the individual in each one of his followers, while bringing the same genial interest and authority to every encounter. In the afternoon he had addressed the campers from an impromptu platform on a trailer in the middle of the field. He could not have inspired them more had he been speaking at the carved lectern of one of the great historic halls of Westminster. No one standing there on the sun-whitened grass was in any doubt that he could lead a proud nation and her dependencies to a bright future. The tragedy was that such a project as his was very far from the nation's heart at present. Everyone at camp believed that here was the one man who could drive a final death blow into the already weak and dying behemoth of the League of Nations; a contemporary Saint George ready to slay the dragon. If only his message could reach everyone in the land!

A renewed spirit of resolve came over the campers. Fresh air and education and good fellowship were all very well, but there was important work to be done. Rumblings as to the likelihood of another continental war could no longer be ignored: all must do their bit. Educational talks were scheduled, every afternoon before tea. In attending these, Phyllis grew to have a deeper understanding of what the Party proposed. First and foremost, there would be no question of participating in any military engagement which did not directly threaten Britain or her Empire. Phyllis believed this very ardently. It was all right for her, of course: Edwin was only a boy. There was no question of him going off to war; he would not be old enough to serve, not for years and years. But her heart went out to other mothers, mothers of older sons. One or two of them spoke, as the campers sat listening on bales of hay. Their conviction and commitment to the cause of peace was very real. Many women would already have lost brothers, uncles, fathers – even, among the older generation, sweethearts – to the dreadful toll of the 1914–18 war. Another such conflict simply could not be countenanced. The path to a lasting peace was clear, as laid out by Mosley.

Like Italy and Germany, Britain must simply withdraw from the struggle for world markets and become self-sufficient, while developing her domestic and imperial resources. The interference of the League of Nations must be brought to an end.

It was agreed that small groups of the more senior officials should set out for neighbouring towns in the coming afternoons, in a drive to enlist fresh supporters. Interested parties would be invited to the camp for an afternoon of entertainment and informal education. It was an excellent advertisement for the cause: well-organized, onward-looking and peopled by enthusiasts of all ages. It made sense to drum up support at such a time as new recruits could observe for themselves the Party machine in its splendid operation. Cadets should also play their part. Julia and the girls she was bunking with were to hand out leaflets on the promenade at Worthing, while other groups of Cadets would be deployed to Bognor and Littlehampton. In their sharp uniforms the young would attract notice, distinct as they would look from the trippers. The handsome Freddy knew how to drive, so he and a couple of the other young men would take a group each, in cars borrowed from the more senior campers. If these lads turned the head of some passing young woman, so much the better.

Hugh had no need to be in London for the next fortnight and he planned to take advantage of his leisure by finding a suitable plot on which to construct a house. He had been drawing up plans, incorporating some of the features of continental property into his design. There would be a veranda along the garden side of the house, where cane furniture could be arranged so as to be able to take tea in the open air. Steps from this veranda would lead down to the lawn. More radically, he intended to install a shower over one of the baths, having acquired the habit from their years abroad. Phyllis interpolated an occasional suggestion, but the project was very much Hugh's own.

'You wouldn't mind if Patricia joined me today, would you? Only she knows some people over at Littlehampton who might be amenable to selling building land.'

'Of course not. Why don't you ask her to stay on for supper, when I get back from camp? I've promised to help Nina with her interminable organizing this afternoon. She's trying to vary the meal rota so that the longer-stay campers don't keep getting corned beef hash.'

When Phyllis returned home she heard her sister's voice through the open door to the drawing room.

'. . . the thing with hydrangeas is that they look rather bedraggled unless one dead-heads immediately after flowering, but I do prefer them, all the same.'

'D'you know, I think I'd really sooner pampas grass,' said Hugh.

'Well, you must do as you like, of course. I do feel the ornamental grasses are rather suburban.'

'Hello darling.' Phyllis went over to kiss her sister. 'Did Hugh collect you? I didn't see your car.'

'Greville's taken it to town,' said Patricia.

'I shan't mind taking you home, after. It's no bother,' said Hugh.

'I do think you might've told me about having dined at the Gordon-Cannings,' said Patricia, turning to Phyllis.

Phyllis wished she wasn't so prone to flushing. People took it as a sign of guilt, when it was much more often the result of a sense of injustice. 'It made me look foolish in front of Tom,' Patricia went on.

'I'm sure it didn't,' said Phyllis. 'I hardly even met him at the dinner, I was right up at the other end of the table. He wouldn't have noticed me.'

'Well, anyway, you should be a bit wary of Venetia. She's tremendous fun, I know, but half of what she says is completely made up. I wouldn't trust her as far as I could throw her, I mean.'

'I wasn't intending to confide in her,' said Phyllis.

'Well, no, why would you? It's not as if you live a life of intrigue,' said Patricia.

When they sat down to dine, Hugh told Phyllis the news. Her sister and himself had visited the chap at Littlehampton and he'd agreed to part with a parcel of land. It was barely a couple of hundred yards from the beach and of a size which would give them a large garden; they might even have a tennis court, certainly a vegetable plot. He hoped to be able to build in an east/west configuration, with the veranda and drawing room looking west so as to get the best of the late afternoon sun. The dining room too would be on this side, while a smaller breakfast room would be constructed off the hall, facing east. In the mornings Phyllis would be able to take her coffee and write her letters there; perhaps they might install a nice little sofa, too, where she might like to sew or read. He had thought of everything. There were already two or three houses going up nearby, of comparable size. There was to be a small private road to the houses, which would number no more than a dozen. Hugh considered the usual north/south aspect a mistake, because it meant one side of a property was always in gloom. It was the devil's own job to find suitable plants for a north-facing wall: even a petiolaris couldn't be relied upon. At this Patricia nodded sagely. The aspect of these other houses might mean that his would have to be constructed side-on to its driveway so as to sit well within its allocated plot, but he foresaw no problem with such an arrangement, albeit unconventional. Patricia could not agree with him on this point, for how would any visitor know which was the front and which the tradesman's entrance? But Hugh would not be budged. Patricia teased him good-naturedly for being so stubborn. Phyllis listened to them talking, relieved that someone else was listening to Hugh's plans.

Hugh was very buoyed up. Phyllis did not wish to dampen his spirits by expressing any reluctance, but she did not look forward to leaving their rented house here at Bosham. She loved the situation, the garden which ran down to the harbour wall and the constant variety of the watery view. She loved the little boats with their sails catching the light, and the parties of children with their shrimping nets who hovered over the shallow pools which appeared at low tide. She loved to walk across the bay when the tide was almost out, when the retreating water created for an instant traceries of foam like lace upon the dark sand.

At least the move wouldn't happen for some time and they'd

be able to see out the summer here. The children would not have to adjust to their new home until the Christmas holidays. A house wasn't built overnight, as Hugh would tell her over and over again in the ensuing months. Nearly every time he said these words he assumed an expression of some portent, as if a great wisdom was to be delivered, before adding: 'Rome wasn't built in a day.' Then he would pause, almost as though he expected to be congratulated. Sometimes her husband struck Phyllis as a rather ridiculous figure. At such times she felt resigned, more than disappointed. He was a decent man, not unkind; it was his seriousness which made him a touch pompous at times, but seriousness was not after all a crime. People often remarked how fine-looking he was and it crossed her mind to wonder whether such expressions of admiration were offered as a sop; whether what they meant was: he may be a bit of an ass, but at least he's handsome. Perhaps what they were really saying was that he was too good-looking for a woman as ordinary as herself. In any event it was an occasional source of mild curiosity to Phyllis that neither his good looks nor others' admiration of them actually brought her pleasure. Her husband's appearance was simply a feature of life, as constant and unremarkable as the curve of a familiar hill. She wondered what people thought her reaction should be when they remarked upon it. Was she expected to be grateful?

The following day Hugh took Phyllis and the children over to see the site where the house was to be built. It was at present a small field with the neglected look of pasture overgrazed by ponies, like a moth-eaten old billiard table. The place seemed very exposed, without trees or features of any kind. Edwin was disappointed because he had been hoping for a tree-house and Julia, who now spent all her time at the camp-site, made no attempt to disguise her boredom. Frances alone expressed enthusiasm for her father's plans, walking slowly around the boundary with him, listening to all his ideas. She suggested that a sunken pond would look nice in the corner where the field dipped slightly.

'We could have goldfish and water-lilies and a little fountain,' she said brightly.

'That's a thought,' said Hugh. 'A flagged path might be rather an idea, with a low box hedge around.'

'I could play hopscotch there if it was flagged,' said Frances.

'Could we have a seat, looking back towards the house?' said Phyllis.

'We might find someone to copy the bench at Rose Green, the one that looks over the rose arbour,' said Hugh. 'It's rather a good shape. I'll ask Patricia.'

'How much longer?' asked Julia.

'Well, these things take time,' said Hugh. 'We haven't even finalized the design of the house as yet. There's the question of sculleries and pantries and larders and so on: they all have to be slotted in somewhere, without taking up all the best views.'

'No, I meant how much longer till we go? It's lunchtime, surely.'

Phyllis found it difficult to envisage them all living here. This bright air would be constrained within rooms, rooms with parquet floors and doors and door knobs, solid and implacable. Sedate clocks would chime the hours, rugs would muffle their footsteps. All the things that went into a house seemed daunting to amass: banisters and stair-rods and light switches and soap dishes and bath-racks and umbrella stands and pelmets, all weighing down upon this empty patch on which they now stood, replacing the fresh smell of the sea with heavy indoor smells of polish, beeswax and wood. This was Hugh's vision, to fashion a house and a garden to reflect himself, somewhere of substance. Phyllis felt a stab of envy that the children would not have to be rooted for ever within this constructed idea of his, but would over time be able to flit in when the weather was fair and then away as it suited them. Like swallows, or bats. Growing up would bring freedom to Julia and Frances and Edwin, but in her own life the reverse had been the case. Age and time had brought greater constriction. She could not help but feel less than thrilled about her life in the new house. It was not her dream, after all.

Phyllis, 1979

Jamie Dickinson. Not that he'd be part of your research: he had nothing to do with politics or any of that. I don't remember ever discussing anything worldly with him, not once. He was rather child-like, in that way. But he was important to me, you see. He liked all of us, my sisters and me: to begin with I think he liked us all the same. His parents farmed a dairy herd to the east of our house; they were much older than our parents even though he was the same age as Nina. He didn't have any brothers or sisters of his own; perhaps the Dickinsons were too old to have more children – it wasn't the sort of thing one inquired about.

Three girls next door with ponies and woods with a stream and a tennis court, of course we were a terrific draw for a solitary boy. If anything he and Nina seemed to make a natural pair, both being the practical ones, not like Patricia and myself. I was rather a dreamer, but now I'd say that Patricia was always scheming, that everything she did was calculated, from her teens onwards. For the rest of her life. But of course I would say that, wouldn't I?

We hardly ever went to his house. It smelt funny, fatty and a bit sour, because of the milking. His mother churned her own butter in the dairy off the kitchen. It had slate shelves to keep the milk cool and one tiny window, high up in the wall like the window in a cell. It had been made like that so the sunlight could light the room but not shine as low as the shelves, so its heat wouldn't spoil the cream and butter. There was tight wire mesh across the window to stop flies getting in. Once he took us in there to see a dead mouse floating on the top of a huge wide pudding basin full of cream: it all had to be thrown out, pints and pints of it. I can't tell you how disgusting the naked tail of a dead mouse looks, in cream: much more revolting than you'd imagine. And on the fur. It took away all the pity of it having drowned.

Our parents tolerated him coming to our house, but there was an unspoken feeling that it didn't quite do for us to go to his over-much. They were tenant farmers, which meant they didn't own their place, you see. I believe Jamie picked it up later, for a song: farmland was cheap, after the war.

Most days, especially on fine days, Jamie would just materialize. I don't think we ever made an actual plan. We'd get to the end of our lessons and he'd just be waiting outside, ready. He wore a squished dark green cap when it was cold. We had all sort of adventures, tremendous fun. We'd dress up as Indian squaws and he'd be a cowboy, coming to rescue us. One year we had a terrific craze for highwaymen and we'd take it in turns for two of us to hold up the other two. We used to take the jewellery Mummy kept in her dressing-table drawers, so we had valuables to relinquish. Someone made us those black eye masks with holes in them; it can't have been Mummy because she didn't sew — perhaps it was our nursery nurse. We had a tricorn, too, God knows where that came from. There was an old velvet opera cape that we used to fight over. It always seemed to be Patricia's turn to wear it.

It was only later that he grew to feel more deeply for me than for the others, I think. By then they had their sights set on other things; their horizons were widening — in Patricia's case, that is. Nina's horizon didn't widen exactly. It sort of slid across, like a photograph in a slide-show.

The others didn't perceive any difference in Jamie, of course. Nor in me. They weren't inclined to notice me very much, I was their younger sister and a bit galumphing and awkward; and I don't think they ever really looked at him, or not in that light, anyway. He was just part of the furniture of our childhood, he had been our playfellow for years and there was no reason for them to suppose he'd ever be anything else. He was like a cousin sort of figure really. That's how they thought of him. Even when we were all grown-ups they never thought I'd have any secrets, that I'd keep anything from them. They thought I was an open book. Patricia

87

believed she was the only one of us who was worth thinking of, the only significant one, if you like. But there were all sorts of things I didn't tell them, about myself and about other people.

There were little signs: he'd often try and bring his pony alongside me if we went out riding and he'd perform small courtesies like holding my pony's bridle when I came to dismount, where the other two were left to slide off unceremoniously. He wouldn't say anything, but he'd be there, holding the cheek-piece so my pony would stay still. Or when Patricia and Nina were expressing their opinions about something, he'd ask me what I thought. Sometimes when we played doubles, the four of us, he'd say a ball of mine was in when one of the others had called it out. Sometimes I knew myself that it had been out. Once after we'd eaten a picnic – I think I would have been about fifteen – we were all four lying on our backs in some long grass and part of his leg was against mine, the part above the knee but below the thigh; and he didn't move away and I could feel a sort of tenseness between us, where our legs met. I shifted my position a little bit so that the rest of our legs touched, all down the length of mine. His legs were much longer, even then. It wasn't that I noticed what his leg felt like so much as that it pressing against me made me acutely aware of my own leg, the heat and shape of it. It almost seemed to prickle, but in a nice way, like pins and needles, only without the hurting part. When we stood up he wouldn't meet my eye.

After that I began to see things about him, to look at him differently. Which is funny, because he looked like a crane-fly, really. Articulated, is that the word? Like one of those rulers with hinges that fold out to a great length. He was immensely tall and lanky and his hands were slightly too big for him, which he must have realized because he tended to wear his sleeves pulled down over his wrists. I don't know whether he had always done this, but I suddenly became aware of it after the time when our legs had touched and it seemed very poignant.

The thought that he might be ashamed of anything about himself made me want almost to cry. It made me want to take one of his hands in both of mine, to pull him in towards me, but of course I never did. Not then, anyway. That didn't happen until after the war. I wouldn't have known how to turn what I was feeling into something that could be communicated to him.

There was a gentleness. It must seem odd, to meet me now, that I should have been fond of someone like that, but I was softer when I was young. Experience hardens you. If it didn't, life could break a person. To look at him you might have guessed that he'd have a stammer, that's the kind of boy he was. He never pushed himself forward, he'd hang back slightly in the same way that a stutterer might. He wasn't like anyone else. Whether it was because I'd known him since he was a little boy, but it always seemed to me that there was something child-like about him. He had a sweetness of nature, a curiosity and naturalness, something so keen and true, almost other-worldly . . . it was as if he'd been touched with angels' wings. As if you could be kept warm on a cold morning by the goodness in him. That will sound fanciful I know, but it's true. What I'm trying to get at is, you couldn't not like him. Or more than that, perhaps, you couldn't not trust him: you could have told from one look at him that he was absolutely honourable and trustworthy. You could have handed him a million pounds and asked him to look after it for you and then disappeared for twenty years and know that he'd have put it somewhere in a safe place and that he'd give it back, untouched. He was the sort of person that if you gave him a sealed envelope it would never even occur to him to open it and sneak a look.

So that was Jamie. I would never have been allowed to what we used to call walk out with him. There wouldn't have been any future in it, my parents simply wouldn't have allowed it. All our county neighbours would have known, you see, that he was the son of the tenants. The only reason that Nina got away with marrying Eric was because he wasn't from the same patch as we were: people weren't so apt to look down on him. And she always had Daddy twisted around her little finger. Anyway, I don't want to talk about it any more now, it's all such a long time ago. Jamie Dickinson. I haven't said his name out loud for years and years.

7. Sussex, August 1938

Julia and two of the older Cadet girls had got themselves into hot water with the officials at the camp. On one of their leafleting afternoons in Worthing they had somehow got hold of a tin of enamel paint and a couple of brushes and had daubed the British Union flash and circle on the side of a theatre, as well as the letters PJ.

'In all honesty, nobody's saying they shouldn't have done it. Nobody's saying that. It was that they were seen doing it, that's the trouble,' Nina told Phyllis.

'But they shouldn't have!' said Phyllis. 'It's completely wrong. It's vandalism. Hugh will be absolutely livid. I can't think what must have come over Julia, she'd never have done anything like this before.'

'Still. People who do amateur dramatics are always such terrible busy-bodies. They've taken over what was the Picture-drome, you see. Nobody going to the flicks in the old days would have reported them. It's called the Connaught Theatre, nowadays: they're all very hoity-toity. It was a group of them coming out after a rehearsal who caught the Cadets.'

'It must have been a dare,' said Phyllis. 'I can't think why ever else she'd do such a thing.'

'They've all got crushes on that boy Freddy. 'Spect they did it to impress him. He was their driver, you see.'

'Julia certainly hasn't got a crush on anyone. She's much too young,' said Phyllis. Nina laughed.

'Why PJ, anyway? What does that mean?' asked Phyllis.

'Perish Judah.'

'Surely that's taking things rather too far? I don't suppose any of them have ever even seen a Jew. Well, I mean Julia will have, when we were abroad. But not so as she'd notice.'

'No one who puts the interests of this country first has anything to fear from our lot, the Leader's quite clear on that. But you can't ignore the fact that they have a great influence: too much, frankly. You have to question whether they're putting their own interests before ours. Industry, the newspapers: they've got their fingers in a lot of pies. Government, too. Hore-Belisha, our Secretary of State for War: he's a Jew. Frightful warmonger. Liberal – need I say more? It's abundantly clear that the Jews and their financiers have a vested concern in trying to goad us into another war against Germany. I've heard many speakers say so.'

'I can't see why anyone would want a war, whatever background they came from. Or religion, or whatever they are. And even if they did, Worthing hardly seems the place to stop them.'

'It's mostly the people from the London branches who get hot under the collar about it all. It's much more in evidence up there. You're not quite up to speed with it all, not that I'm blaming you or anything. It's because of you living overseas while all this has been building up. People feel there's a strong threat to British jobs, British businesses. There was some trouble in the East End a couple of years ago which became rather notorious. They're terrible trouble-makers, these Hebrews, especially at some of our London meetings: they come along just to stir things up for us. And as you know we've got a tremendous amount of supporters from those parts: you've met many of them at camp. Anyway, this'll blow over. I don't believe anyone's actually cross with Julia and the others for the doing of it, as I say. It's the being seen. It's just unfortunate they were in uniform. We don't want people around and about thinking we're hooligans.'

Phyllis wondered whether she could keep this incident from coming to Hugh's attention, and asked Julia not to mention it unless he did. There were only a couple of weeks of camp left to run and then Julia and the others would be off to school not long afterwards: it was entirely possible that he need not hear of it. Now that work on the house was beginning he was preoccupied with building matters and unlikely to come to the camp-site, but on the other hand he had become something of a figure in the Union locally and word would probably get out. People gossiped. Julia was, after all, the daughter of two active and by now fairly senior members. And Nina and Eric were well-known at London HQ and beyond, through their work at camp and on Party communications and printing; while Greville was an actual friend of the Leader's. An errant child with such relatives would be a gift to the newspapers. It would be a disaster if the press got hold of it. Phyllis's heart sank at the thought of having to tell her husband. Hugh had a great respect for other people's property and this was vandalism, when all was said and done. He would be furious with Julia and possibly displeased with Phyllis for having allowed their daughter the freedom of camp life, with its emphasis on people from all backgrounds mingling together.

She judged it wiser to say nothing. Of course there was the possibility that tongues would wag and Hugh would hear of it. But there was also a fair chance that he would not, in which case there was little sense in her bringing it to his attention. As it transpired, he did hear about the incident, but his response was not at all as Phyllis would have predicted. He laughed it off.

'You're not angry?' Phyllis asked.

'If Julia were the sole culprit I'd be of a mind to give her a ticking off, but I believe she was only one among a little group of them. Put it down to youthful high spirits,' said Hugh.

'But she can't go about daubing walls. It's barbaric.' Phyllis was surprised to find herself annoyed at her husband's unexpected clemency.

'We don't know for certain that she actually wielded the brush herself. And no harm's been done, to speak of.'

'Well no, but . . .'

'As a matter of fact – and I don't believe the young people concerned were aware of this – the theatrical troupe operating out of that place are frightful people. Not all of them, perhaps, but the folk in charge. Truculent. Apparently they refused us the hire of the place, a year or so ago. And not for any old meeting, either: the Leader himself was coming down to give a talk. A couple of the chaps in the office told me about it; the theatre people were quite rude. Said our views were against the principles of common decency, anathema, that sort of thing. The men in our office actually seemed rather pleased that Julia and her chums had made our presence known over there. Serve them right.'

'Yes, but even if the owners of the building are difficult or unpleasant, it's still not right to deface the place. You can't just go about painting slogans everywhere. I don't care for the sentiment they expressed, either. We don't want anyone to perish, surely? We simply want to put our own interests first. I do think we must impress that on Julia. It's a matter of right from wrong.'

Hugh put his hands on his wife's shoulders. 'They got a dressing-down at the camp, let's just leave at that shall we? It doesn't do to overreact.'

Phyllis thought of refusing to allow Julia to attend camp for the remainder of its tenure, but what would the girl find to do by herself all day, alone at Bosham while the others were out? Gating her seemed more trouble than it was worth. She would soon in any case be removed from the Cadets and reunited with her school-fellows; a placid group of girls they were, from nice families scattered about the Home Counties. These school-friends would have less of an influence upon Julia, or a better influence. Phyllis asked Nina to ensure that Julia made no further forays outside the camp-site. Instead she would help with the organization of the final week, when various send-off celebrations were planned, including an archery competition and a donkey derby along the beach.

But Julia had her heart set on joining the others for a final evening out. There was a plan for the youngsters to go to a dance-hall in Bognor. She begged to be allowed to go.

'Please, Mummy! It's my last chance to say goodbye to everyone.'

'We'll have to ask your father,' said Phyllis.

'He's already said I can go,' said Julia. 'It's just you, now.'

'Has he? When did this happen?'

'Earlier on. Yesterday, in fact.'

'Well, I see you are presenting me with a fait accompli. I can't very well refuse if your father has already given you permission. But you must be back at camp by ten o'clock.'

'I will, I promise,' said Julia.

Julia was true to her word, but the evening did not end when the group returned to the site. Instead, a gaggle of the boys led by Freddy raided the canteen, taking all the sausages which were earmarked for breakfast the following morning, and made a bonfire down on the beach. But no one took them to task. There was so little time left before they disbanded, and with the uncertainty and ill-ease of the situation in Europe some of the older campers had an unspoken sense that the young might not meet again in such carefree times. In earlier years there had always been lively talk of plans for the following summer, but this time everyone was more subdued.

'I gather there was singing around the fire until the wee small hours and then a few of them went bathing in the sea, with nothing on,' Nina told Phyllis.

'Not Julia, I'm sure,' said Phyllis.

'The girl's not a child, you know. She's rather more grown up than you think,' said Nina.

'She is only fourteen years old! We were still having supper in the nursery at her age,' said Phyllis. Nina often sounded rather knowing when she spoke about Julia. Phyllis blamed her brother-in-law for this unfortunate tone. Before Nina had met Eric she had never been coarse like this.

'I'm sure we'd have liked to have some fun, if there'd been any other children round and about,' said Nina.

'Well, there weren't,' snapped Phyllis.

'Only Jamie,' said Nina. 'And he didn't count.'

Neither sister spoke. Eventually Nina broke the silence.

'There's to be a meeting on Thursday to go over camp funds, make sure we've settled with all our suppliers and logged everyone's subscriptions. Will you come and lend a hand?'

But Phyllis felt cross, still.

'I'm not terribly good where accounts are concerned, I rather think I won't,' she said.

In any case Phyllis would be glad to have Thursday to herself, for she had people coming to dinner the next day: the Templetons, Patricia and Greville and the Gordon-Cannings. If it was fine she planned to serve drinks on the lawn first, so that her guests could make the most of the harbour view. An extra woman was coming in to help in the kitchen and to serve at table. Then on Wednesday Venetia rang and asked if she might bring her sister, who was staying. This meant they were a man short, so Phyllis telephoned Patricia's friend Pea-Brain, who seemed quite unperturbed at the lateness of the invitation. She was beginning to understand the man's popularity, for he was always so pleasant and affable. She was rather excited that they would be ten, now: a real party. She thought she might wear the good bracelet Hugh had given her as her wedding present, since they had such a crowd.

Once she'd made sure the glasses were set out for their after-dinner drinks in the drawing room – tumblers in case the men wanted whisky, as well as the little engraved glasses for liqueur – Phyllis went up to her room to dress. Hugh had already changed and was downstairs in the drawing room with the paper. Edwin and Frances came in and sat on her bed, watching as she brushed her hair and dabbed the cool glass stopper of her scent bottle against her wrists and throat.

'Can I try on the bracelet, Mummy?' asked Frances.

'Not now, darling, I've got to get back downstairs. If you're good and read your brother a story I'll let you have a go with it tomorrow. Where's Julia?'

'I think she's gone for a walk.'

'What a silly time to choose! She knows we've got people. I don't want her trudging about looking sorry for herself while they're arriving.'

The evening went well. Hugh and Greville greeted each other cordially and by tacit agreement they kept off politics. Hugh and Sarita talked about South America. Fergus Templeton and Andrew Gordon-Canning and Venetia's sister became happily animated about horses. There was county gossip and during the first course Pea-Brain flirted amiably with Phyllis, before addressing his attentions during the rest of dinner to Venetia's sister. After they'd eaten the women went through to the drawing room and Venetia regaled them with risqué stories. Even Patricia was in stitches. Before the men came in to join them, Phyllis asked if anyone wanted to go upstairs. Only Patricia did.

'I'll look in on the girls, say goodnight,' she said.

'Do,' said her sister. 'Edwin'll be asleep, but they'd love to see you.'

Patricia came back directly, unsmiling. It was futile trying to take Phyllis aside; the others were sure to overhear.

'Darling, I'm sure there's nothing to worry about – only Julia's not here. Frances tried to cover up for her but she burst into tears when I questioned her and gave the game away.'

'But where can she have gone?' cried Phyllis. 'Oh Christ – you don't think she's fallen into the water in the dark, do you? I'd better go and get Hugh.'

'Of course not. She'll be fine. I'll fetch Hugh, you go and see whether you can get anything out of Frances. She may know where Julia's got to.'

But Frances only cried and said she didn't know where Julia had gone. As Phyllis came down the stairs, Hugh and Greville were in the hall, ready to go out and start looking for the girl: Venetia and the other guests were all standing by the drawing-room door, offering to help form a search party. Phyllis protested: the women were in evening shoes. Sarita came and put her hand on Phyllis's arm. Hugh took charge. The men would split up, one group to go west towards the church around the bay while the others headed east. It would be better if the women stayed put, in case there was a telephone call or she came back. He went to find a torch.

'There hadn't been any cross words?' Patricia asked Phyllis.

'No, no, nothing,' said Phyllis.

Just then the headlights of a car flashed through the hall window. Phyllis rushed forward to the front door and out into the drive. Julia, head bowed, got out and her mother ran to embrace her. From the driver's side came a man.

'Eric! For heaven's sake, what are you doing here?' cried Hugh.

'We didn't like to telephone in case you hadn't noticed she wasn't at home,' said Eric. 'Thought it would be best to just bring her back, directly. No harm done.'

Under the light of the hall it was evident that Julia had been weeping. There were black smudges like ash at the top of her cheeks. It took her mother a few moments to understand what the cause of these marks could be, before it came to her that her daughter had been wearing make-up. Looking at Julia more closely, she now saw that her daughter's mouth was smudged with lipstick and that she was wearing a sundress, her shoulders exposed. Her hair was neat and there were no scratches on her bare arms, yet she produced a picture of dishevelment.

'Come on, darling, let's get you upstairs and into something warm,' said Phyllis. It was such a relief that Julia was all right. She felt a rush of love and pity for her daughter. She put her arm around her and led her up.

The dinner guests were all in the hall now, observing the scene with some curiosity.

Pea-Brain spoke: 'Thank you so much for a lovely evening.'

The others took their cue and began to assemble themselves ready to leave. Only Patricia and Greville made no sign of departure.

'It's coming on a spot chillier now, of an evening,' observed Eric cheerfully, to no one in particular.

'Terribly nice that you could come,' said Hugh to the backs of his departing guests.

'Who is that funny little man?' said Venetia's sister, audibly.

Once the dinner guests had gone and Phyllis had taken Julia out of the way, Hugh addressed Eric. 'What on earth is going on? Turning up like this in the middle of dinner in front of all our friends with Julia dressed like someone going to an amusement park! We'll be a laughing stock. It's really too bad.'

'He's brought your daughter back safely, as you can see,' said Greville. 'A word of thanks might be in order.'

'I'm sure no one will gossip,' said Patricia. 'We've all got children. Well, except Pea-Brain and that woman, whatever her name was.'

'Venetia Gordon-Canning does nothing but make up stories about people. I daresay she'll have told half the county that Julia came back half-naked with a strange man by tea-time tomorrow.'

'Julia is safe, that's the main thing,' said Patricia.

'It was just a stroke of luck that I went to the site this evening at all,' said Eric.

'Would you like something to drink?' Greville offered, since Hugh had not. 'It's very good of you to have come out. You could have just told Hugh to come and fetch her.'

'I'll take a glass of whisky, yes, thank you,' said Eric.

Greville went into the drawing room and the other three followed. 'I still don't see how you came to find Julia,' said Hugh.

'Well, as you know, the camp has packed up, they've all gone now. But I thought it would be an idea just to nip down there, make sure the Leader's hut is secure and in order and the place hasn't been left too untidy. Just as well I did, because there was your daughter, bawling her eyes out. She'd fixed to meet up with one of the lads, Freddy. He's the son of the chap who does the catering, bit of a heart-throb, or so they tell me. Apparently he'd told her he was staying on for a day or two. Anyhow.'

'I think you must be mistaken,' said Hugh.

'I'm just reporting as I find,' said Eric. 'That's what she told me and that's all I'm telling you.'

'Oh dear,' said Patricia. 'I'm sure this wouldn't have happened if Phyllis had only got her a pony.'

'Well, it can't be helped now,' said Greville.

Hugh turned to Eric. 'I have to say I wish your wife hadn't insisted on involving my family in this wretched camping-ground business. Julia should never have been allowed to mix with people of that sort. Nina can be very overpowering and I do think she took advantage of Phyllis's better nature.'

Eric looked at Hugh mildly, without rancour.

'What's done is done. I don't know what else your wife and kids would have found to do with themselves all summer. They've had some first-class entertainment and learnt a fair bit too: got themselves a political education.'

'Only goats have kids. We have children,' said Hugh.

Eric smiled. 'I should count yourself lucky the lad wasn't there to meet her this evening. Could have been far worse if he'd kept his word.'

'Are you implying that my daughter . . .'

'Well, I think it's time to call it a night, don't you?' Greville interrupted. 'Eric? I'm afraid your car is blocking ours in, if it isn't too much trouble.'

'I'll be getting along then,' said Eric, standing. He put his half-finished whisky down on a side table. Hugh didn't respond. He made no move as the three left, not opening the hall door to see them out nor stepping out on to the gravel driveway to watch them away. When his wife came down after settling Julia to bed, she found him still standing in the drawing room. Motionless with his arms by his sides, he suddenly looked his age.

8. Sussex and Paris, autumn 1938

Poor Julia had been made miserable enough by the disappointment and humiliation. Hugh had taken her into his study and closed the door behind them on the morning after the dinner, but Phyllis hadn't had the heart to remonstrate with her. In any case, discipline had never been Phyllis's strong suit. Julia surely would have learned her lesson, and anyway, no further opportunity for capers of this sort would arise once she was back at school. The routine and the better company of her school peers would do her good.

Since the evening of the dinner party, relations with both her sisters had been rather chilly. Patricia seemed to be sulking, which was typical. She sometimes seemed to Phyllis to be one of those people who court umbrage, searching it out in corners, like cobwebs, where it was imperceptible to anyone else. She had muttered something about Hugh's dreadful behaviour towards Greville, but beyond that Phyllis could not see why the matter was any business of Patricia's at all. Nina by contrast had never been a sulker, but had always been the most fiery of the three of them. She had rung up the next day and given Phyllis the most terrific earful. Hugh had been unforgivably rude to Eric, she said, and in front of people: not just Patricia and Greville, but the county people Eric had to encounter at Party functions and meetings. It was really too bad. Eric had been kind enough to bring Julia home, and this was all the thanks he got for his troubles!

Phyllis had hardly had a chance to get a word in edgeways. Both her sisters laid the blame for Hugh's behaviour at her door.

Neither of them seemed to realize that her chief concern should be for her daughter.

Hugh had given her a very different account of things. His view was that Eric and Nina had known full well that they had people to dine and, miffed at being excluded, had timed things so as to disrupt the evening as much as possible. Eric could easily have telephoned discreetly to let them know he had found Julia: it was quite unnecessary to make such a drama out of things and to bring her home when the house was full of their friends. It had shown them up in front of people, making such a theatrical entrance with poor, disgraced Julia. The girl was only half dressed! There was ample room at Nina's house, the sensible thing would have been for the girl to stay the night there. Then she would have had time to calm down and collect herself before being picked up by her father the following morning. The fact that Eric and Nina hadn't even taken the trouble to give Julia the chance to wash her face or put on some kind of coat or wrap was further grist to his mill.

'I don't know that the blame can be laid quite so squarely at their door,' said Phyllis. 'After all, it is Julia who started all this, by going out in secret to meet that wretched young man.'

'I was getting round to that point,' said Hugh. 'She'd never have come into contact with a boy of that sort if she hadn't been press-ganged into going to Nina's bloody camp-site in the first place. I shouldn't be surprised if Nina and Eric didn't engineer the whole thing. They must be rubbing their hands with glee, to've made me a laughing stock in the county.'

'I think that's taking things rather too far. I don't believe they'd ever be malicious. Clumsy, perhaps,' said Phyllis. Uncomfortable though it made her to hear her husband do her sister down, she was relieved that he at least didn't seem to be angry with her for taking the children to the camp. Hugh could be slow to let a grievance go: she was only glad that he was not berating her on this occasion.

'I thought you approved of camp, in any case.'

'I did, for the rank and file. Build up a sense of camaraderie among them, that sort of thing. It's very useful for morale-building, I see that. I'm not convinced it's really for people like us though. Even the Old Man himself didn't actually stay there. If it hadn't been your sister's operation the children would never've got so involved.'

Phyllis supposed the ill feeling would blow over, given time. Eric and Hugh would be bound to run into one another at some meeting or other. The politics they shared and their sense of the urgency of the cause would surely help to rebuild bridges.

With camp finished and all the children now away at school and building work underway at the site of the new house, Phyllis would have found herself rather alone had it not been for Sarita Templeton. She missed the children dreadfully. Hugh still went up to London for a day or two in the week, to see to business affairs and visit Party HQ. On those days when he was in Sussex he busied himself with paperwork connected with committees and other local Party matters and with overseeing the construction at Littlehampton. Phyllis was not very involved with plans for the new house. Every now and again Hugh would show her a drawing in one of his catalogues and ask if she approved: a door knob or some fire-irons or some such. She never found any reason not to. In the afternoons she walked by herself around the harbour and along the lanes. There were blackberries plumping in the hedgerows now and buddleia, giving off a faint scent like pencil sharpenings.

She was grateful to be able to go to the Templetons'. Sometimes she and Sarita went riding, cantering up on to the Downs: on the warmer days in September they sat by the pool in their bathing dresses, taking the occasional dip. It was such fun to talk silly talk together, rather than the relentless politics that

Nina went in for, or Patricia's competitive social prattle. Often they chattered about favourite books. Who did they like best, of the fictional detectives: Hercule Poirot or Miss Marple; Lord Peter Wimsey or Roderick Alleyn? Phyllis confessed that she sometimes found Poirot insufferable.

'I met a man at a dinner in London who had been on a dig with the husband. You know, he is a famous archaeologist, I think?' said Sarita.

'Max Mallowan, yes. What was he like, did your friend say? I don't suppose he met her, too?'

'I think only him. But apparently he told this man that Agatha herself sometimes gets annoyed with Poirot, because he is too smug.'

'No! Do you think she'll bring him down a peg or two, in the next book?'

'I don't know what this means,' said Sarita.

Phyllis giggled as she tried to explain. While they were on the subject of the pitfalls of language, Sarita confessed that she had never known how to pronounce the name Ngaio, even though she adored Ngaio Marsh's books and, on balance, thought she preferred Marsh's Roderick Alleyn to all the others. When she went into a shop to get one of her books, she wrote the name on a piece of paper and handed it to the sales-girl, so she wouldn't have to say it out loud.

'It's knee-argo, I believe,' said Phyllis. Sarita repeated the syllables.

'Why? Why is it so funny?' asked Sarita.

'It's your face. You looked as if you were trying some horrid new kind of cough sweet.'

Sarita's daughter Emilia was taught by a governess, with a music teacher and French master brought in to augment her lessons. There had been vague talk of finding a school for the girl, instead of the home-tutoring she had at present. Perhaps she might go with Julia and Frances, but it had come to nothing: Phyllis thought her friend preferred to keep her daughter close by, at home. Then Sarita had the idea that it might be rather fun to ask the French tutor to stay on for an hour or so of informal conversation and she asked whether Phyllis would like to join them. It was a way of keeping up the French she had learned during her time in Belgium and it provided her with something to do, something of her own. They were to meet at eleven o'clock on Wednesdays, so that their lesson would finish at noon or so; then the tutor would leave and they would have luncheon. Perhaps, if Fergus wasn't there and there was no one else present, they might even continue to talk in French while they ate. From the first it was evident that Sarita's French was excellent, a legacy of the time she had spent in Paris with her first husband. Phyllis felt self-conscious and couldn't remember the right words for anything. She would begin a sentence and then break off halfway, while Sarita and Monsieur Hubert waited politely. By the time she had found her feet the hour was almost up. Afterwards, French phrases kept jumping into her head: *lorsque, il me semble, j'ai aucune idée.* They must have been in her memory all along, forgotten, like an odd glove at the bottom of a drawer. As the weeks went on she became more fluent and more willing to speak: the words began to follow one from another almost automatically, like footsteps. Instead of coming to an end halfway through a sentence, unable to think how to phrase her thoughts, she was able to keep up with herself. Retrieving the words was fun, like remembering the rules of a childhood game.

At lunch they were joined by Fergus, who sometimes had company of his own, friends he played polo with or who were otherwise involved with horses. Phyllis noticed that he tended to be rather short with his wife, which led to occasional moments of awkwardness at the table. Sometimes his rudeness was sharp enough to create a palpable intake of shocked breath from the other guests. But Sarita never gave any sign of being ruffled. She seemed to glide through everything with a permanent half-smile, as if she had received some good news in the morning's post. Her manners were not the same as English manners: they were not invisible. Although there was no ostentation, there was nevertheless something pretty about her manners, like the steps of a formally restrained yet elaborate dance. Phyllis was always intrigued to observe the effect this had upon people. Sarita seemed to drain anything irritable or coarse out of people, to raise them towards her own standard. Men, especially, were charmed. With the apparent exception of her husband.

It was at one of these lunches that the subject of the ball was first raised. The Templetons were known for their parties, which were the most lavish in the county and also had the reputation for becoming boisterous. The story of the pig which went over the parapet had passed into local legend; to some a source of horror, to others of amused indulgence. Disapproval of such antics tended to be greater among those who were not invited to the Templetons' parties. Insiders were always more forgiving. Sarita herself had never passed comment, but Phyllis could not imagine that her friend could have found such a thing very funny.

It was over lunch one Wednesday in early October that Fergus brought up the idea of their giving a winter ball. There was cause for celebration, he said: the Prime Minister had successfully averted the threat of war.

'I don't have a great deal of respect for the man, but when he got off the aeroplane from Germany waving that piece of paper, I must say he won me over,' said Fergus. 'This'll shut the socialist warmongers up, for good.'

'Better a strong Germany than the bloody communists in Russia taking over,' said Fergus's friend.

'Quite,' said Fergus. 'A fair number of my pals are in the Anglo-German Fellowship, as a matter of fact. They're thrilled with the Settlement, say it will put an end to any hostility between our two countries.'

'My husband's frightfully relieved, too. We both are, as a matter of fact,' ventured Phyllis. 'He fought in the war, you see. Naval intelligence.'

'Good man,' said Fergus.

Sarita, who loved clothes and dancing, needed no persuasion about the party. There was talk of bringing in a dance band from a London club; they all agreed that really good music made a party so much more fun.

'Do people like to dress up, do you think?' Sarita asked Phyllis.

'In fancy dress, do you mean? Costumes?'

'Oh God, not fancy dress again,' said Fergus. 'Last time everyone had to come as someone from the court of one of those French kings, powdered wigs and painted-on beauty spots and all that. It makes it all such a performance. People don't want to have to go to Morris and Berman's every time they come to a party. It's just a nuisance.'

'I think people love it, the opportunity to dress up,' said Sarita.

'I don't really know,' said Phyllis.

'Perhaps just a colour would be better. More simple,' said Sarita.

'That's a much better idea,' said Fergus. 'Then the men can just wear white tie and get a cummerbund made in whatever the colour is. Blue, or what-have-you.'

'White!' said Phyllis. 'Wouldn't that be lovely for a winter party, like snow or frost? Everyone's got white evening gloves after all. And I love grosgrain, don't you? One could get a white grosgrain ribbon and turn it into a sash.'

'Or ermine,' said Sarita. 'It's not too much trouble to get your dressmaker to put a little ermine trim around the neck of a dress, or a collar. So pretty, like a skater. Or an evening cape, perhaps. It would look very nice. Very nice. It's a good idea, Phyllis, thank you.'

'I should think you could run the Foreign Office,' Fergus turned to Phyllis.

'Oh, but I wasn't trying to be diplomatic,' she said.

'White Ladies! They're terrifically good,' Fergus's lunch guest interjected.

'Of course! Very important to give everyone a really stiff cocktail, get the thing going,' said Fergus.

'Gardenias,' said Sarita. 'We must get gardenias, then everything will smell delicious.'

'How lovely that will be,' said Phyllis. 'Perhaps it will snow! Then everything outside can be white as well.'

'Steady on,' said Fergus. 'People might not be able to get here, if it snowed, they'd be slithering all over the lanes. We don't want a party that no one can come to.'

Parties weren't the sort of thing Hugh was very enthusiastic about. Phyllis had gone back to Bosham full of chatter about the ball, but he'd given her a blank look and changed the subject. Only when she mentioned the reason Fergus had given for the party did he become a little more enthusiastic. Just a couple of weeks before, Hugh had attended a demonstration for peace in Shepherd's Bush, at which Mosley and his followers had been refused permission to march, much to their indignation. 'They forbid us to demonstrate for peace, but they're only too glad to permit the Labour Party to demonstrate for war,' Hugh had said. 'If German-speakers in some remote corner of Czechoslovakia wanted to be reunited with their fellows, what business is it of Britain's?'

Mr Chamberlain's journey to Munich had been a rare act of courage and commonsense, they both agreed.

Phyllis went upstairs to change out of the good shoes she had worn to the Templetons'. But instead of going into her own bedroom, she found herself continuing along the landing and into her son's empty room. She could smell his little-boy smell, slightly bitter, like the shell of a cracked nut. On the chest of drawers was a pile of name-tapes, with 'E. C. Forrester' embroidered on each in scrolling blue thread. They looked very small. She had been sewing them into his things the night before he went off to school and then ticking them against his trunk-list:

pyjama tops and bottoms x 2
Aertex short-sleeved grey shirts x 4
grey knee socks x 6

. . . and so on. Edwin's name was how he would be recognized in this new, strange place; whereas here at home he was known by his scampering steps on the stairs or running in and out of the hall; by his gappy grin; by the little hollow at the nape of his neck where Phyllis liked to plant a kiss when he got out of the bath before bedtime, his young limbs slippery until the towel smoothed them dry. With a pang she remembered that he wouldn't in fact be known as Edwin at all, but as Forrester, the new boy among many other new boys, all with their ears slightly red, their hair newly cropped; all of them eager in their slightly stiff new uniforms, all trying to be brave. A couple of days before term started he had said: 'Do I have to go, Mummy?'

And she knew she'd hesitated a moment too long before responding, that she should have answered straight away, so that he wouldn't see the doubt in her.

'Everyone has to go to school, darling. I'm sure you'll meet all sorts of nice and interesting boys. And it won't be long until first exeat.'

'That girl doesn't. The one in the big house.'

'Emilia, do you mean? But her mother's not English, you see, she probably has different ideas about things. And anyway, Emilia's a girl. Girls often don't go away to school till later. It's the same for Frances, after all. She'll be a new girl this term, too, remember. She's in the same boat as you.'

But Frances was older and would be joining her sister; she wouldn't be the only one at her new school. The girls had each other. Phyllis could see that, although neither she nor Edwin had said so. He hadn't answered her at all. Now she opened the top drawer and tucked the unused name-tapes on one side. A folded vest or two lingered, with some slightly too small flannel pyjamas. When they'd arrived at Bosham she had lined all the drawers with new waxed paper. The futility and optimism of that act now seemed faintly absurd to her.

Hugh hoped the new house would be ready by Christmas, but the building work was held up – partly, so far as Phyllis could see – by the fact that he kept changing his mind about the plans. Exasperated, he laid out the revised drawings on the dining-room table at Bosham one afternoon, and asked his wife to cast her eye over them.

'I don't think it really matters whether the scullery has a window or not,' she said.

'That's where you're incorrect, I'm afraid,' said Hugh. 'Any room where steam is generated requires ventilation, or one can get terrible problems with condensation. There's quite enough water outside, frankly. One doesn't want to risk trapping vapour within.'

'Oh. Well, do you think we could take a bit off the downstairs cloakroom for the scullery, then?'

'Is that wise? We need somewhere for boots to go.'

'But why? It's not as if we have a huge collection of boots, I mean we don't hunt or anything. It's only five pairs of gumboots we need to make room for. And actually neither of the girls ever wear theirs, so it's really only yours and mine and Edwin's. You'd still have plenty of room for them along that wall, look, with coat-hooks above. All you'd have to do is to move the washbasin in with the loo. Then you could take that bit off and incorporate it into the scullery. The two windows would balance, from the outside, they'd be the same size, I mean. I don't know, it's just a thought.'

'I rather think you may have solved the problem,' said Hugh. But he still sounded doubtful.

At the beginning of November, after their French conversation class, Sarita had a proposition to make to Phyllis. Suppose Phyllis were to accompany her to Paris, just for two or three nights: Sarita wanted to have a dress made – something lovely – for the White Ball in December and Phyllis would be doing her the most tremendous favour if she would agree to come too; otherwise Sarita would be lonely by herself. They could practise their French and Sarita could show her friend some of her old haunts.

Phyllis felt herself pinken with excitement.

'I don't know what Hugh would say, I'll have to ask him first,' she said.

'Please explain to him that you would be coming as my guest, as a personal favour to me,' said Sarita. 'Or would you like me to telephone to him, perhaps?'

'Would you? I think he couldn't possibly say no to you. He shouldn't mind too much; as a matter of fact, I don't imagine he'd even notice I wasn't there. And I should so love to come.'

Phyllis couldn't resist ringing Patricia to tell her about the jaunt.

'But what on earth for? Do you suppose she's meeting a lover?'

'I don't think so. I think she just wants to go dress shopping and see the sights.'

'Yes, but one can do that in London.'

'If she was meeting someone, why on earth would she drag me along?'

'As an alibi, silly. She thinks she can buy your silence.'

'She wouldn't have to pay me for it. But she's never mentioned an admirer. I really don't think you're right.'

'Well, why would she, mention someone I mean?'

'Because we're friends. We talk about things.'

'You are funny, Pill. You can be so naïve sometimes.'

Patricia hadn't called Phyllis the long-ago nickname – Pill – for as long as she could remember. At one time both her sisters had called her this, partly in mockery, partly from affection. She had almost forgotten about it. It took her by surprise to hear it again and she knew it meant that Patricia's huff following the dinner party row was over. The relief at their new détente made her choose to overlook the fact that Patricia was being frankly patronizing. Sarita was a polished flirt, but she had never so much as hinted at anything more. Really, Patricia was almost as bad as Venetia Gordon-Canning! Some people just had a one-track mind.

Hugh hardly so much as murmured about the trip. It would barely inconvenience him, since their cook would come in as usual and do his lunches, as well as dinner for the one evening he would be at home. He planned to attend a Party meeting in Chichester on the final night, so he'd dine at an hotel then; and Patricia said she'd ask him on the middle night, so he'd at least have had one properly cooked dinner during his wife's absence. The women were to sail from Newhaven; Sarita had taken a cabin. They would go on by train and a driver would be waiting for them at the Gare du Nord.

★

Phyllis's room at the hotel had a vast kidney-shaped dressing table with billowing chintz skirts that matched the curtains and the bedhead and the little bedroom sofa. The room had its very own bathroom, full of marble, with enormous chrome taps. The carpet throughout was as soft and cushiony as moss. She had never stayed anywhere so grand in her life and would have been perfectly happy to stay put for the whole three days: luckily Sarita turned out to be a late riser, so she was able to enjoy a good couple of hours alone in the mornings, luxuriating.

'An old friend is going to join us for a drink tomorrow, you don't mind?' said Sarita, on the first evening.

Phyllis's heart sank. She had been so sure that Patricia was wrong. 'No, no, of course not. Would you sooner I was out of the way? You've probably got things you'd like to talk about.'

'No, not at all. He will just come for half an hour before we go in to dinner.'

The man was not what Phyllis had been expecting. She had pictured a continental matinée idol type, with brilliantined dark hair and a heavy gold cigarette case and a knowing sort of charm. This man wasn't the least bit attractive, but had a chalky kind of pallor, like blotting paper. His mouth was colourless, and his hair was pale without being fair, nor quite grey. He was the colour of a cigarette. He was very much less attractive than Fergus Templeton. When he first appeared, Phyllis felt something approaching embarrassment for her friend. But he and Sarita behaved stiffly, as if they barely knew one another. He brought as a present a flat box of marrons glacés wrapped with a brown and gold ribbon: the box was made of splintery pale wood, a miniature replica of a packing crate. Sarita and he seemed to have nothing much to say, but exchanged pleasantries, as if they had only just met on the deck of a liner. After he had finished his glass of champagne, he stood up to go: Sarita did not press him to stay. Phyllis supposed he must have been an old friend of Sarita's first husband, seen now not for pleasure but as an obeisance. She felt something approaching relief that he was so evidently not her friend's lover.

The afternoons passed in a blur. They visited a museum called the Jeu de Paume and the cathedral of Notre-Dame. They looked at pictures, but not too many: Sarita announced that she never spent more than half an hour in a museum because after that she didn't really take anything in. There were gauzy mauve paintings of bridges which seemed to float on a cloud of mist and wisteria; and tranquil ponds with vast and placid lily pads, all in a haze of summeriness. Phyllis thought Hugh on the whole wouldn't have liked these pictures, despite their horticultural themes, for he appreciated precision in art. What he liked was realistic detail. Sarita smiled when Phyllis said so. They walked along the river but not for long, for there was a sharp little wind on the Quais. They repaired to a steamy and jostling *salon de thé* and drank hot chocolate served in tall glasses on which floated tiny Alpine peaks of white cream. While Sarita went to her dressmaker in a little street near the rue St Honoré, Phyllis wandered alone along the Jardins des Tuileries before making her way back to the hotel to write cards in her room. She sent pictures of the Eiffel Tower to Julia and Edwin and her parents, and one of a boat on the Seine to Frances; to Hugh and both her sisters she couldn't resist showing off by using the picture-postcards provided by the hotel. For their lunches they ate out at brasseries and then dined at the hotel each evening, making up stories about their fellow diners.

At a neighbouring table sat a dapper little man with a moustache, who was a good head shorter than his stately and much bejewelled wife: they became convinced he had been a fortune hunter. Among the other notable occupants of the dining room were a young, very fair couple who looked Scandinavian and who never exchanged a word during the whole three courses; while in the corner were an elderly pair who Phyllis thought were impoverished Russian grandees, although Sarita was convinced from their drooping lips and deep eyelids that they were minor members of the Spanish royal family.

'I think the Scandinavians are brother and sister. That is why they never speak,' said Sarita.

'Really? I'd have thought they'd have masses to say, in that case. I think they're an arranged marriage and that's why they're so silent. They're furious to have been forced together. And they don't even know each other, yet.'

Sarita laughed. 'But who arranged this marriage? And why?'

'Their fathers are businessmen together. They run a huge . . . a huge . . . pilchard factory. It's essential they should marry, to secure the dynasty.'

'Of course. Without this marriage, there would be no future of Norwegian pilchards. It could be finished. Kaput.'

'No wonder they don't talk to each other,' said Phyllis. 'Do you think their pillow talk is all about the fishing fleet?'

'The mind baffles,' said Sarita.

'I think it's boggles, actually. The mind boggles.'

'Oh.'

They both fought to suppress giggles.

When after a rather rough crossing the two had to part at Newhaven, Sarita had taken both Phyllis's hands in hers and thanked her. Touched by the gesture – it was after all she who had reason to be thankful, not the other way around – Phyllis felt that she might cry. It was silly, really. She'd only known Sarita since the summer, after all, and yet it was a tremendous wrench to part from her now, as if they were childhood friends, or close relations.

'We'll go again, next year, yes?' Sarita said, luggage loaded, stepping into her car.

'Do let's! I should love to,' said Phyllis.

As soon as she was back at home, before she'd even taken her things upstairs, she telephoned Patricia to report about the trip.

'Was it fun?'

'Such fun; so lovely. I can't remember when I've enjoyed myself so much. Sarita was so kind. Do you know, she even offered to get a dress made for me?'

'Don't tell me you said no!'

'Of course I did. It was very generous of her to pay for my room, I wouldn't have dreamed of accepting any clothes as well.'

'I don't suppose Sarita would even have noticed.'

'She can be rather vague, it's true.'

'I didn't mean that. I meant, she's got so much money, she wouldn't miss the price of a frock for you.'

'You're probably right. All the same.'

'And was there any sign of a lover?' Patricia asked.

'Absolutely not,' said Phyllis. But something made her refrain from mentioning the ashy man with his pale box of marrons glacés. He had been so insubstantial, she almost wondered if he had existed at all.

Phyllis, 1979

I know you're here to hear about my being one of the female followers of Sir Oswald Mosley and not my private life. But it all gets muddled up together, the political and the personal. I'm rather enjoying telling you about it all, actually. I'm glad you didn't take no for an answer that first time and that Antonia persuaded you to write again, gave me the chance to change my mind. I can't see what harm it can do, now, to tell you about those days. I don't get much of a chance to talk about myself, so a lot of this is things I've never told anyone before. You won't want to put any of these private things into your book, only I can't really get at my association with the Party without explaining things about my family and friends.

I couldn't swear that Hugh slept with Patricia while I was in Paris. Not in a court of law. There wasn't anything remotely different about him, when I got back. He didn't look furtive or buy me guilty flowers. It wasn't as it is in those songs, lipstick on his collar or her scent on the pillow: nothing of that kind. I just had a sort of hunch.

Have you ever come back from abroad and had a secret hope that something very exciting will have happened, while you were away? Even something rather awful, like a fire or a flood; but something that will in any case make things be different from how they were before? We lived overseas so much, as you know, that I grew very accustomed to this feeling. I've never heard it mentioned, but I don't imagine I'm the only person who's ever felt like that. Because what's so odd is that one longs for home and for home to be the same as it's always been, as it is in one's imagination and memory; but yet there's the most dreadful sense of disappointment when it is. The same. When everything is unchanged you can feel terribly crestfallen. Especially when you have the idea – perhaps wrongly, who's to say – that you are altered yourself. Inevitably, you don't feel as if you're quite the same person, coming back, not when you've lived abroad for years at a time. It's the same thing when you come out of prison, as a matter of fact. You feel full of things, of all the sights you've seen and the ideas you've absorbed and people you've met. It can be so dreary to find that no one else has had a single thought outside of their run-of-the-mill lives. They're still just blathering about their cooks or gardens, or the price of paraffin; things as trivial as that. People always talk about how lovely it is to get home, but they don't mention this thing, how flat and disappointed it can make you feel.

Of course now that I live alone there's absolutely no chance of anything being different to come back to. I can go out for hours at a time, days even – not that I do, not often – and when I come back everything is exactly where I left it, exactly the same. It ought to be reassuring, but somehow it isn't. It's like being stuck in a peculiar dream.

When I got off the boat at Newhaven, Hugh was there waiting for me with the car. Everything was as it always was: road-map in the glove compartment, a cold fug inside the car misting up the windows, slight smell of barley sugar. I might be embroidering, about the barley sugar: he always had barley sugar twists in the car, but I couldn't really be sure they had a smell. Anyway, it was the same thing when we got back to the house. Nothing had moved, not even an inch. His book on the table beside the sofa. Even the hand-towel in our bathroom was folded, just as I had left it. You always recognize your own folding, have you noticed? You can tell it's your own, like handwriting. And you can tell when someone else has touched it, it just looks different. So when I went upstairs after telephoning to Patricia – oh, the irony! – and I saw the hand-towel and realized he couldn't have used it at all while I was away, I had a feeling as if a trapdoor had opened in my mind. There was something just too . . . would the word be scrupulous? Too exact. And Hugh was exactly as he always was, too. Asked me the minimum of questions and then started

118

banging on about the house. Not the house we were living in; the house he was getting built at the time.

I knew that something wasn't quite right. Some instinct, I suppose. After I saw the hand-towel I went down to the larder and looked at the eggs. Hugh always had two eggs for breakfast and the farm boy came every Thursday, I think it was, or it might have been Friday; in any case, by the time I got back there would normally have been a certain quantity of eggs in the larder. There was a farm about a mile up the road where they kept hens, everyone in the village got theirs from there. They had a slightly peculiar daughter, she'd had some sort of illness in childhood. Funny-shaped head. So there should have been however many eggs they normally delivered, minus the two he had every morning. Possibly another couple might have gone into a cake. I can't now remember how many I worked out there should have been, but anyway there were at least four too many. Even if the cook had made a cake or scones while I was away, there were too many left.

So I realized he hadn't been at home while I was in Paris and yet he hadn't mentioned anything about a visit to London. I asked him. I said: 'Were you in London while I was away?' and he looked rather taken aback and said that he hadn't been. But he didn't venture that he'd been elsewhere, either. I didn't fully put two and two together until I saw my sister and she happened to let slip that Greville had been in London the night she'd had Hugh over to Rose Green for dinner. And the one after. As a matter of fact he'd been away all week. Of course Antonia was off at school by then, too.

They'd have been better off at our rented house in Bosham if they'd planned to be alone, the two of them, because we didn't have living-in servants, whereas Patricia did, at Rose Green. So I don't think they'd plotted it in advance or they would have thought of that. Mind you, in those days people were loyal and wouldn't have gossiped about an employer, and even if they had it would never have reached the ears of anyone we knew. She wouldn't have wanted any raised eyebrows from the housekeeper or the cook; it wouldn't have done for anyone to know. Whatever they may or may not have done, Patricia wasn't stupid; she would have covered her tracks, where the servants were concerned. I imagine she'd have put Hugh in the spare room or at least made it look as if he'd been in there, just for form's sake. They may have concocted some story to explain his staying there. I don't know.

I don't think they were madly in love with each other or anything like that. I never thought for one moment that I had anything to fear. Hugh would never have left me – if I was being critical I'd say he was just too straitlaced, but to be fair he valued having a family of his own tremendously and he wouldn't have wanted to destroy that. And Patricia was too attached to the life Greville gave her to rock the boat there.

I'm sure they hadn't been waiting like racing greyhounds to spring out of their traps. I don't believe they'd been pining for one another for years, ever since Hugh first clapped eyes on her; that is to say, I don't think it was anything terribly romantic. I think it was just a case of happenstance: Greville and myself being away and Antonia out of the house and no doubt a gin and tonic or two, and somehow one thing may have led to another. Hugh was very keen on that sort of thing, you see. So was Patricia, I happen to know. She'd grumbled to me and Nina over the years about her husband not being so interested as she was. It's so often the way, in a marriage – you get one person who wants to, and the other not. Anyway.

I couldn't face asking her. If I'd asked, she'd have felt she had to lie and I couldn't stand the thought of that. I didn't want to be put in a position of having to make her tell me an untruth; it would have embarrassed her and then she'd have got cross. People often get angry after they've been cornered into a lie, I've noticed. The person who has done wrong can end up getting far angrier than the one who's been wronged. We'd only just made up after the slight falling out we'd had over the dinner party and I didn't want to create any more unpleasantness. I always wanted to be friends with both my sisters. Perhaps that was the source, really, of all the troubles of my life.

I was piqued, I will admit. My pride took a bit of a denting. But I didn't mind as much as you might think. It may seem peculiar to you, but I shouldn't have minded if she'd wanted to borrow my coat and I didn't particularly mind if she'd borrowed Hugh, not really. It wasn't as if they were going to run off together, or anything like that. Patricia cared terribly what other people thought. To be fair, you wouldn't have said the same of Nina; Nina was always much more her own person. If she wanted something, she went after it, and hang the consequences. She didn't care what people made of her. She couldn't have married Eric if she had.

Infidelity is much more wounding to the young. I'd been married for years; I felt like a middle-aged woman at the time, even though I hadn't left my thirties. So we didn't fall out over it, because I never let on that I knew. Well, knew is too strong a word: that I had my suspicions. Our great quarrel came much later, after I got out of prison. I never forgave her for what happened then. Which is peculiar really, because she'd already done me a great kindness and was only offering to extend that kindness, in a way. You'd think I'd have hated her when I thought she had been sleeping with my husband, and been grateful to her, later, for what she did for me. But it was the other way around. Funny, isn't it? They say no good turn goes unpunished. And that's how it was, you see, with us.

9. Sussex and Buckinghamshire, November 1938

A few days after Phyllis returned from Paris, a call came in from Nina. It was the first time they had spoken since the incident with Julia.

'You didn't tell me you were going abroad,' she said.

'Oh good, you've had my card,' said Phyllis. 'Oh Nina, I can't tell you what fun it was! We . . .'

'Daddy's been taken into hospital,' Nina cut in.

'Oh no! What's happened? Is he all right?' said Phyllis.

'His heart, they think. Mrs Manville's going to ring me this afternoon, when they should know more.'

'Should we go?'

'I'm not sure. What do you suppose would be best?'

Phyllis dithered. 'Shall we wait until Mrs Manville's let you know, would that be the thing?'

'Yes, let's. I'll ring you again, when I've heard. Could you let Patricia know?'

'Haven't you told her?'

'No. I thought you could.'

'Of course,' said Phyllis.

Patricia said they must go at once. Of course she was right: it wouldn't do for Mrs Manville to be the only person at his side, and anyway their mother could not safely be left alone in the house for any amount of time. But Greville couldn't spare Hitchens at such short notice, so they agreed that Nina would drive. They would go straight to the hospital and then stay the night at the Grange.

Mrs Manville hadn't sounded too keen to prepare supper for them, but Nina had reassured her that they'd only want something light so she need not go to a great deal of trouble.

Patricia automatically installed herself in the front passenger seat. Phyllis was relieved to have the back to herself, so that she could look out of the window without having to engage in much conversation. She was worried about her father and not in the mood for chatter and gossip. Every now and again one of her sisters would say: 'Don't you think, Phyllis?' and she would have to pretend to have been following what they'd been talking about. Before they arrived at the hospital Patricia brought out her lipstick and compact and dabbed her nose with powder. Even from the back of her head Phyllis could tell that this small display of vanity was annoying to Nina. 'Will I do?' she asked Phyllis, turning her head. 'No smudges?' In actual fact she had applied the powder more thickly on one side of her nose, but Phyllis did not say so.

The corridors in the hospital were of highly polished pale green linoleum, and shiny paint in the same colour came halfway up the walls, where it ended at a dado rail. The rest was a custardy colour. A nursing sister took them to their father's room. Beneath the thin cotton blankets the outline of his legs seemed too insubstantial, and his shoulders and chest and arms looked wrong: too narrow, too concave, too spindly. The familiarity of his face hardly registered above the shock of this sudden diminishment. For a moment Phyllis thought they must have gone into the wrong room. But when he spoke his voice was their father's voice.

'Hello, darling. How good of you to come.'

It was Nina he was addressing, of course. Illness had compromised his ability to be democratic with his affection. She went at once and took his hand – it looked not like a living thing, but as veiny and papery as a fallen leaf – and sat herself on the bed.

Patricia stood to the other side, while Phyllis hovered at the foot. After an interval of a few minutes, Patricia removed herself, tip-toeing with some theatricality from the room. This they had agreed in the car: that the younger two would stay with Daddy while she went to talk to the doctor.

'How are you feeling?' Phyllis asked.

'Oh well, you know, could be worse,' said her father. 'Rather a fright.' He seemed to be very short of breath. The effort of even these few words made him seem to sink back into his pillows. He seemed to shrink still more. He was less than himself, like a half-plucked bird.

'It must have been dreadful,' said Nina. 'Did you fall or did you just come over all peculiar?'

Mrs Manville had found him on the floor in the hall. The dog had been sitting beside him, a detail which, talking things over later, had made all three daughters cry; not because it was typical of the dog, but because to have induced such loyalty towards his master was typical of their father.

'I fell, I think,' he said, his voice now barely above a whisper. He closed his eyes.

Phyllis and Nina looked at each other. Their father's breath made a rasping noise in the quiet of the room. Phyllis felt oddly embarrassed by the sound; it was so bodily. Their father had always been rather formal. It was rare to see him even in his shirt-sleeves, let alone a dressing gown: throughout their lives he had appeared at the breakfast table fully dressed, shaved and with his hair pomaded; his cuff-links just so, his shoes always polished. He wore a wool tie on days when he wasn't expecting to see anyone and a silk one when there was company, or on those days when he was appearing in court as a Justice of the Peace.

Patricia came back.

'We must let you get some rest,' she told her father. 'Doctor's orders.' He didn't seem to have heard her.

'Daddy?' said Nina. 'We're going to go now. We'll be back in the morning.'

He opened one eye. 'Tell your mother not to . . .'

'We will,' said Nina. 'Don't worry about a thing.'

'I loathe the smell of hospitals,' said Patricia, once they were back in the car. 'You'd think they'd invent something to mask it.'

'I think they have,' said Phyllis. 'I mean, I think what you're smelling is the smell that hides the other, worse smells.'

Patricia shuddered at the thought.

'What did the doctor say?' asked Nina.

'It's his heart. He's going to have to rest. Stay in bed. Trays. No gardening.'

'Crikey,' said Phyllis, aware that someone was going to have to prepare those trays and take them up and down the stairs.

'But is he going to be all right?' said Nina.

'He said it's too early to say.'

'Oh God. How will Mrs Manville manage, with Mummy as well?' said Phyllis.

At this they all fell silent, while each of them wondered whether either of the others would volunteer.

'Let's just get home and see how the land lies,' said Patricia. They each knew that by home she meant the Grange.

It was evident that one of them would have to stay on. While they were sitting with their mother, Mrs Manville dropped several saucepan lids on to the stone floor in the kitchen, always a signal that she felt she was being overworked. As girls they had stifled laughter at the expressive sound effects which came from behind the kitchen door, but now they felt weary and exasperated.

'Honestly, what is that woman paid for?' said Patricia in a sort of hiss.

Their mother, meanwhile, seemed elated. The excitement of

their father's fall appeared to have given her a temporary reprieve and she seemed to speak quite normally, asking what the doctor had said and whether her husband had seemed comfortable. Her eyes were bright. It was only when she repeated her questions immediately that it became apparent that no real change had taken place.

'We ought to draw up a rota, work out who can be here and when,' said Nina, after supper.

'That sounds like a good idea,' said Phyllis. 'I won't be able to stay next week, because it's half-term and the children will be back. But I can manage the week after.'

'I don't see why you have to turn everything into a committee,' said Patricia. 'There are only three of us, after all. We can perfectly well decide what the best course of action is, without rotas and lists. Anyway we're all very busy. I think we should be considering a nursing home. For Daddy.' Their father had always been adamant that their mother should not be sent to rot in a nursing home. Nina took no notice.

'I'll stay on tomorrow, if one of you can drive the car back after breakfast?'

'I'd like to see Daddy in the morning, first,' said Phyllis.

'Right-o,' said Nina.

'We don't know how far their finances stretch,' said Patricia. 'I think I should look through Daddy's desk, try and get an idea of things, before we look into a nursing home.'

Her sisters regarded her with open hostility. Their father's study was private, a sanctuary of leathery maleness. It was to this room that he repaired every morning after breakfast, to attend to his affairs and enter figures into mysterious ledgers. There was a heavy silver inkwell, inscribed to him from his regiment, and an ivory letter-opener. Its blade was too wide to fit into an envelope, but it had always lain across the desk in a ceremonious way, a small enamel box – for postage stamps, an early gift from his wife – at its side. His desk was implicitly out of bounds, like an altar. It would no more have occurred to Phyllis to look inside the drawers of this desk than to poke about in a sacristy.

It was mid-November when Phyllis came to take her turn at the Grange. The house had a dejected air, as if the people who lived there had gone away. For the time being she and Nina had prevailed: their father was to be looked after at home, at least until the New Year. After that, Patricia had insisted that they must return to the question of what would be best for the long term. They couldn't keep taking it in turns to stay with their parents in perpetuity: they had their own lives to be getting on with. The spectre of putting both parents into nursing homes loomed.

Hugh drove his wife back to Buckinghamshire. It had been wet for the past few days, so that even the trunks of the trees were stained, darkened. Now a pale sun broke through the cloud, making the surface of the road and the trees gleam with the muted, warm colours of metals: branches catching the light glowed in patches like unpolished brass and the lanes shone a dull pewter. It sometimes seemed to Phyllis that she was never more content than when looking out of a window at the endless variety of England's countryside and light. Nature was such a consolation.

Hugh was to stay the first night. It was clear that his mother-in-law had no notion who he was. 'Could you just put the card table over there by the window, if you don't mind?' she asked him.

'It's not a removal man, Mummy! It's Hugh.'

Her mother gave her a blank, owl-like stare. 'I think the secretaire would be best in the drawing room,' she replied firmly.

For dinner Mrs Manville served consommé, followed by a chicken dish with mushrooms. The chicken seemed to consist mostly of bones, with no meat adhering to them. Without her father guiding things at the table, conversation was impossible. Their spoons made an amplified noise against their soup bowls in the silent dining room, as if they were unhappy diners in a dingy hotel.

Now that her father was out of commission, Phyllis realized what a lot of looking after her mother required. Once she was up and dressed and installed in her chair she more or less stayed put, but she needed to be reminded to go to the loo and to be escorted there several times a day. It didn't do to be entirely sedentary, so a little turn around the lower garden took place in the early afternoon, which meant wrapping her up against the cold. Her feet and ankles were now too swollen to fit into boots or shoes. She had two pairs of tartan slippers, one for inside, one for the garden. With her memory had disappeared any sense of the minute-by-minute continuing passage of time, and she never complained of boredom, although she barely moved from one hour to the next. She had forgotten how much she had loved riding, and never mentioned her horse – the culprit of her present condition, now long deceased – nor asked after any of her companions from the old, hunting days. It had been a miracle that she had survived the fall, the doctors had said. Her body had recovered, more or less intact. Phyllis supposed that they should be thankful for this miracle, but it was not easy to feel gratitude at the sight of this poor simulacrum of a mother. Her mother didn't read, or even seem to think; she just sat. She didn't seem happy, but she didn't exactly seem unhappy either. She was like a well-mannered child, sitting politely in a waiting room.

It was difficult, now, to recall what her mother had been like before, when they were children: her animation and low laughter, the tilt of her head when she read bedtime stories aloud to them; the reassuring flat of her hand against a forehead hot from fever. As a child there had been nothing Phyllis loved more than the smell of her mother's skin, when she bent to kiss her goodnight: the smell of orange-flower water and distant cologne.

Now getting her up in the mornings and down the stairs took

ages. She sat limply while her swollen feet were inserted into her rolled-up stockings. When required to she lifted her arms obediently but without any spontaneity, with no apparent memory that this was something she did every morning in order to have her nightgown removed and her wool vest put on. Mrs Manville helped her mother dress, muttering short phrases of encouragement: 'That's it, put your hand in there'; 'Leg in, there you are.' A different and kinder side of Mrs Manville emerged, without impatience or irritability.

Phyllis, having glanced into her mother's room, next went to collect her father's breakfast – the things arranged already on a tray on the side in the kitchen, awaiting toast and boiled egg – and take it up to him with the newspaper. She drew back the curtains and asked him to lean forward in his bed so that she could plump the pillows. Even this small effort brought a flush to his cheeks, as if after some great exertion.

'Would you like the wireless on?' she asked. Patricia had bought him a set, especially for his bedroom, to keep him entertained while he rested.

'No, thanks. I'm very happy with just the paper. Later, p'raps,' he answered. Phyllis went down to the dining room, where Hugh was waiting for her.

'Doesn't seem to be a paper,' he said, looking rather put out.

'Daddy's got it,' she explained.

Hugh did not like to talk in the morning and generally retreated behind the pages of *The Times*. Now they were obliged to exchange mild pleasantries whenever they caught each other's eye. Afterwards Hugh went to fetch his case down to the hall, ready to go. As he stepped out of the door, Jamie appeared.

'Hugh, how are you?' he said, extending a long arm to shake hands. 'I've come to see your Pa,' he told Phyllis. He did not say hello to her.

'Oh good, he will be pleased, do go on up,' she said.

'Odd-looking sort of fellow, isn't he?' said Hugh, once Jamie was out of sight. Jamie's frayed shirt, open at the neck, and his uncut hair were very much outside his own standards of dress.

'Ssh,' said Phyllis. 'He'll hear you.'

Hugh said he trusted that Phyllis had put arrangements in place with their cook, before she left, so that he wouldn't be left to starve. In any case he planned to spend the next several days in London: Party membership was growing thanks to the peace campaign, with which he was closely involved. It was essential that the government now adopt a programme of economic appeasement in order to continue to extend the hand of friendship to Germany. Hugh was among a small group entrusted by the Leader with the task of gaining influence with certain key members of the Conservative Party. Such allies would bring respectability to the cause. Once he came back to Sussex he would be alone at Bosham for only three nights before Phyllis joined him. It occurred to Phyllis that Hugh would have ample time in which to see her sister, assuming Greville would be in London.

She waved him off. Going back into the house she was aware of a lightness, a feeling as if something burdensome had been lifted away. She lingered in the hall until Jamie sprang down the stairs, two at a time. She imagined that the stair carpet at the Dickinsons' farmhouse must be worn in strange uneven patches, for Jamie never took each tread individually, but leapt up two and three steps at a time, and down in the same way, pell-mell.

'Would you like to come for a stroll?' he asked.

She said she would. 'Come back to the farm with me and I'll give you morning coffee,' he said. 'I've got some things I'd like you to see.'

As they made their way up through the garden and across into the wood that fringed their two parcels of land, Jamie talked excitedly. He planned to turn the long low building, once part of the dairy, into a studio for his sculpting and pictures. The old farm buildings made a perfect place to work, at least until the weather turned, when they might prove too cold.

'I didn't know you were artistic,' said Phyllis. This new side to Jamie made him suddenly seem unfamiliar to her. She felt shy, as if she were walking beside a stranger.

'Mum and Dad weren't especially keen on my painting: they didn't feel I'd be able to make a living at it. But I learned a lot, during my travels. Don't look so surprised! You're not the only one who's been abroad, you know. I was in Italy for a couple of years, in Florence. I think it was when you were in South America. When my grandfather died – Mum's father – he left me some money and I used some of it to go off and study art. I've been drawing for years,' he said. 'I've got some sketches of you, as a matter of fact. I was thinking of seeing if I could translate them into a head. In clay, I mean.'

'Goodness. Can you draw from memory, then? I thought you had to have the person in front of you.'

'Well, you have been in front of me. In the front of my mind, anyway,' said Jamie.

Phyllis looked down at her feet in their sensible lace-up shoes. 'I can't begin to imagine how you would go about turning a lump of mud into something that looked like someone,' she said.

'Well, that's the challenge. That's what makes it interesting,' he grinned. They had reached the farmyard. 'Come and have a look.'

A long low shed that had been used for calving had been cleared and repainted with whitewash. Jamie had installed a wide wooden counter all down one side, on which were ranged some eight or nine sculptures, some of them concealed under cloths, which looked wet. There were three finished portrait heads and some abstract sort of shapes, carved in wood. A long table was covered with drawing books and glass jars full of pencils and charcoal.

'Goodness!' said Phyllis. 'You've done so much.'

'Well, it's not a new hobby,' said Jamie. 'I've been making maquettes for years. The wood carving's a new thing, but actually I don't believe it's working: it's too difficult to get it to do what I picture in my mind. I think I may abandon those.'

Phyllis was relieved to hear this, for most of the wood pieces were rather peculiar.

'And drawing. Don't you remember, I did drawings of you and your sisters, ages ago. I even did one of your pony,' said Jamie.

'Do you know, I've quite forgotten.'

'So, what do you think?'

'Well, I don't really know anything about art, much less sculpture. Although I did see some wonderful things only a few weeks ago, in Paris. But they were all marble. Greek goddesses, nymphs, that sort of thing.'

'But do you like them?'

'I think I do. I'm not sure, yet. I like the way this one looks a bit like driftwood and a bit like a person lying down.'

She walked very slowly along the length of the counter. 'This head is very life-like, you've got the hair exactly. Who is she?'

'Her name's Clemmie. I got to know her in Italy.'

Phyllis couldn't help feeling pleased that he didn't seem at all interested in talking about the sitter.

'A man from a gallery in Bruton Street in London has been down to see my work. He likes them very much. We're talking about an exhibition in the spring. It's a well-known gallery.'

'But that's wonderful! When will it be? You must tell us, so we can all come and cheer you on. Oh Jamie, is that why you've got such long hair, now? Because you've turned into a professional artist?' She couldn't resist teasing him.

He batted her on the arm. 'There's nothing professional about it, I just haven't got round to going to the barber. Come on. Let's go into the house and warm up. I might even have a biscuit to offer you, somewhere.'

After this her days at the Grange took on a routine. Phyllis would get her father's breakfast in the mornings and then take his dog out for a morning walk. The distance to Jamie's house was just right: enough to give the spaniel a good run, but close enough to be back at the Grange in plenty of time for lunch. Each morning he made coffee for her and they drank it in the kitchen, talking. They reminisced, or told each other about their travels: something made Phyllis hold back from telling Jamie about all the meetings and things she had got involved in. Then in the early afternoons she sat with her mother while her father had what they all persisted in calling a rest, as if the whole of his day was not also made up of resting. At four o'clock Phyllis took him up a cup of tea and drew the curtains and read to him for an hour or so, something out of Kipling or from a funny little book of country reminiscences an old JP friend had brought, called *Small Talk at Wreyland*. At five he liked to switch on the wireless. A couple of times Jamie came over to the Grange, ostensibly to see how the patient was getting on. One evening he stayed on to dinner and afterwards got out a pencil and a pocket sketchbook in which he made several rapid little drawings. She didn't like to ask to see them in case she sounded vain. Phyllis's mother had always been fond of Jamie and his presence seemed to calm her. Other visitors tended to make her agitated, but in Jamie's presence she sat quietly, smiling her empty smile.

On her last evening, as she made her way up to bed, Phyllis saw a sliver of light at the bottom of her father's bedroom door and knocked softly.

'Hello, Daddy. Just come to say night-night,' she said.

'Thank you darling. It's been lovely having you here. Very peaceful. I don't imagine things will be so nice and quiet with Patricia next week. You know how she likes to rub Mrs Manville up the wrong way.'

'She doesn't mean any harm, she just wants you looked after properly.'

'As long as Mummy is all right, that's the thing. Nothing wrong with me that a few days in bed won't sort out.'

'No, of course not,' said Phyllis. 'Well, I'm off to bed, then. Anything you'd like, before I go?'

'No, all's well,' he said.

She wondered whether to go and give him a kiss and decided against it. Her father had never been one for displays of emotion.

On her way home Phyllis was to spend a night in London with Hugh and then they would take the train down to Sussex together. He wanted her to join him at a dinner, to hob-nob with some of the London Party people. He hinted that the Old Man himself might be coming. Phyllis hoped he would appear. She was eager to see him again, now that she was so much more engaged with Party matters. If there was time in the morning she rather thought she might look for a new pair of shoes to wear for the Templetons' ball, now only a couple of weeks away. Nina would then take her turn at the Grange, since she hadn't been asked to the party. Patricia, on the other hand, had already devoted some energy to her dress for the night and had unearthed an ostrich feather fan that she planned to suspend from her waist with a rope of artificial pearls. They had both bought new evening gloves for the occasion.

The French conversation Phyllis had been taking with Sarita had gone into abeyance since her father's illness and had also been put off for the following week, because of getting the house ready for the ball. This Wednesday, with Phyllis back at Bosham, they had decided to invite Monsieur Hubert to start an hour early so that they would have a longer lesson, giving them the chance to discuss their Paris trip.

'*Je regrette que je suis comme le jeu de serpents et — comment on dit "ladders"?*' Phyllis ventured.

'*Echelles,*' said Monsieur Hubert.

'*Alors, comme le jeu des serpents et d'échelles, j'ai gagné un peu de Français quand j'étais en France, mais maintenant je tombe par les serpents encore.*'

Sarita was trying very hard to keep a straight face.

'*Il faut pratiquer. Qu'est-ce que vous avait fait, à Paris?*' asked Monsieur Hubert.

Sarita was much better, able to speak fluently about the Parisian visit. Afterwards they lunched in the little morning room, since Fergus was away for the day. Sarita asked all about Phyllis's father and Phyllis thanked her for the Muscat grapes she'd had sent to the Grange for him, from Harrods. After their coffee they went up to see the dress that Sarita had had made for the ball. By luck, it had arrived that very morning. It was palest mauve velvet, with hundreds of little pearl buttons down the back and a scooped neck, trimmed with ermine. With it was a little evening cape in ermine, lined with glossy silk a shade darker than the dress itself.

'It's the colour of a shadow, yes?' said Sarita. 'Like a shadow on the snow.'

'What a clever idea,' said Phyllis. 'I'd never have thought of that. You're going to look so beautiful.'

10. Sussex, December 1938

The stone-floored entrance hall had four enormous arrangements of white flowers on waist-high Doric pillars made of plaster, brought in by the London florist: one to either side of the main door, with a mirroring second pair flanking the way through into the large drawing room. Each of the four arrangements occupied several yards of air, the blooms appearing to soar upwards and then to cascade extravagantly down, like a burst of fireworks. The scent from the tuberoses and lilies was sticky, intoxicating; while white freesias, tucked in low, gave off a smell half citrus, half peppery.

A tall blaze in the vast hall fireplace added to the sense of occasion. Phyllis and Hugh had been asked for dinner before the party along with other close friends of the Templetons. Some of them, having come from London, were staying at the house. Four round tables, each set with ten places, had been arranged in the smaller drawing room, so as to keep the dining room clear. There the long table and its many leaves had been taken down, and all the chairs and side tables removed and the rugs lifted so as to clear the floor for dancing, later. The Templetons were expecting more than two hundred guests. They'd had fifty more than that at their last ball without crowding, but that had been a fine summer's evening and people had spilled out on to the lawns. On this occasion Fergus had insisted that anything less than a hundred and sixty wasn't a proper party; the more people you invited, the more fun they were likely to have, was his view. Sarita protested mildly: there had been a lot of talk about where the coats would go. In the end it was decided to put them in the morning room, ticketed. A couple of girls would oversee the operation and hanging rails of the kind found in shop storerooms were procured for the purpose. Fergus hadn't been happy about this – it was a private party after all, not the cloakroom of a railway hotel – but at this time of year everyone, but everyone, wore an overcoat and all the men's were heavy dark tweed and all the women's were heavy dark fur, so short of getting people to spend hours fishing about for their own coats at two and three in the morning, no other solution for their retrieval had presented itself.

'Do look,' said Patricia, coming to stand by her sister at one of the pillars. 'How many different kinds of flowers can you count? I can see freesias and gardenia and these trailing bits are jasmine and that other wonderful smell, what do you think it is? Oh look, and stephanotis, that must be the scent. Wherever did she get them from, do you imagine? They can't have been grown in England, surely, not even in a hot-house. They must have cost the earth.'

'I think she said she'd had them brought down in a van from Moyses Stevens.'

'I ask you,' said Patricia.

'I hope I don't look as if I'm wearing a nightie, do I?' Phyllis said. She was dressed in a pale duck-egg blue silk dress, with a white silk ribbon threaded around the neckline and a wide belt of white petersham, fastened with a jade and diamanté clip. It was an old dress and she felt now that it was rather too young for her, but she'd replaced the original turquoise ribbon and belt with white and worn her pearls, to fit in with the party's theme. Sarita had insisted on loaning her an ermine tippet, to keep her shoulders warm.

'No, darling, you look lovely. That dress has always suited you so well,' said Patricia. 'What about me, do I look silly? God knows who dreamed up white, it's impossible not to turn out like some ghastly Miss Havisham.'

Venetia Gordon-Canning waved from across the hall and after leaving her coat made her way straight in the sisters' direction.

'Don't tell a soul, but it's rabbit,' she announced, holding up the corners of her evening stole. 'They just take little pinches of the fur and dye it darker, to look like ermine. Clever, isn't it? You'd never guess.'

'Most effective,' said Patricia. Venetia pulled a comic hoity-toity face at Phyllis while Patricia scanned the room. No one spoke for a moment while a waiter glided up with a salver of champagne, ready poured into tulip glasses.

'Is Andrew with you? I didn't see him come in,' said Patricia.

'Oh, he's here somewhere,' said Venetia. 'Quite honestly I couldn't wait to give him the slip. I'm hoping to have some fun once the dancing gets going, and he can get a bit huffy. Husbands can be the most frightful bore, can't they?'

Phyllis laughed, but Patricia made no sign of acknowledgement. 'What did you have for the dinner?' asked Patricia.

'Partridge and bread sauce and then some sort of thing with meringues. Then cheese.'

'No first course?'

'Oh yes, I'd forgotten. A fish mousse and melba toast. All white, you see. Then they had lots of little silver dishes with white mints and sugared almonds with the coffee.'

'I'm not sure that I'd find white food very appetizing,' said Patricia.

'I love Melba toast,' said Venetia. 'It's one of those things that's much better than it's got any right to be.'

'Isn't it?' agreed Phyllis, smiling.

Their hostess had never looked lovelier. In her hair she wore a simple diamond tiara; a matching pair of long earrings trembled between her ear-lobes and her neck like tiny waterfalls. At dinner the gleam from the candles glanced off the diamonds, making small white polka dots of light dance on the damask tablecloth in front of her whenever she moved her head. Phyllis was touched to have been put at Sarita's table for dinner. On her right was a much older Italian gentleman, whose name she failed to register; on her left was the ubiquitous Pea-Brain, whose nonsense always made him the easiest of dining companions.

'Phyllis,' he said, pulling her chair out for her to sit. 'You look especially ravishing tonight, if I may say so. A man's heart could shatter at the sight of you.'

'Now, now,' said Phyllis. 'There's no need to take it that far.' Pea-Brain grinned.

Phyllis leant in close to his ear and whispered. 'Do you know the name of the fellow on my other side? I didn't catch it, quite.'

'Haven't the foggiest. The Count of Monte Cristo, I daresay,' said Pea-Brain. 'But look, you're in luck, he hasn't pocketed his place-card. It's just there, just by the wine glasses, do you see? You can crib off that.'

As it turned out, the gentleman was indeed some sort of Count. During Sarita's youth he had been Italy's ambassador to Brazil, where he had become friends with her family. Later he had been posted to Paris, where he had again coincided with Sarita, during her first marriage. He was now retired and resident in London.

'Do you not miss your own country?' asked Phyllis. 'I know when we were overseas I used to long to get home. I even missed things I don't like, like tapioca.'

'Home becomes internal when you have been abroad as long as we have,' he said, with a certain mournful politesse. 'In any case it is not possible for us to return at present. My wife's family are not welcome in Italy and I must be at my wife's side. Perhaps one day. London is very congenial; we have been fortunate to find friends here in England. We walk every day in the park.'

'How nice,' said Phyllis. 'Do you have a dog?'

'We do not,' said the Count.

A silence began to settle between them. 'Is your wife musical?' asked Phyllis.

The Count smiled ruefully, whether at the limitations of her conversation or of his own responses she could not determine. 'She is fond of the ballet, but no: music is not especially important. Her family are academics.'

'Oh dear, I fear I made a bit of a bish, talking to the Count,' Phyllis murmured to Pea-Brain, after the first course was cleared, when it was time to turn to her other side. 'All I could think of were the most stupidly obvious things to do with Italy, like opera and gondolas. He was terribly sophisticated – even seemed to speak much better English than I do. He must have thought I was very silly.'

'No one could possibly think you anything other than delightful,' said Pea-Brain. 'Anyway, he was probably so mesmerized by your shape in that dress that he didn't hear a word.'

Phyllis giggled, a result of the champagne she'd been drinking before dinner and the wine since. 'Don't be ridiculous. He's about a hundred.'

'What makes you think men grow out of such things?' asked Pea-Brain.

Once all the after-dinner guests had arrived, the dancing began. Phyllis took a turn with Greville and another with Hugh: Pea-Brain disappeared into the throng almost at once, despite having spent half of dinner begging her to dance with him. Andrew Gordon-Canning was a very rigid and silent dance partner who spent the whole tune looking over Phyllis's head, presumably in the hope of finding his wife, who was nowhere to be seen. Hugh, on the other hand, was a surprisingly good dancer; or at least, it was surprising to Phyllis how fluid and smiling he looked, when she sat out a dance and watched him twirl across the floor with their hostess. Presently Hugh came away from the music and suggested that they go in search of a glass of something. In the hall they found Greville and Patricia and a small circle of their friends, all very animated.

'Shall you mind if I steal Hugh for a dance or two?' Patricia asked her sister. 'Only Greville's had enough for the time being and I so love it.'

'Of course not, darling,' said Phyllis. 'I was going to sit out for a bit in any case, catch my breath.'

It occurred to her that the small sitting room would have been cleared of tables by now and would provide a comfortable sanctuary in which to find a seat. There she found Sarita and a group of the less boisterous of the Templetons' friends, talking. The Count and his wife were among them, as well as a woman with a long face like a melancholy fox terrier. Phyllis felt rather unsteady. As a rule she wasn't much of a drinker, but she had had wine with dinner and then two glasses of the delicious pudding wine – it was like cough linctus, only nicer – and she'd lost count of how many glasses of champagne since. All of a sudden, seated in the warm room, she felt terribly hot and urgently queasy. She smiled vaguely in Sarita's direction and made her way out into the hall and on to the steps outside the house.

The sharp night air was refreshing. The sky was clear and dark and full of stars, but Phyllis reeled a little when she looked up, which made her aware how tipsy she was. A frost had not yet formed, but the tang of frost was already in the air. If she breathed through her nose and kept her gaze level she would be all right, but it felt important to be cold. The best thing in the world would be something cool directly against her skin. Cold could forestall the nausea and bring her back from the sense of tilting. If she could only press her face against something smooth and cool, that would solve everything. She half thought of lying down there and then on the stone steps, but someone might see her, or trip over her. Instead she made her way down the steps and across the gravel in the direction of the old stable-yard, where the cars had been parked for the evening. She could see the outlines of the vehicles, standing in lines on the hard ground. Some of the guests had brought drivers, but no one seemed to be about: on such a cold night they had surely come inside to smoke and wait it out in the warm until they were called to take people home. At first Phyllis thought she must find their own car, but it occurred to her that this wasn't neces-sary. Any one of the vehicles would serve, all she had to do was drape her shoulders across the cold metal of a car bonnet, to cool her cheeks and her forehead. Then she would feel better.

She had enough composure to realize that she would make an absurd figure if she were seen, and so she stepped gingerly past first one and then two rows of cars, further into the darkness. Here. But the car was too tall to incline against: she would have to kneel on the grass, and the damp might mark her frock. She decided instead to step up on to the front fender, so that she could bend from the waist on to the soothing surface of the chilled metal. It took a few moments to manoeuvre herself. The cold of it was far colder than she'd anticipated and made her gasp a little, like walking into sea-water. As the coolness spread across her arms, she laid first one cheek and then the other against the car. She hummed a little, half under her breath. The strange cold compress was working, she was beginning to feel less giddy and the nausea was evaporating. She didn't want to overdo it and catch cold, but she knew she wasn't yet steady enough to go back into the gaiety and heat of the party.

Phyllis had no sense of how long she had been upended there when she heard the sound of a woman's laughter. At first she supposed the person must be laughing at her expense – she must look like a madwoman after all – and she jolted upright in an attempt to recover some dignity, rearranging her dress. She looked around her, but couldn't see anyone. She stood very still. Now she heard a man's voice, a low rumble, before the woman's laughter came again. She knew that laugh well. Venetia. Now Phyllis felt sober and alert. The male voice was indistinct, but whatever he was saying must evidently have been very funny, as peals of laughter punctuated the low tones again and again. Then there was silence. Perhaps the two were now making their way back towards the house? Phyllis hesitated to take the same course herself, lest she run into them, for she was sure that the man with Venetia was not her husband. The return of sobriety made her aware now of how cold she had become, out here in the night with no coat, and she began to shiver quite violently. All at once a noise came, a kind of deep moan, answered in turn by a high, breathy sound like a contralto practising a downward scale. These were not sounds meant for other ears. Phyllis didn't want to hear. She slipped away into the enfolding darkness, towards the welcoming lights of the house.

'Whatever's happened to your dress?' Patricia asked her.

Her sister had found her standing by the fire in the hall. She still had goosebumps all along her arms, but her teeth had stopped chattering. Phyllis looked down and saw that there was a dark patch below her bosom, where she had leant against the car. Moisture had darkened the material. 'Oh Lord, does it look dreadful? I went out to get some air and I must have brushed against something.'

'Well, where's the tippet Sarita lent you? You could just hold that – fasten it over – till it dries. I don't think it'll have marked the fabric, will it? It's only water, by the look of it.'

'I think I left it in the little sitting room, earlier.'

'Shall I go and fetch it for you?'

Phyllis felt a rush of warmth towards her sister. 'Would you? Thanks so much.'

Patricia duly returned with the fur and suggested that they go back to the small sitting room, where various of their friends – Pea-Brain and Fergus and Andrew Gordon-Canning among them – were holding court.

Phyllis squeezed in between a couple of them so as to keep thawing out. The men were in high spirits, flushed from dancing and wine. In due course Fergus stood and reached out his hand to her. 'Dance?' he asked.

Phyllis did not really want to dance with him, but Fergus was her host; it would have been churlish to say no.

He led her through into the dining room. The room was long and slender, hung with pearl-green silk. Pairs of gilt swans necked at the top of tall ornate mirrors which stood at either end of the room, reflecting the distance between them again and again in the candlelight. A five-piece band installed at the far side were playing a slow tune. Phyllis hoped Fergus wouldn't attempt conversation. It was so embarrassing, trying to talk small-talk and keep in step at the same time. In the event he did not speak. Instead he held his face so close against her head that she could feel the warmth of his breath on her hair, close to her ear. Fergus was a good dancer, she could tell, and the fact that he was on the short side allowed the rhythm of his body to awake her own. Some men were entirely stiff and only moved their legs, but he was different. There was a lilt in his torso and an ease in his arms, as if dancing came as readily to him as any other kind of movement. She wondered whether it was because he was an expert horseman that he seemed so natural to dance with. She thought of asking him as much, but she was enjoying herself and didn't want to break the mood.

As they shuffled about on the parquet, the pressure of his hand against the small of her back intensified. His hip touched hers. He shifted his face very slightly so that his breath was now against the naked skin behind her ear, as if he might be about to whisper, but still he said nothing. When the music came to an end Fergus made no sign of bringing their dance to a close, but carried on idly turning, as if in a dream. And yet there was a sense almost of purpose about him, despite the languor: a feeling that all his interest and energy were secretly aimed only at her, as if no one else in the world existed. Again she thought of riders. Adepts could urge a horse over a jump or around a tight turn without giving any apparent directions – no kicking, no yanking of the reins – just by turning their own face a little or with some invisible tightening of the legs against the flanks of the animal. Now a new tune started up and Fergus made the merest of adjustments, so as to keep in step, but still he did not speak. She was surprised to find that she was glad he had not let her go and that he meant their dance not to end just yet; she was surprised to find she liked being held by him. In real life she had never cared for him very much: he had never seemed to her to be worthy of Sarita.

Phyllis felt her ribs against his, the softness below her ribs flattened against him. He was clasping her. His hand in hers was dry and smooth. He dropped his head very slightly and she thought she felt for an instant his mouth, the softness of his lips, brush against her throat. Still they slowly circled. His hand moved a little lower on her back, pulling her in. They seemed to be moving in slower and slower circles. Again the tune came to an end; again he gripped her against him, waiting for the next to begin. And there it was, suddenly, like the hilt of a dagger. Pushing, pushing against her. Like an insult. A nasty, sinewy accusation. A gizzard. She felt it against her stomach, almost pulsing; insistent and sharp. Every part of her recoiled with revulsion. The swoony feeling evaporated at once and she made to pull away, but Fergus had her, as if in a clamp. Now he took his face away from the nape of her neck and looked at her with a knowing, unashamed frankness.

She could feel her face and throat burn with shame and fury.

'No, I don't want . . .' she hissed. She would have shouted, but she did not want to alert the other dancers.

Fergus smiled a slow smile, but maintained his grip. His arms were very strong and she found she could only wriggle. He put his mouth against her ear.

'Shall we go somewhere?' he said in a low voice.

His mouth was level with the side of her throat. Earlier in the evening she had applied scent to the spot of skin just below her ear. It was one of the little rituals of going out for the evening, a pleasant feeling as the coolness of the glass scent stopper deposited its floral trail on her throat. Now, in that same place, something warm and wetly sticky slithered across the skin. For a moment the sensation so repelled and confused her that she almost thought the emission had somehow worked its way up from his groin on to her neck. Then she realized that it was his tongue. Fergus had licked her. If an eel or hagfish had deposited a trail of nacreous slime on to her body she could not have felt a more visceral disgust.

'Let go of me!' she hissed. She tried to lift her hand in order to wipe the smear he had left upon her neck, but he had both her hands in his, and would not yield. She pulled her head away from his and saw the look of challenge on his face.

'Let me go!'

'I can't do that for the moment, I'm afraid,' he said. 'Got to wait for things to die down.' Still he pressed himself against her.

'Keep that . . . keep to yourself. I don't want to dance with you any more. I want to stop,' she said.

'Steady on. All in good time,' he said. Fergus didn't seem at all riled. If anything he seemed amused. He continued to hold her, but less tightly. Now the supple rhythm of his dancing seemed disgusting, as if he were some sort of pantomime snake charmer. He still moved to the music, but all the concentration he had fixed on her had departed. Now she felt as if she were just an inanimate thing he had to move around, like someone's coat. Phyllis willed the music to come to a stop, but it seemed to drag on and on. She could feel tears pricking in her eyes. All she wanted was to go home, away from here.

At last the tune died away and she was able to break free. She tried not to run. She must find Hugh. In the hall people were standing about in twos and threes, some of them evidently the worse for wear: faces were flushed and voices raised: a roar of vowel-sounds seemed to issue from these people, as if they were all shouting the word 'hour' over and over again. One man stumbled as he progressed towards the door. She went to the little sitting room, but there was no sign of her husband. Perhaps he was dancing and she had not seen him. She didn't want to go back towards the music, but the desire to get away was stronger. In the vestibule outside the dining room she bumped into Venetia Gordon-Canning.

'Come back for another round?' she asked.

'I'm looking for Hugh, actually. Have you seen him?'

'I think he's dancing with your sister, down by the band. If you were trying to make him jealous just now, he won't have seen. You were at the wrong end of the room.'

'I don't know what you mean,' said Phyllis.

'Egging Fergus on like that. I didn't know you had it in you.'

'I wasn't egging him on! I find him creepy, to tell you the truth,' said Phyllis, lowering her voice.

'Well, it didn't look as if you did. Everyone saw you, practically having it off on the dance floor.' She leant in towards her friend's ear and whispered: 'You could spot his stiffie at twenty paces, so you must have been doing something right.'

'Who saw me? What do you mean?' said Phyllis. She felt panic-stricken.

'Sarita and I came through to watch the dancing.'

Phyllis's heart plummeted. 'Where is she?'

'Gone upstairs, I think. She said she was just going to go and get something. Probably felt embarrassed. Rather shows her up if her great friend gets off with her husband at their own party.'

At this Phyllis burst into tears. 'Honestly, Venetia, you think you're so smart and amusing, but you're just cruel. I heard you outside, earlier on; what you were doing with some man in the back of a car out there. Someone's husband, I daresay. Just because you go on like that doesn't mean other people do. You shouldn't have let Sarita be upset like this, it's too unkind.'

'Ooh, tra-la! The pot and the kettle spring to mind. It's a bit late now, to be so sanctimonious. What were you doing out by the motors, in any case? I bet you were spooning too. With Fergus, were you?' said Venetia.

'No, I wasn't, I . . .'

'Well, if you sneak on me I'll certainly tell on you,' said Venetia. She strutted off.

Phyllis tried to collect herself. She could feel her heart pounding against her ribs, like a trapped bird flapping at the bars of a window. Her nose was running. She turned to face the wall, pretending to examine a little painting of what looked like a Dutch landscape, flat and straw-coloured. Just then she heard Patricia's voice and Hugh's. She sprang round and clutched at her husband's arm.

'Oh, thank goodness, I've been looking for you everywhere! Can we go now? I'm terribly tired, suddenly: I don't think I can go on for another minute.'

'But we haven't had breakfast yet,' said Hugh.

'We can have breakfast at home. Only I really must go,' said Phyllis. 'I'm going to wait on the steps, while you fetch your coat.'

'Are you all right, darling? You don't seem quite yourself,' Patricia asked, following her sister through the hall towards the door.

'I'm not ill or anything. I think I've just overdone it.'

'Let's telephone in the morning so we can have a post mortem,' said Patricia. 'Not too early, though. Greville never likes to leave a party until the last crumb has been swept away.'

'I will,' said Phyllis. 'I promise.'

Phyllis cried silently all the way home, allowing her tears to fall unchecked. She kept her face averted, so Hugh wouldn't notice. The effort of not making any sound gave her a sore throat. She could hardly bear to think she had upset Sarita, who had always been so very kind to her. Her dearest friend, really; the person – even more than her own family – she was most herself with.

Phyllis didn't know how she could make things right, but she knew she must try. A letter or a telephone call wouldn't do: she would go and see her in person and just hope that Fergus wouldn't be about when she called. She didn't know how she would be able to face him, after this. Almost the worst thing had been that way he'd looked at her; the ghastly assumed complicity in that look. Hugh gave no sign of noticing her distress, he was concentrating on the road. It was bitterly cold and he rather thought there might be black ice: he drove slowly.

The following morning was bright and clear, with air so cold and fresh it almost stung to breathe. The sky was remote and very blue; the horizon a distinct line where the dark sea met the sky, as if a child had drawn it with a ruler. The bare elms cast long shadows. Phyllis took her morning cup of tea and stood under the cedar, looking out across the horseshoe bay towards the village church. The low sun revealed frosted cobwebs, strewn over the empty rose bushes. They looked as intricate and easy to tear as old frozen lace. Hugh was already up and dressed and freshly shaved. He came and stood beside her on the grass.

'Do you think it's wise to be wearing gumboots with your

dressing gown? You do look eccentric,' he said. He sounded more doubtful than chiding.

'I don't suppose there's anyone much about,' said Phyllis. 'I didn't want to ruin my slippers, you see.'

From inside the house came the sound of the telephone ringing.

'Could you go?' Phyllis asked Hugh. 'If it's Patricia will you tell her I'll ring her back in an hour?'

She was enjoying the sun on her face and the glittering water. It was a new day after all and in the brightness good humour was restored. Gossip could wait.

After a time Hugh came out to her and took her by the elbow. When he spoke it was with such exaggerated calm that she knew he was about to impart something very terrible. She felt an almost physical coldness, like opening the door into a deep cellar. She thought her father must have died. 'You'd better come in and sit down, Phyllis. I'm afraid there's some very sad news. It's Sarita.'

Phyllis, 1979

When I heard about Sarita of course my first thought was that she had taken her own life. I suppose in a way she had. It was devastating: there's no other word for it, really. It would have been terribly upsetting to have lost such a dear friend under any circumstances, especially someone as young as Sarita still was. And at that time I'd never lost anyone close to me: she was the first. Until someone you're really close to dies, death is something that happens to other people but you don't truly take in that it'll ever happen to you. I felt not just grief but the most awful, searing guilt. And shame. Guilt and shame are not quite the same thing, that's something I have had a great deal of time to think about and I am quite sure of the difference. I should be, because I am very familiar with both. My children think I'm shameless – that's one of the things they can't forgive me for – but they're wrong about that. They're wrong about quite a number of things, as a matter of fact.

On that morning I couldn't stop thinking how ghastly it must have been for her to see me smooching with her husband, how alone she must have felt at that moment. You must remember that she was a foreigner: she didn't really fit in with English life. It might have been better if she'd been in London, with more sophisticated sort of people. As it was I think she always felt very much the outsider. I believe she was lonely. Especially in the horsey and rather coarse circle her husband mixed with. Everything about her was the opposite of that: she was a very refined sort of person. An extraordinary person, really. She was curious without ever being indelicate and she had this tremendous natural elegance. That was the word people always used to describe her. She was elegant in a very un-affected way, all her gestures and the way she dressed and moved and spoke. Her hands. She just couldn't help it. And she had such a pretty laugh, which made people want to please her, because it was like a beam of light when she laughed. Grace, that's what Sarita had.

I blamed myself, of course I did. And what made it even worse was that I couldn't tell anyone. I certainly couldn't tell Hugh and I felt too wretched and ashamed to tell my sisters. The other friend I had at the time – her name was Venetia – had seen me dancing closely with him: the husband, Fergus. It sounds so trivial now. She'd been standing with Sarita: in fact it was she who told me that Sarita had seen us on the dance floor. She was a spiky sort of girl. My sister Patricia had tried to warn me off her, but I'd put it down to a spot of sibling jealousy, because this woman Venetia was rather a figure in county circles and my sister always minded about that sort of thing. But actually I think Patricia had had my best interests at heart, that Venetia actually was a trouble-maker and a gossip. Anyway. Venetia had seen Fergus and myself in this sort of clinch, you might call it, and I lived in dread of her broadcasting it. She might have exaggerated, claimed he and I were having an affair, she was the sort of person who piled it on for fun. It would have been the most natural thing in the world for her to spread it about that poor Sarita had been broken by the sight of her husband and her dear friend together. I never really knew whether Venetia did talk in this way, because I stopped seeing her after the Templetons' dance.

It was morphia. I only learned years later that Sarita'd been taking it in secret for years, even before she'd married for the second time. The first husband knew about it and had tried to get the little girl to live with him because he didn't think Sarita was reliable. I imagine Fergus must have known, but I don't suppose it troubled him too much: he knew lots of people who did rather rackety things, and if anything he seemed to relish that sort of behaviour. She let him do as he liked – she had deep enough pockets for his ponies, all that – which presumably was the main thing.

No one had gone up to bed that night until God knows when. Fergus hadn't slept in their room but had gone to bed in his dressing room – which had its own bathroom – otherwise he'd have noticed that she wasn't there. One of the house guests had got up in the night and afterwards they said that they'd stepped in something wet on the landing outside their bathroom but that they hadn't thought too much about it. Everyone was pretty drunk and a soggy patch of carpet could have been where someone had spilled a drink, or a dog had peed. It wasn't the sort of thing that would cause a guest to wake up the whole household after a party.

It was fortunate that the plaster didn't come down on someone's head or they'd have had another corpse on their hands. As it was, it was a lump of heavy cornicing in the bedroom below that fell. Luckily it was in the room of an elderly Italian couple – friends of Sarita, not Fergus – and they did bother to switch the light on and get out of bed and when they saw that there was a huge brown mark spreading across the ceiling and water dripping they went to investigate. There was water trickling through the landing ceiling outside their room, too.

Naturally they thought it was a cistern in one of the attics. The husband went down to the servants' quarters and fetched someone, while various others brought up buckets to put under the leaks. By then the house was waking up and Fergus appeared. He sprang up to the attic where the water tanks were and shone a torch around and couldn't see anything amiss. Everyone was groggy with hangovers I suppose; anyway it took them quite a while to think of looking in the bathrooms.

Sarita's bathroom door was locked. Apparently she was in the habit of having a bath at night, before she got into bed – you may not remember, but big houses were so fearfully cold in those days. You'd get into bed and your feet would be freezing. Anyway. From the water coming through the floor it seemed likely it was still locked from the night before. By then the little girl had appeared and was by Sarita's bedroom asking for her mother. A bleary gaggle of them had congregated on the landing outside her bathroom and hovering by her bedroom. It was lucky that Fergus had the presence of mind to guess what might have happened and he ordered them all off and got someone to take the child downstairs. It was just him and one of the servants. They had to break down the door.

She was in the bath with the taps running. Everything was drenched. They had to lift her out. They carried her through to the bedroom and covered her up.

Of course the doctor must have known. Women in their thirties don't just die of nothing. They don't just see their husband trying to get off with one of their great friends and then go upstairs and lie down politely in their bath and expire from a broken heart. It's not like The Lady of Shalott. But I never thought of that at the time. I believed that she must have had a weak heart already and that the upset and the hot water brought on an attack. There may have been marks on her skin, from the syringe, I don't know. If there were, they weren't on her arms: I remember her arms in her evening dress and they were quite smooth and unmarked. Years afterwards, when I found out, I was told that something similar had happened during her first marriage when they were living in Paris, but she'd been found in time and they'd been able to revive her. That was why the child's father didn't want Sarita to be left alone with the little girl, at any time. Well, presumably it was all right in the daytime.

I don't know whether drug addicts observe some sort of sun-over-the-yard-arm ritual, like six o'clock drinks time, but I don't suppose they're taking things at all hours, are they? Although when I think back on it, there were times when she seemed very vague, even in the middle of the afternoon.

I don't know what I felt about the fact that she hadn't told me, when we had confided with one another about so much else. I suppose it must have been something she wasn't proud of. It's pretty sordid, after all, and Sarita was the opposite of that in every other respect. She wouldn't have wanted people to know. Anyway Fergus stopped it coming out and there was nothing in the papers. The official line was that she'd had heart failure and that that's what killed her. I know I've said it before, but people of that kind observed a sort of code of silence, so that nothing ever got into the papers. Their GP would have been in cahoots as to the cause of death. No one would've wanted to upset the child or the servants.

I only found out by accident, after the war. We were dining with my sister Patricia; it may have been one of the last times we went there. She put me next to her friend Pea-Brain and he let something slip about Sarita's death. I think he assumed I already knew. Then he told me the whole story. He said Sarita and Fergus hadn't been sleeping together for some time before then, which may explain why she'd taken to having baths at night – for a little comfort, perhaps. Of course it was a terrible shock.

Afterwards, when we got home, I remembered the grey man in Paris and how he'd brought the box of sugared chestnuts to our hotel. It had always struck me as odd, the way she'd hardly spoken to him. I wondered if he'd really been bringing her morphia. It would have explained why she was so late coming down in the mornings.

The awful thing is that in all the upset I did nothing for the little girl. I couldn't face going to the house and I was so miserable and ashamed of myself . . . in those days people didn't take children to funerals, so I don't believe she was even there. I didn't see her in the front pews and when Fergus followed the coffin out to the churchyard he walked alone, head bowed. I didn't go back to the house afterwards, I just couldn't bear to revisit the place without Sarita there. And I didn't want to come face to face with Venetia and have to talk to her, either. I suppose the child must have gone to her father, perhaps before the funeral. I told myself that I'd get in touch with her in due course, once she was settled in her new life. I believed her father lived in London for at least some of the year, and I vaguely imagined I'd write and arrange to take her out for tea somewhere, perhaps taking Frances and Edwin with me.

In the time that followed, when I was in prison, I had plenty of cause to consider how much it mattered to me to believe that people were being kind to my children in my absence. It was the only thing I hoped for.

But I wasn't kind to Sarita's child. It makes me feel awful to tell you this, but you may as well know the truth, for what it's worth. I'd like to think I'd have more moral gumption, now. I didn't go to see her or to offer her any comfort or consolation. The truth is I never saw her again and now I find I can't even remember her name.

11. Sussex, March 1940

By the time war was declared, Phyllis was an altogether busier and more important person. Had she still had her women friends – Sarita, principally; but Venetia, too – she might still have been content with French conversation, with riding and lunches and picnics, with ferrying the children to and from their schools for half-terms and exeats, and with arrangements in the new house. As it was, she found herself perforce more and more involved with Nina and her political work. Seeing how low her sister was after Sarita's death, Nina had taken Phyllis under her wing. She couldn't just mope about in the house for ever; what she needed was something useful and constructive to do. It was all too easy to simply sit in the morning room, writing a letter or two; missing the fine open view she'd so loved at Bosham, missing the children now they were away at school for the greater part of the year, missing Sarita. It was Hugh who always proudly referred to it as the morning room, but it was really just a little sitting room, rather dark, on the east corner of the house.

Privately Phyllis thought of it as the mourning room. In years to come, when she had so much more to mourn, she thought back on this and considered herself to have been very spoilt.

There was a view that in these urgent times women must not be simply tea-makers and note-takers and general dogsbodies, but a great force within British Union. It was true that a quarter of Mosley's supporters were women, more than in any other political party. As the threat of war with Germany became more real, that number grew, and then again, when war was declared, there was a surge of women members: many of the new recruits were wives and mothers who didn't want to see another generation of their young men slaughtered in Europe. A good portion of the key speakers for the overall Party Peace Campaign were women. When the Party's Women's Peace Campaign was launched in February, Nina and Phyllis went up to London on the train for the meeting in Holborn, to sign up. The Leader had given the enterprise his blessing, even pledging to come and address them. There were rallies at weekends. At the Women's Peace Meeting in April, there was a turnout of almost a thousand. Phyllis found it electrifying to be among such a number of fellow souls, all united in their passion for the cause. It was a wonderful feeling, to belong. When Sir Oswald took to the stage to address them, she joined the others in giving him a standing ovation. He brought such force, such hope! It was clear that he was the only politician who had the strength of character and of argument to redeem Britain from this futile and needless war. If, before she became involved in the Women's Campaign, there had been some aspects of British Union policy Phyllis didn't wholly applaud, now against the fervour of the peace initiative these reservations shrank away.

Nina had already made something of a name for herself as a public speaker, so much so that she had been asked to address meetings in London, Birmingham and Manchester. She had spoken on a range of topics, and had caused something of a stir when she addressed a Kensington meeting on the nuisance of society women. Her contention was that such women contributed nothing to the wider world, but frittered their evenings in night-clubs and languished their mornings in bed, telephoning: whereas the industrious and resourceful women of BU put such useless females to shame. This was bold, given that such types abounded in the very constituency where she was speaking, and one or two Party eyebrows were raised, given that the Leader's own wife was of the kind. Nevertheless, Nina gained a reputation for the force and reason of her speeches. Buoyed by her success, she encouraged her sister to obtain her own speaker's licence, also. But Phyllis didn't want to tread on her husband's toes. Hugh was very proud of his platform position and she had no craving for the limelight. She preferred to work behind the scenes. She found plenty to occupy herself with. There were branch meetings in Chichester and Bognor and along the coast, all of which required organization. Study circles were set up. Speakers needed to be booked, halls hired, pamphlets written and distributed. Then there was the money side of things: subscriptions to be collected and sent on to London, printers to be paid.

Once men began to be called up, women became ever more essential in keeping Party business going. The nearby Bournemouth branch was now run solely by women, who had been having a dreadful time of it: local thugs had daubed their office with paint and then returned to throw bricks through the windows. There was shattered glass all over the room, tiny splinters worked their way into files and the women complained of cut fingers for months afterwards. This was the trouble: people outside the Party were apt to mistake the Peace Campaign for a lack of patriotism, little understanding that those within it felt a passionate loyalty to the very notion of a Great Britain. A war with Germany was simply not in Britain's interest. So long as the Kingdom and her Empire were unthreatened, it was folly to take up arms. Everyone Phyllis knew shared the conviction that Germany would never attack England. When ARP volunteers started to hand out gasmasks to use in the event of enemy gas attack, Nina and Eric refused to take them. Phyllis and Hugh followed suit. It was on the same grounds that Hugh declined to install an air-raid shelter in the garden of the new house, certain that such a thing would never be necessary. Covering the nearby beaches with barbed wire and defence lookouts was blatantly ridiculous.

Hugh's age meant he would not be required for National Service. Greville and Eric, though, were both called up; somehow Greville managed to land on his feet and secure a desk-job at the Ministry. Eric went into the Air Force – if the Flying Corps had been good enough for Sir Oswald during the last war, it was certainly good enough for him – and was sent off to somewhere-or-other for training.

Phyllis could see that her husband was restless, now that work on the house was complete. There was the garden, of course, but his London post seemed to have fizzled out altogether. Phyllis did not like to enquire too closely, as Hugh was apt to become irritable. The logical thing for him to do, he now assured her, was to stand in a local council election as a Party candidate: this he intended to do as soon as a suitable seat became vacant. When Eric asked whether Hugh might be able to help out at the garage two or three days a week while he underwent his RAF training – strictly behind the desk, of course, not with the donkey work – he assented. Such work was rather beneath him, but at least it was local.

In the second week of March, the telephone rang early one morning, while she and Hugh were having breakfast. It was Mrs Manville, to say that her father had died. She had gone up to take him his tray and found him stone dead in his bed. The words stone dead somehow struck Phyllis as absurdly funny and she struggled not to laugh out loud while Mrs Manville went on. The doctor had been called, but had not arrived as yet. Her mother had been told, but she was not having one of her better mornings and she appeared not to have been able to take it in. Phyllis said that she and Hugh would come at once. She thanked Mrs Manville, although it wasn't clear to her what she was thanking her for. No sooner had she put the receiver down than the telephone went again. This time it was Patricia.

'What on earth is going to happen about Mummy, now?' she said, without preamble.

'I know. She won't be able to stay at the house, I shouldn't have thought; not unless we engage a nurse,' said Phyllis.

'With the best will in the world, I can't have her here. We've just got a new puppy.'

'Have you? You never said. When?' said Phyllis.

'Oh, a fortnight or so. The Tuesday before last, we collected him. Don't know that we've spoken since then, that's why. Wire-coated fox terrier. Absolutely the sweetest thing you've ever seen, but I fear he's going to be a yapper. Rex. Antonia chose the name, rather silly but there you are. Children are so fearfully unimaginative when it comes to naming their animals. When we got her a rabbit she wanted to call it Bunny. Anyway, I couldn't possibly cope with Mummy as well.'

'No,' said Phyllis.

'Nina's good at organizing things.'

'Yes. I'm not sure she'd have the patience, though. Or the room, in that little house.'

'Well, we'll have to talk it over. But I just thought I should make my position clear from the beginning.'

'Poor Daddy. I shouldn't think he ever said an unkind word to anyone, not in his whole life,' said Phyllis. Now that she was talking to her sister, she felt as if a huge bubble of sorrow was beginning to rise through her chest and up into her throat.

'It's been expected,' said Patricia.

'Yes,' said Phyllis. The grief was forming itself into a sob. She felt she might choke on it at any moment. She rang off abruptly and stood by the telephone table and wept, her face in her hands.

★

Nina and Eric were already installed in the kitchen at the Grange by the time Phyllis and Hugh arrived. An armchair had been brought through from the sitting room and placed in a corner, near the stove. In it sat their mother, her swollen feet as ever encased in a shabby pair of slippers. She looked no sadder than the last time Phyllis had seen her, when her father had been alive. Phyllis did not know whether to feel relieved or exasperated that her mother seemed so blithely unaware of her own widowhood.

'Where's Mrs Manville?' asked Hugh.

'Gone into the village,' said Nina.

'Should you like a cup of tea? I daresay you're thirsty, after your journey?' asked Eric.

'We've only come from home, not halfway across Europe. It's hardly an ordeal,' snapped Hugh. His wife knew that he found Nina and Eric's habit of drinking tea at all hours of the day an annoyance. Tea was for tea-time, in his view.

'That would be lovely, thank you so much,' said Phyllis.

'We stopped at an hotel for a sandwich, in any case,' said Hugh, relenting.

It felt peculiar to watch someone other than Mrs Manville fill the kettle and use the old tea-tin, the pattern on its lid almost worn away from years of handling. She realized that the kitchen was a room she never lingered in, generally. It was just the place where trays were collected and deposited. She noticed, now, how shabby it looked. Half the things in here were chipped or dented.

'What's that chair doing there?' asked Hugh.

'I think Mrs Manville brought it in,' said Nina. 'So she can keep an eye on Mummy while she's cooking. And anyway, it's warmer in here. Might as well.'

'Are you all right, there?' Hugh asked his mother-in-law. He raised his voice as if to be heard over the noise of a loud engine and said the words very deliberately, as he always had when talking to a foreigner.

'Very nice,' she replied.

'Well, I don't know what Patricia will say,' muttered Hugh.

'Patricia doesn't have the last word on everything, you know,' said Nina.

'Is . . . is Daddy still upstairs?' Phyllis asked Nina, in a whisper. She didn't want to alarm their mother.

'Yes, of course. They're not coming to take him until later this afternoon. The doctor's already been, though.'

'Have you been up?'

'Yes. He looks very peaceful.'

'Oh dear, will I be able to face it, d'you think?' Phyllis caught her sister by the arm. 'I've never . . . well, you know.'

'Honestly, there's nothing to fear. He doesn't look spooky, or anything. I'll come in with you, if you like.'

'Did you say it was time to get ready for dinner?' asked their mother. She looked worried by the thought.

'No, Mummy, it's only just after lunch,' said Nina.

'Patricia will be here shortly,' Hugh told his mother-in-law, in the same loud voice he had used before. This was intended to console her, for her eldest daughter had always been thought to be her mother's favourite. She laughed wanly in response, as if humouring a stranger.

In the event, Patricia did not arrive until after nightfall: Greville had been in London and they hadn't been able to set off until he got home. The undertakers had been told – by Mrs Manville, presumably – not to remove the body until such a time as all the daughters of the house had had the chance to pay their last respects, and so Eric had telephoned to postpone them until the morning.

After supper, once their mother had been installed in her

bedroom for the night, Nina suggested it might be the moment for Patricia to go up to her father's room. But she told her sisters quite bluntly that she had no intention of doing so.

'I just can't manage it,' she said with a shudder.

'He looks a bit like something from Madame Tussauds,' said Phyllis. 'Not really like Daddy at all. Not frightening, but just not the same.'

'How anyone can confuse a dead person for someone asleep is beyond me,' said Nina. 'I mean, they're nothing alike. You can tell straight away.'

'Sort of waxen,' said Phyllis.

'Of course, Patricia's very sensitive,' said Greville, in order to call a gentle halt to this line of conversation.

Nina and Phyllis exchanged a glance. Well-meaning though Greville was, he had never made any secret of the fact that he considered his wife to be cut of finer cloth than the rest of her family.

'Should you like me to go and sit with him for a bit?' asked Eric.

'You are a love,' said Nina. 'But there's no need. It's not as if he'll miss the company. Anyway, I thought I'd tell them, and I think you should be with me.'

'Tell us what?' asked Patricia, rather sharply.

'That Eric and I have got some news. I'm expecting.'

'Nina! That's wonderful!' said Phyllis.

'Very good, very good. Wonderful news,' said Greville. He stood up and went to embrace Nina, before shaking Eric warmly by the hand.

'Yes. Excellent,' said Hugh. He did not follow his brother-in-law's lead, but stood holding his little coffee cup and saucer.

'Are you sure?' asked Patricia.

'Of course I'm sure, you ninny! I've been hoping for long enough, haven't I?'

'Well, we never knew,' said Patricia. 'We didn't know whether you both wanted to have children.'

'Of course we did,' said Eric, beaming.

'Such a shame that Daddy couldn't have known,' said Phyllis. 'He'd have been so thrilled.'

A sad little silence settled on the room, before Nina spoke again.

'The only snag is, I'd been asked to stand for election. Up in Warrington, there's a seat coming vacant. But I shan't, not now. It would mean such a lot of travel and exertion.'

'Very wise,' said Greville. 'You just put your feet up and let your kind husband here wait on you hand and foot.'

'Don't be ridiculous,' said Patricia. 'There's nothing actually the matter with her.'

'Are you sure you've got that right, about Warrington?' Hugh asked. 'Only no one at HQ mentioned it to me and I rather think they would've.'

'Quite sure,' said Nina. 'Sir Oswald spoke to me about it himself, as a matter of fact. He said that he thought my manner of speaking would go down especially well in the north. I don't know that that's much of a compliment, actually.'

At this they all laughed.

'Well, I'm going to turn in,' said Greville. There was a general murmur of assent.

'We ought to have a talk about Mummy, tomorrow, once we're all feeling more refreshed,' said Patricia.

Nobody answered.

Various neighbours appeared over the course of the following days, Jamie among them. Letters of condolence arrived. It surprised them all, the quantity of post; people they had never heard their father mention now expressing such affection for him. Since their mother could no longer write with any coherence, it was agreed that Patricia, who had the nicest writing, would respond on her behalf. Nina and Eric took charge of the funeral arrangements. Phyllis would help Mrs Manville to prepare sandwiches and fruitcake for the mourners and to lay out tables with cups and plates and so forth: on the day, Mrs Manville's niece and sister-in-law would come in from the village to help hand round sherry and tea, as well as the food. The conversation about their mother's future kept being put off. Now, the day before the funeral, Mrs Manville raised the subject with Phyllis. The two women were in the kitchen by themselves, hard-boiling eggs and slicing cucumber.

'I don't know what you're all planning to do concerning your mother,' she said.

'No,' said Phyllis. 'I don't think we're any clearer ourselves. It's such a worry. I think we all felt we'd get the service today over before we really address it.'

'I've given it some consideration and I just thought I should let you know that I'd be prepared to stay on with her, if you wanted me to. She's used to me: we rub along. I understand what she's trying to say, most of the time. Routine is important for her, familiarity. She gets unsettled very easily.'

'That would be wonderful!' said Phyllis. 'It hadn't occurred to any of us that you'd even countenance it, with all the extra work it'd mean now that Daddy won't be here to keep an eye on her in the afternoons and early evenings, when you're not usually about. To be honest we thought you might be considering retirement. That would be really wonderful. Much the best solution. It would be lovely for Mummy to be able to stay here, with all her things around her.'

'I'd be expecting some consideration, for the extra responsibility and hours.'

'More money, do you mean?' said Phyllis. 'I can't see that anyone would object to that. I'll take it up with my sisters, of course.'

'And I'd be wanting one weekend off a month,' said Mrs Manville. 'As well as a fortnight in the summer.'

'Well, I'm sure we could cover for you during those times.'

'You wouldn't be covering for me. You'd be covering for your mother,' said Mrs Manville crisply. Phyllis felt herself colour.

'While we're having this little talk, I feel I should tell you: my sister-in-law, her nephew went down with the *Courageous*. Five hundred of them, killed.'

'I'm heartily sorry to hear it. That was a dreadful thing.' The ship had been sunk off the coast of Ireland by a German U-boat, almost as soon as war was declared.

'All those sailors, our sailors. Boys, a lot of them, all perished. What I wanted to say to you is: it's no thanks to any of you lot.'

'Mrs Manville, of course I understand you'd have very strong sentiments, having lost someone. I may remind you that I've just lost someone myself: I know what it is to be bereaved. A nephew, did you say? But I fail to see how my sisters and myself contributed to this.'

'Not my nephew, my sister-in-law's: it was her brother's boy. Anyway, Patricia, she's all right: I've no quarrel with her. She doesn't parade about the streets in uniform, like your children and your sister Nina. It's you two that need to look to your consciences, following that wicked man. He'd have us taken over by the Germans in a trice. You with your salutes and uniforms and speechifying: you're nothing better than a bunch of traitors. Thugs they are, most of them. Just because you don't bring your flags and banners here, don't think word doesn't spread. I've got family on the south coast, you know, they tell me all sorts of things as to what your lot get up to. I know all about your camping parties, brainwashing the young. You and your husbands, you're just idling about, promoting these odious ideas while others are laying down their lives for this country. It's a disgrace. That's what it is: a disgrace. There, now I've said my piece. I had to say it. If you shan't want me to stay on with your mother, then so be it.'

Phyllis noticed that Mrs Manville was still holding the little peeling knife in her right hand. Someone had wound twine around and around its handle, presumably to bind some crack where the wood had split. For once she wished that her husband was with her to back her up, although Hugh certainly would not ask this woman to stay on after such a tirade. In her heart Phyllis knew that she lacked both the will and the strength of character to dismiss her. Her sisters would be so relieved that their mother was to be taken care of without a great deal of extra effort on their part. They might blame her, if Mrs Manville were to leave; although, Lord knew, this outburst was no fault of her own. She knew she must be conciliatory, however riled she felt. Nevertheless, such impudence could not be allowed to stand. She tried to imagine what Hugh would say and to summon up some of his hauteur.

'Mrs Manville, our politics are no concern of yours; nor yours of ours. We vote by secret ballot in these islands for this very reason, so that neighbours and friends shall not be divided by their beliefs. You clearly have no idea of what British Union stands for or you would know that we are deeply, deeply patriotic; more so, I'd wager, than any other group in this country. We more than anyone wish to preserve the lives of our young men. You seem to have forgotten that our family had its own tragedy: Daddy's nephew, our cousin Timothy, was killed in 1917. But I realize you can't be expected to understand politics and that you are speaking in temper, because of your nephew.'

'I've told you, he wasn't my nephew. But I'd known the boy since he was knee high to a grasshopper. A lovely lad, he was.'

'I'm sure he was a delightful person, but this dreadful . . .' here Phyllis struggled to find the right word, 'occurrence was not brought about by anything that Nina or myself stand for. Quite the reverse, in fact. If our Peace Campaign had been put into operation, this calamity might have been averted.'

'That's balderdash!' said Mrs Manville. 'You're talking through your hat, you are.'

'That's quite enough!' said Phyllis. 'I appreciate that this is a trying time for us all, very trying. We are all upset about Daddy. What I suggest is that you take the rest of the morning off, to compose yourself. I will see to the sandwiches. Then let's put this behind us and say no more about it. I will not insist on an apology, provided this is not brought up again. Is that clear?'

Phyllis felt a surge of exhilaration. She felt she had spoken with real force and dignity. Mrs Manville made no reply, but put the knife down on the table and left the room. As soon as she had gone, Phyllis picked up the knife and took it to the sink and held it for a long while under the tap, the hot water running white down its blade. Then she dried it carefully with the tea towel that hung over the rail of the stove. The string around the handle was still damp when she replaced the knife in the drawer.

12. Sussex and London, May to June 1940

Phyllis answered the door herself, because the girl who came in to do the beds and the grates was having her day off and the cook hadn't yet come in to start lunch. Before her stood a uniformed policeman and just behind him were two men in ordinary suits, whose bearing nevertheless suggested that they too were police officers of some kind. One of them closely resembled Fredric March, the star of a film Phyllis had especially enjoyed, *Dr Jekyll and Mr Hyde*. She found herself grinning rather stupidly at him, as if he really were the actor and she a star-struck autograph hunter.

'Mrs Forrester? May we come in?' said the uniformed man.

'Of course,' said Phyllis, opening the door to allow them to step in.

What followed passed in something of a blur, so that Phyllis afterwards could not recall who had said what, nor how long the men had spent in the house. Someone asked if her husband was at home and she said that he was; she installed the three men in the drawing room and went to find him. Once Hugh appeared, one of the men in civilian clothes – not, she thought later, the one who looked like Fredric March – told them that he had reason to believe that they were both close associates of Sir Oswald Mosley. Hugh confirmed that this was so. In that case, the man went on, his two colleagues would now make a thorough search of the premises, while he and his wife remained here with him, to answer a few more questions.

'But this is ridiculous!' Phyllis objected. 'My husband is a distinguished man, he was a Naval Commander in the last war.

You can't just come into our house and rootle through our things.'

'I'd like to speak to your senior officer,' said Hugh. 'If you'd just come with me to the telephone in the hall, perhaps you could ring through to him, and we can sort things out without these gentlemen needing to look through all our possessions.'

But this hadn't worked. Nothing had worked. Instead they had both been asked questions, a great many questions, about meetings they had attended and people they knew and their roles within the Party. When Phyllis had made to stand in order to propose that she make coffee for their interlocutors and themselves, the man had only smiled and asked that she remain seated and in the room: coffee would not be necessary. At length the questions dried up and the three sat in silence, while the uniformed officer and the other man continued to go through all the drawers and cupboards. Their tread could be heard overhead, as well as the closing of wardrobes and doors.

'You don't need to go in the children's rooms, surely?' said Phyllis.

'We're conducting a thorough search. Won't be too much longer, now.'

'I shall be lodging a complaint,' said Hugh. 'This is simply . . . simply monstrous. You've absolutely no justification for coming into a man's home and rifling through the entire contents. It's an affront.'

The man only smiled, unperturbed.

After what seemed like an eternity, the two men came back to the drawing room.

'We found this, in what looks like one of the youngsters' rooms. Back of the wardrobe, in a shoe-box,' said the uniformed man. He was holding what looked like a revolver.

Phyllis cried out. 'Hugh, what is that? Tell me it isn't anything to do with you! You couldn't have kept a gun in . . .'

'It's an old service revolver I was asked to keep in case of an emergency. But I shall say nothing more until I have legal representation,' said Hugh. 'I should like to use my own telephone in my own house now, if you please.'

''Fraid there won't be time for telephoning,' said the man who looked like Fredric March.

'So, who asked you to keep this firearm, then?' the second officer asked.

'As I've told you, I am not prepared to say more. Kindly allow me to use my own telephone in my own house.'

'As I say, there won't be time for that. You'll need to come with us, now.'

For the first time, Phyllis felt afraid. The fear came with a jolt, sudden as nausea. It was one thing to be interviewed by the police, to have your house crawling with policemen; but to be taken, removed from the sanctuary of your own home like a piece of evidence, wasn't a thing that happened to people like her and Hugh.

'Well, and how long do you propose to detain us? We've things to do, you know. We can't simply place ourselves at your beck and call,' said Hugh.

The man only smiled.

Somehow Hugh and Phyllis found themselves out on the drive. Phyllis had the presence of mind to bring her handbag. There were two cars on the drive: a second uniformed officer sat behind the wheel of one, while the other was empty. The uniformed man who had been inside the house now took Phyllis by the elbow and led her towards the car in which his colleague was waiting, while Hugh was ushered towards the other vehicle. Phyllis felt too bewildered and afraid to protest.

Only once they were under way, Phyllis installed on the back seat, did she ask where they were going.

'Are we going to the station at Bognor, or at Chichester?' she asked.

'Neither. It's your lucky day, you're going up to London,' the driver replied.

'To London? But what on earth for? I've already told you – the other man who was with you – all that he asked.'

'Ours is not to wonder why,' said the driver. 'I daresay they've got their reasons.'

There was a sweet smell in the car, a mixture of the leather tang of the seats and some sort of cheap, soapy odour that she couldn't identify.

'May I open the window a little?' she asked.

'You do what you like, Missis. Enjoy yourself. If I were you I'd sit back and enjoy the view while you can.'

Phyllis did not know what he meant. It was all so bewildering and frightening and strange. The indignation she'd felt when the policemen arrived at the house had faded and now she felt only helpless and pathetic. She wished that Hugh were in the same car with her, instead of being alone with these unknown men. They drove on through the Sussex lanes lined with great elms, through the little towns; Horsham, Dorking, Epsom. In the streets the shoppers were blithe and busy, going about their morning chores: ordinary everyday tasks like buying liniment or bread or gardening twine for the canes of their tender sweet peas. It was like a bad dream to be moving unseen among them, effectively being taken hostage. She wanted to cry out to the passers-by to help her.

The car came into the southern suburbs of the capital, mile after mile of monotonous buildings, only punctuated by the odd church or war memorial or the gates of a crematorium. She did not recognize any of it, for she generally took the train when she came to town. No one had spoken for the past hour.

'Tell you what, we'll take mercy on you.' The officer who wasn't driving turned to face her. 'We'll stop off for a cup of tea, so you can stretch your legs. There's a place on the common, just up here.'

She smiled thinly. 'You certainly seem to know your way,' she said.

'We're Metropolitan, see. We're not from your part of the world.'

'Oh, of course. I hadn't thought,' she said. She had been too fraught to notice the accent. They drew up at a small tea-room.

'Fancy a bun? They do a nice rock cake,' the driver asked. 'It may be a while until you next get something to eat, by the time they process you. It's gone dinner-time.'

The waitress came and took their order. If it seemed peculiar to her to see a respectable woman in the company of two police-men, she gave no sign of surprise. The rock cake was the size of a fist. It was crumbly and rather dry, with little pebbles of dem-erara sugar on top. Phyllis felt she had never eaten anything so good, never enjoyed a combination so felicitous as the scalding, metallic tea and this sandy, sweet bun. She hadn't even known she was hungry.

'Will my husband be with me, when we get there?' she asked.

The two officers exchanged a smile which she could not interpret. 'No, not your husband nor anybody else's. It's women only.'

Phyllis felt a flash of alarm. What kind of police station was divided in this way? 'When you said they'd process me, earlier on: what did you mean?'

'Well, they'll have to take down all your details, won't they? And make a list of all the personal items you've got with you.'

'You make it sound awfully sinister. It's as if I'm going to prison,' said Phyllis. Once again, the officers exchanged smiles.

'You just enjoy your cup of tea. Have a little wander, after, if you feel like it. You've been cooped up in the car, you look a bit green.'

'I should like a moment in the fresh air, yes. Thank you.'

'Jack will accompany you, won't you, Jack?'

'That's very good of you.'

They all three finished their tea. The driver pulled out a packet of cigarettes and a matchbook with 'The Flamingo Club' printed on its cover. The man who hadn't driven, the one who she now knew to be called Jack, got up. He extended an arm, as if inviting her to dance.

'Shall we?' he asked.

Phyllis stood. She found she was unsteady, as if she'd received a physical blow. The two of them came out of the tea-room and made towards the common. It was a still, clear afternoon. Wood pigeons were murmuring their soft call. On the common a handful of boys were playing an informal game of cricket, using their blazers for wickets. Their school satchels lay in a bundle on the fresh grass, with one or two jerseys strewn among them. This early in the year their knees were still pale below their grey shorts. With a stab of longing Phyllis thought of Edwin.

'I will be home before too long, won't I? Only my little boy, it'll be his exeat, you see,' Phyllis said. She thought she might cry.

The man turned to her and regarded her face to face now, not unkindly. 'Ours is just to deliver you, that's all we're told. The non-uniform boys make the decisions, not us. We're just cabbies, really, when all's said and done. We're just along for the ride, to drive you from A to B. You're only the second we've had under our custody. It's a new power of detainment they've got for you lot: God's honest truth, I've no idea how long they'll keep you. I doubt they even know themselves.'

This made Phyllis feel a little calmer, although there was nothing in his words to reassure her. But the fact of his looking directly at her, talking to her as a fellow human, stilled the panic that was threatening to engulf her.

'Where am I being taken?' she asked him.

'Other side of London. Holloway.'

'But surely you can't take me to prison without arresting me, without putting me on trial? I haven't done anything wrong! I must be allowed to speak to a solicitor first, surely?'

'I'm afraid I don't know anything about it. No doubt someone will explain things once you get there. You won't be by yourself, they're picking people up from all over the South East. Your husband being in possession of a firearm isn't too clever, though. That won't help.'

'I've never seen that gun before in my life, you must believe me. I had no idea it was there. I should never have allowed him to keep it in one of the children's rooms.'

They had come to a standstill.

'We'd best be heading back to the car,' said the officer. 'We've still got a ways to go.'

Phyllis didn't answer. It didn't seem to make any odds, what she said; whether she spoke or not.

The rest of the journey passed more or less in silence. Phyllis felt very tired. By the time they arrived at their destination she was too exhausted to be any longer afraid, or even indignant. Once she had been brought inside she resigned herself to the small series of indignities to which she was subjected: her belongings removed, the lining and hems of her skirt and light overcoat ripped unceremoniously before they were returned to her, so that she looked as scruffy as a ragamuffin. She was weighed and measured, like a parcel. Then she was issued with a pair of coarse sheets and two thin blankets with a stiff, close texture like cardboard. After all this – which seemed to take an eternity – she was required to wait in a small locked room, little better than a cage, until such a time as someone was free to escort her to F Wing. Here, at least, she was not alone. There were three other women already in the tiny space: one of them was plainly a tart; one a young woman of a mousy, clerical-worker type; while the last was an older woman with wire-framed spectacles and hair in a tight grey perm. The latter two certainly did not look as Phyllis imagined criminals might look: they were women who would attract no attention whatsoever in a railway waiting room. The tart jiggled her crossed leg as if listening to a dance tune, but the other two sat still. It had been a warm day outside, but now Phyllis felt cold.

They introduced themselves. The tart said her name was Diane, but that they shouldn't trouble themselves to remember what she was called, because she would most likely be let out within the hour. She explained that on Fridays and Saturdays she was sometimes kept in, because these nights in detention cost her trade; it was intended to be a deterrent, yet what it really meant was that she had to work twice as hard the next weekend, to make up for loss of earnings. But on a weekday such as this they generally didn't bother, and let her go after a few hours in the cage. She had been brought in umpteen times, she announced. They weren't bad people, who worked here, if you didn't cheek them. The food was filthy and there wasn't much of it. The tea wasn't made with tea at all, but with iron filings: it'd never so much as seen a leaf. Everyone knew that. As for the stuff they gave you to put on your bread! Car-grease, it was. Not even lard and certainly not margarine. She spoke in a harsh monotone, without smiling or even really looking at the others, yet Phyllis felt grateful to her for prattling on so, covering her own awkwardness. All the time her leg fidgeted.

When Diane stopped talking, the office-worker-looking girl said her name was Kathy and the older woman introduced herself as Jill. Phyllis noticed that Jill hesitated for just a moment before saying her own name and guessed that in ordinary life she would introduce herself not by her Christian name, but as a Mrs So-and-so. Under normal circumstances, she would do the same herself. They did not shake hands, but nodded cautiously.

Phyllis didn't like to ask what had brought these women here, but at length Kathy spoke.

'It must be a mistake, my being here. No offence to you, of course,' she said, glancing at the others.

'You didn't do it, I'll wager. That's what everyone says,' said Diane.

'Well, that's just it. I didn't do nothing.' The girl went pink. 'Anything, I mean.'

'Well, you must have done something, or you wouldn't be in here, would you?' said Diane.

'They came and searched my flat – it's more of a bed-sitting-room, really – went through all my things. Even my smalls drawer. Do you know what they did, as well? They took the lids off my saucepans. I've only got two. I don't do a lot of cooking, just potatoes, the odd bit of greens to go with a fried chop. Anyway, they took the lids off the pans and looked in them. And the tea-tin. The worst of it was, they shook out my talcum powder. All over the linoleum in the bathroom, the place looked a tip. I share the bathroom with two other girls. My landlady'll kill me. What on earth do they expect to find, in a tin of talc?'

'But why, dear?' asked Jill.

'It's my boyfriend they're interested in. He's Italian. Works at the Italian Embassy. I met him at a church social. We're Roman Catholics, see.' She looked slightly defiant at this, as if she expected the other women to take issue with her religion.

'Good heavens,' said Phyllis. 'They can't just lock you up because of your friend. That's not right, not right at all.'

'That's what I kept telling them, all the way here in the car from East Sheen. That's where I live. They kept asking if he'd left anything with me, any papers or letters. Why would he do that?'

'What about you?' Phyllis asked Jill.

But before the older woman could respond there were footsteps, a rattle of metal on metal. A warden Phyllis had not seen before signalled to them to follow and they traipsed after her, along corridors and up flights of cast-iron stairs. The last was a spiral staircase leading to a short, broad landing. Phyllis had completely lost her bearings and had no notion what storey she was on, nor where she was within the building. A dozen or so doors gave off the landing into cells. The doors were open and Phyllis saw that each was identically furnished with a washstand, a wooden chair, a small table and a very low, narrow bed. The windows were tiny and high: a smudge of London sky was visible but nothing green, no grass nor even the branches of distant trees.

'Here you are, Madam,' said the warden with a false flourish. 'Your room awaits.'

Seeing the naked alarm on Phyllis's face, she added: 'These good ladies will be just along the way, so you won't want for company. Lock-up's not for another half hour or so, give you a chance to find your feet. Toilet's down there on the right if you're feeling brave enough; otherwise there's a po in your cell.'

Phyllis went into the cell and sat down on the bed. It was almost a relief that there was no give in the mattress: any semblance of comfort would have mocked her. Seeing now the back of her thick cell door, how it had no handle on the inside, gave her a jolt of fear. Before long the older woman, Jill, came in.

'Kathy's breaking her heart in the cell along from mine; should we go in to her, d'you think, or give her some privacy?'

'Well, I suppose we'll have plenty of time to be on our own, once they lock us in for the night. I rather think we should go to her.'

'I agree. We don't want her getting hysterical.'

★

And so Phyllis's life in prison began. There were two things above all other things: the cold and the dirt. Phyllis had never in her life been anywhere so grimy. Fat eels of black dust lay coiled beneath the legs of chairs and tables or nestled in the crooks of walls and the elbows of steps. When the air was stirred, if someone walked by or opened a door along the way, these moved sluggishly in response, like dead things adrift underwater. Something worse than dust – an almost oily dark film, a sort of sweated, acrid soot – lay over everything. The smell was at once sharp and yet with a cloying undernote of foul sweetness, catching in the nose and at the junction of the throat, so that the constant presence of nausea threatened to mature into actual sickness. The lavatories and adjoining washbasins were unspeakable. Phyllis thought she would never get used to the dirt, the smell. The cold was more difficult to comprehend. It had been a fine day when she arrived, and the dry, warm spell of the late spring endured. In the building, though, a damp chill seemed to dwell in the very fabric of the walls and floors, in the ironwork and the fetid air. Long hours of inactivity slowed the circulation: often her toes and fingertips were the colour of candle wax, until she rubbed and pummelled the blood back into them. She had left home in only the clothes she stood up in and it took more than a fortnight before she was permitted to receive a few more things: spare stockings and knickers, a couple of warm jerseys. It was the sort of cold that gets in deep to the bone, the kind that can only be resolved by long immersion in a hot bath. But the prisoners were allowed just one bath a week and that was a scant few inches of water. She was cold all the time. It was hard to get to sleep at night, shivering.

The day after she arrived and the one after that and throughout the ensuing weeks the cells filled. It was impossible to get information about what was happening to families and husbands, although a rumour spread that some of the male internees had been taken to Ham Common. The women were already frightened and anxious and many of them feared for their husbands' lives. If it was possible to lock people up like this, without trial, anything could happen. The sound of weeping could be heard in the corridors at night.

By the end of June there were almost seventy women under custody in the wing, all but three or four of them political affiliates. One of the women, Rita, came from a village not far from Manchester, out on the moors. Somebody had informed the police that Rita and her husband went to meetings once a week, which was true. When the police came knocking they went through everything in their cottage and found their membership cards and some printed leaflets they'd been asked to distribute. But, Rita said, the thing that had really interested the plain-clothes people who'd come with the local bobby was her husband's diary. He'd written 'Remove British Queen' and then a few days later 'Install Italian queen', and so they'd got it into their heads that this was an Italian fascist plot to overthrow the monarchy. In actual fact, the man kept bees: that was what he'd been referring to. All the women enjoyed this story: there was a bitter sort of comfort in illustrating how unreasonable and pointless their incarceration was.

Phyllis had met a few of her fellow inmates before at meetings and rallies and it was a huge relief to see familiar faces. She liked young Rowena Bingham, who'd worked at London headquarters, and June Driscoll seemed a lively sort of person, with a wide smile. For the first month or more no one received any information as to how long they might be detained and Phyllis got only muddled snatches of news of Hugh. She heard nothing from him directly, but incomers brought rumours of the detention camp at Ham Common, where the men had supposedly been taken. A newly incarcerated branch secretary from Surrey caused an outbreak of near panic when she announced that gun-shots had been heard from Ham: there was talk of the detainees facing firing squads. This couldn't be true, surely? This was England. Things like firing squads simply didn't happen in England, least of all in the affluent suburbs. And yet, with no way to quell the rumour, it somehow caught light. Cooped up with no access to outside events, gossip and hearsay assumed the force of doctrine. Phyllis didn't really believe that her husband had been executed; yet if she could be taken from her home, locked up without trial, without committing any crime, without explanation, perhaps anything was possible after all. She had never been a smoker, but now she found that tobacco calmed her frazzled nerves, as well as staving off hunger pangs.

The women began to organize themselves. Each morning they were woken at 6.30, when their cells were unlocked. An hour later, half a dozen of them had to troop across to the kitchen to fetch breakfast for the wing: by the time they got back the porridge would have congealed into a grey paste, like papier mâché. Between them they arranged a roster, so that everyone would take their turn on the meal-runs to and from the kitchen three times a day; they set about cleaning the wing as best they could. Squabbles broke out here and there, but mostly there was a spirit of shared defiance which bound them together. Some chafed at being bossed about. In any case, Phyllis did not mind being told what to do: it meant she never had to think or plan.

To begin with they weren't allowed parcels, but once these were permitted people began to share out cigarettes and squares of chocolate and books. Each inmate was allowed to write and to receive just two letters a week. For Phyllis this was agony, since she always wrote to the children at least twice a week each, and sent them tuck on Fridays: a tin of butterscotch, or a box of fudge or Edwin's favourite mint humbugs. Now she had to make do with a shared letter to the girls and then a separate letter to Edwin. If she wanted to correspond with anyone else, it meant missing a letter to the children. It seemed cruel to make them wait a whole fortnight to hear from her, and yet she desperately needed Patricia and Nina to champion her cause. The long school holidays would shortly begin, and she needed to get out in time to be at home for the children. Much as she'd have wished to have kept her incarceration from the children, there was no way of writing to them which did not reveal her true whereabouts: her letters were censored and bore her prison number and Holloway postmark. She couldn't simply stop writing to them. It was better that they should know where she was than imagine that she had simply disappeared. She hoped that Greville, with his friends in high places, would be able to wield some influence.

Lady Mosley was brought in. The Leader's wife tended to keep herself to herself up in her third-floor cell. It was odd to think of someone with as much warmth and charm as OM being taken with such an absurdly drawling-voiced, brittle sort of a woman, although she was certainly beautiful. You had to give her that. Not without a sense of humour, either, although she didn't look the type. And you had to take your hat off to her; she bore her imprisonment without complaint. It must have been very hard on her, being carted off to jail leaving her newborn behind; and his small brother. Just babies, both of them. Nevertheless it embarrassed Phyllis, the way some of the other women fawned over her, at mealtimes and about the place. Like the rest of them Lady Mosley was always cold: more so, being such a wraith. For the first few weeks she wore a raccoon jacket all the time, and when parcels were allowed she must have got one of her sisters to send in a fur coat: after that she was never seen in anything else. It set off a fashion among the wing, for those of them who had furs.

There seemed to be no rhyme nor reason as to who was

detained. The woman in the next cell, Margaret Thomas, for instance, had only ever been on the periphery of things. Here too were little nobodies like Kathy, while key personnel walked free. And Nina. When Phyllis thought about it, she could not understand why it was she who had been incarcerated and not her sister. Nina had been involved so much longer than she had. She was on the approved speaker list and had been asked to stand for a parliamentary seat, by the Leader himself. She had run the summer camps all but single-handedly and been active in every aspect of Union business, from handing out leaflets to collecting subscriptions. She had come into contact with almost all of the top brass, at one time or another. So had Eric. His not being detained was also deeply puzzling. More so even than his wife, for Eric had been in charge of printing and publicity material for the Southern region and several of the pamphlets he'd produced had been distributed nationwide. It was a mystery.

Phyllis, 1979

Patricia didn't offer to have the girls. I think that's where the rot started to set in, between the two of us. There was plenty of room at Rose Green, you see; she could easily have fitted them in. She wouldn't even have had to give up one of the spare rooms; there was the nursery she'd used for the monthly nurse when Antonia was born, where the toys were kept, that would've accommodated them. It wasn't as if she'd never had anything to do with girls, she had Antonia, and Antonia was always rather a lonely creature, I never saw her have a friend of her own to stay. Don't repeat this to her, but we all felt rather sorry for her. She'd have loved to have had the company, I expect. You might think. She was always very precious about Antonia, everything had to be just-so: the perfect nursery with the perfect doll's house and of course the perfect clothes. Her dresses were stiff with organza lining and she wore hair-bands to match and those grand coats with velvet collars that the two royal princesses had worn.

It was because of the incident with Julia at the summer camp, I knew that. Well, after the summer camp, as a matter of fact. Not that anything did actually happen, but that wasn't what it looked like. The point was that, to Patricia, Julia was tarnished after that. She'd run off one evening in secret, you see, to try and meet a boy. And not even a boy of the right kind. Patricia had always made a terrific song and dance about the sort of people who attended the camp; she didn't want Antonia mixing with the hoi-polloi and was forever warning me of the dangers of allowing my children to mingle with them. As if class was something that could be caught off people, like nits or pink-eye.

Her not having Julia meant that Frances couldn't go, either. Patricia couldn't have one sister and not the other. I think she thought no one would surmise the reason she didn't want Julia, if she refused them as a job-lot. So she took Edwin. That's how it began. Greville was always terribly soppy about children; he borrowed a pony from someone or other so that Edwin would feel he had the same as Antonia. And they had a dog, which of course Edwin had always wanted. Antonia was grateful for the company, she was nice to him. He liked it there, it was an adventure. Greville got it into his head that archery was the thing to amuse a boy, got him a bow and arrows – a proper big archery one, I mean, not one of those toys with rubber suckers on the ends of the arrows – and put up a target in the orchard. They'd go out every day and practise. Well, he was just the sort of age when he was mad on Robin Hood and William Tell and knights of old, all that sort of thing. It doesn't require too much imagination to turn a boy's head.

It was all very unsettling for the girls and I worried about them a great deal. First they went to Nina's, but of course their house was right on the main road and tiny – more of a cottage, really – so it was quite unsuitable, especially after the baby came along: there was nowhere for them to go. After the baby was born, the girls got carted off to my mother's. Well, of course there was plenty of space there to run around and explore, but Mummy was off with the fairies, to be honest, she couldn't supervise. She was looked after by this Mrs Manville, a dreadful woman, who at least was devoted to my mother. So devoted, actually, that she didn't trouble herself with my daughters any more than she had to. I always imagined that the girls must rather have loved staying there, because no one kept much of an eye on them. In fact years later Julia complained that they'd been terribly lonely at their grandmother's, but that's Julia for you. I wasn't sure I believed her: she had her sister for company, after all.

In the end Nina had the brain-wave of moving into our house, for the duration. Clever, practical Nina. She took the baby – his name was George, after our father – and decamped with Julia and Frances. Eric joined them when he wasn't working in Portsmouth or Southampton, or wherever it was. None of us had a clue how long it was all going to go on for, that's what's so hard to fathom now. Neither the war itself, nor Hugh and myself being in jail. If I'd been guilty of a crime I'd have had a sentence imposed on me, a know-able amount of time; but as it was I hadn't committed any crime and yet neither I nor anyone else had the fog-giest idea how long I'd be detained. For those first weeks I truly thought I'd be let out any day. It was only later, once the children had gone back to school and the autumn set in, that I resigned myself to the long haul. The uncertainty, that's why it was so difficult to make arrangements. I had to accept that my sisters would take charge of the children and do things for the best. There was simply no other way.

Going back to the house, our house, was by far the most sensible plan because the girls had all their things and their own rooms and so on; and there were tennis courts just down the lane and croquet in the garden. They would have felt happy and at home and relatively settled. They couldn't bathe in the sea because of the barbed wire and defences all over the place, but I don't know if they realized how lucky they were to have their liberty and their youth and their health; to have the sea-wind in their hair. But I don't believe the young ever really understand how free they are. What I'd have given, to feel that salty summer air on my bare legs and on my face.

Is this of interest to you? I'm not telling you much about Sir Oswald's followers, although none of this would have befallen my children had I not been a follower myself. In any case, Edwin joined them at the house, just for the last week or so of the holidays. I think he was rather tickled not to be the only boy in the family any more, now that Nina had baby George. He'd never really met a new-born before, being the youngest: he may have hoped his new cousin would be ready to play cricket straight away. Anyway, Nina wrote to tell me how sweet he was, with the baby. I'm sure he would have been, Edwin always was the sweetest boy.

13. Holloway, September to December 1940

Some things were better in prison after the Blitz began in September, but others were far worse. The fear made it especially grim: the fear and the cold. Halfway through November, B wing was hit by two bombs; by some miracle there were no fatalities, but many inmates had cuts from the broken glass. Everyone was very shaken. The noise had been terrifying, as if the earth itself was exploding, opening up; as if the end of the world had come. Women screamed from their cells, terrified they would be burned alive. The building was a panopticon, the wings arranged like the spokes of a wheel around the central area, which was entirely roofed with glass. This roof had somehow survived the attack intact. The bomb hit an empty wing, but the roof's transparency made the building a target. The strictest blackout conditions now applied: no more torches for reading under the bedclothes. People ducked down to light their cigarettes under the rickety washstand tables in their cells. They learned to hold the lit ends inwards to conceal the glowing tip, as well as the tiny flare when they inhaled. Some of them struggled to get the hang of smoking in this way and made self-conscious jokes about turning into navvies or coal miners. Their fingers began to be stained with nicotine.

The improvement the air raids brought about was that the prisoners' cell doors were kept unlocked at all times, so that they could follow the evacuation procedure if need be. This was freedom on a heady scale, after the oppressive schedule that had operated previously. A festive, slightly frantic atmosphere broke out, as if they were girls at boarding school. People darted in and out of each other's cells at all hours of the day and night, sitting on each other's beds smoking and talking, or played cards at the long table for hours at a time. But once darkness fell – earlier each day – the mood became more sombre. Many of the women on F Wing came from the East End of London. Every night they flocked up to the third-floor cells and took it in turns to stand on chairs and tables, craning to see if they could judge where the bombs were falling. Numbers of them sobbed through the dark nights, terrified of what might be happening to their homes, their families.

Word filtered down that OM was campaigning from his own prison cell for the women in Holloway to be protected in Anderson shelters during the nightly raids. He was said to be outraged that these women, innocent of any crime, should be denied the basic safety measures available to the rest of the population. His own wife was among them, after all. It was comforting to know that he was speaking out on their behalf, even at a time when his own wings were clipped. The very thought of him brought them strength. At the summer camp there had been much talk about the fact that his visits always coincided with fine weather, as if his charm could work its magic even on the recalcitrant English sun. The air raid on Holloway had hit just two days before OM's birthday. Among the women on F Wing there was a general feeling that the luck he brought in his wake had somehow prevailed here, too. No one had been badly hurt! It was in this fervent, slightly giddy spirit that they arranged a tea-dance of sorts to celebrate the Leader's birthday. Someone got hold of a gramophone and another detainee, Lady Domvile, obtained a tin of biscuits. To Phyllis it was wonderful, the way her fellows pulled together and made the best of their situation and jollied each other along. No matter the difference in their backgrounds, they were all in this together. It was only their courage and camaraderie which made the days bearable.

Phyllis found the boredom was easier to manage than the uncertainty. There were frightening and persistent rumours that all the women detained under the same terms as herself might be deported, perhaps to the colonies. Obtaining any information as to how long her imprisonment might last was all but impossible, nor did anyone seem to know what steps she might take in order to be released. There was talk of having to appear before some sort of judging committee. From October the women were allowed to write to their MPs to appeal against their treatment, but since it was Parliament which had put them in jail in the first place, the gesture seemed pretty futile. The not-knowing made everyone jittery and corroded hope as surely as salt water rusting metal.

Although she never believed that her convictions were reason enough for her incarceration, Phyllis could not help but see her imprisonment as something she deserved, a punishment she had brought upon herself for her carelessness regarding poor Sarita. As well as having been a bad friend, she had been a neglectful daughter to her poor dear father: these thoughts tormented her. She thought of the words in the General Confession: We have left undone those things which we ought to have done and we have done those things which we ought not to have done, and there is no health in us. There is no health in us. The phrase caught in her brain, like the chorus of a popular song. Many times a day it came to mind and repeated itself. If it had not been for the friendship she found among the other women, Phyllis would have felt as though she was thoroughly rotten.

By now the prisoners were allowed short visits. Greville wrote a brief note to say that he would be coming: Phyllis guessed that he and her sisters and possibly Eric too had agreed that it should be Greville who would be the first visitor. She imagined that he wouldn't have countenanced Patricia making the trip:

Holloway was in the back of beyond, and he would have insisted that prison was no place for a woman, notwithstanding the fact that Phyllis was a woman herself. The visit took place in a room Phyllis had never seen before, filled with scuffed tables and oddly low chairs, the height of chairs in a nursery school. It was humiliating to sit so close to the floor, making them all look knock-kneed and out of proportion. Four or five warders stood about, presumably to make sure no one passed contraband. Phyllis took a seat and waited for her brother-in-law to be brought in with the other visitors. He was not quite able to conceal his shock at his first sight of her.

Greville began speaking almost before he had taken his seat, she guessed in a gallant bid to hide his dismay at her gaunt and pallid appearance.

'You must try not to worry, we're doing all we can. We're in touch with the Advisory Committee and it seems they're aware of you and will call you to speak in due course. There doesn't seem to be a way of hurrying them along, although,' and here Greville lowered his voice, 'I did drop some names which I thought might help. Made it clear that you're not without connections. So much for habeas corpus! It's like something out of Lewis Carroll, dealing with these people. You know, the scene in *Alice in Wonderland*, Who Stole the Tarts? I have pointed out that you are guilty of no crime and therefore should be the equivalent of a remand prisoner, with the privileges that that entails. I've been quite insistent on this, both in private interviews with one or two people and by letter with several others. But of course one has no way of knowing if anything gets through to them. They are treating you decently?'

Phyllis did not know how to answer. It wasn't how she was treated that was of concern to her: it was that she was locked up in the first place.

'We manage. There's one rather annoying thing: they do

insist on distributing things that come in our parcels, sharing them out. Not clothes, but toffees, cigarettes, tea; that sort of thing. You might tell Patricia, so she could put in a few extras. Otherwise I end up with just one biscuit or whatever it is, out of a whole packet.'

'But that's monstrously unfair!' said Greville. 'A package sent to you ought to be your own property. The sole property of the addressee. That's behaving like socialists.'

Phyllis smiled wanly.

'Anything you need, in particular? Books?'

'Books are always a great boon. Anything by Margery Allingham would go down well, if you wouldn't mind. We've got some Agatha Christies, we pass them around once we've finished. It's rather fun, actually, because it means we've all read the same things, so we can discuss them together. We all got a terrific craze for *Murder is Easy*, we couldn't talk of anything else for a fortnight. Rather suitable, for a bunch of jailbirds.'

'I don't know it,' said Greville.

'Oh, well. It's a potboiler, as Patricia calls them. Probably not your sort of thing.'

'I don't care for stories. I tend to read history. Mark you, I hardly do read: two pages and I'm out like a light. Takes me months to get through a book.'

'How is she? And Antonia?'

'The tiddler is doing splendidly, by all accounts. Seems to be getting on very well at school.'

The idea of Antonia being splendid at anything was hard to fathom, but Phyllis nodded as if he was only reporting something she had expected all along.

'Patricia's got some chickens, for the eggs, you know. She's rather taken to them, goes out before brekker every morning to see what's what in the hen house. But of course she's sick with worry about you. We are gunning for you, you know.'

'Thank you, Greville. I know you are. It makes such a difference, to think you're trying to get me out. I simply couldn't bear
not to be with the children for Christmas. For their stockings.'

'No, of course. Well, we'll do all we can to make sure you're
home by then.'

'Is there a chance, do you suppose? It's less than a month
away.' Desperate, Phyllis made to clutch at her brother-in-law's
arm across the narrow table.

Greville recoiled. The gesture, almost imperceptible, was all
the more wounding for having been involuntary. It was a tiny
movement, but to Phyllis it was devastating. She felt it as a physical sensation, as if she had been winded. In the moment of his
drawing back from her Phyllis understood that she had crossed
an invisible barrier which set her apart, now, from the people
she loved. They were on one side of this line and she was on the
other. All that was to follow revealed itself to her in that split
second with a terrible force and clarity.

At just the same moment a warden came across and told Phyllis that touching was forbidden. Phyllis was sure that Greville
felt the same rush of perverse gratitude for this intervention as
she did. It was merciful that someone else had spoken before
they had to face each other again. She saw that her brother-in-
law at least had the good grace to look embarrassed. He was a
kind man, she knew that.

'Well now,' he said, recovering himself. 'Is there anything
else you'd like, any little thing we can send?'

'You might tell Patricia that if she scribbles a note on the
flyleaf of a book or the inside lid of a box then it doesn't count
as a letter. Just as long as it's light newsy things, they let it
through. Nothing about the war. We're only allowed two letters, you see, and I try to keep channels open for the children. In
case they write.'

A hooter sounded, signalling the end of the visit. Chairs

scraped back from tables all at once, as at the end of a school lesson. In the slight flurry as she stood, Phyllis noticed a sharp, oniony sort of smell. She wasn't sure if it was coming from her, or from the others. It seemed to fill the room, as if a pan of stew was being heated nearby. It wasn't the smell of ordinary sweat, the sweat of exertion; it was the sweat of unease and fear. She recognized it, now. Perhaps it was the smell of dread, the dread of being locked up once more, separated from families and sweethearts. Or perhaps it was the visitors who were perspiring, made nervy from the unfamiliarity of the hostile surroundings and abrupt goodbyes. And yet for all their pity and even sorrow, they would be returning to the outside world. They would feel fresh air on their faces, the wintry cold pinching at their noses. They would be able to turn up their collars against the chill, blow on their wool-gloved fingertips while they stood in little groups at bus stops; make their own way, each of them, to their own homes, their own familiar things. It seemed to Phyllis that she would never again take for granted the comforts of home: the soft blankets with their fraying satin edges, her favourite rose geranium soap, the soft rich glow of a table newly polished with beeswax and turpentine. In the time it took her to imagine such things, the visit was over, a hasty leave had been taken and she was trudging back along the narrow corridors to her cell.

In early December Phyllis was called to appear before the Advisory Committee to consider appeals against orders of internment. To everyone in prison this had by now become known as the tribunal, even though there were usually four officials on the other side of the desk and not three. A couple of dozen of the women had already been through such hearings and reported the absurdity of the proceedings. They said that members of the tribunal seemed to think they could ensnare them by getting them to admit to being fascists, forgetting that the word – which to outsiders was pejorative – had been used among them as commonly as Mr or Mrs, especially among the older stalwarts who had joined before the Party changed its name from British Union of Fascists to British Union.

Several women had even been before the tribunal more than once, to no avail. Only three or four had been released after appearing before the Committee, but it wasn't known how they had obtained their freedom: whether they had confessed or repented or denied. Most accepted that their activities had been too well-known – public meetings, pamphleteering – for any attempt at minimizing them to be believable. In any case, it was a matter of principle: there was personal loyalty to Sir Oswald to consider. It was known that the Leader was campaigning for their release: it would be an act of treachery to repay him with disloyalty. They certainly would not have sneaked on anyone else: there was a strict unwritten code of loyalty among them. Whether they had said the right thing, whatever that might be; or whether the grounds on which they were being held were too flimsy to prolong their incarceration, was much discussed. Was there, could there be, a correct thing to say, some kind of open sesame? No one knew. It became something of a point of honour to try and outwit the panel, to cheek them. There were so few opportunities for the women to assert themselves. Several of the prisoners had been asked if they loved Germany, which struck them all as a very stupid question. In any event, only two or three of them had ever set foot in Germany. One woman had been required to say what she would do if a German airman with a parachute fell at her feet. Her response became more and more outlandish in the retelling. The others chimed in with humorous suggestions, some of them ribald.

'I'd have my clothes off – and his – quick as a knife. He could wrap us both in the parachute, then, and do me on the spot,' said one.

'Well, I'm fluent in German and I'll tell you, ich lieber dick,' said someone, with a music-hall roll of the eyes as she pronounced the last word.

'Don't we all, ducky,' said someone else.

'I'd make him lick my fanny and then sew me a nice frock out of the parachute silk,' said another, to whoops of laughter.

Phyllis had seldom heard this sort of talk before, apart from the odd coarse remark of Venetia Gordon-Canning's. Even her outspoken sister Nina did not go in for such banter, while Patricia would have considered it beyond the pale. One or two of the officer's wife types didn't join in and Phyllis was aware that in ordinary circumstances she would have been expected to be among them. Hugh had been a Commander of the Royal Navy, after all. But any laughter was a respite from the boredom and anguish, a chance to forget the time.

The tribunal Phyllis was called before consisted of three women and one rather tired-looking man. The youngest of the women asked almost all the questions. Since Phyllis did not know what Hugh had told the police, nor any tribunal he'd been put before, she thought honesty was the best policy. What was Phyllis's opinion of the war? Had she ever visited Germany? Had she visited Germany in the twelve months leading up to the declaration of war? Was it her belief that a wife owed complete loyalty to a husband? That she should obey her husband in all things? If asked to decide between loyalty to her country or to Sir Oswald Mosley, which would she choose? To this last she gave an answer she was proud of: that there could be no such choice, for Sir Oswald would never be disloyal to the interests of Great Britain. They pressed on, questioning her about Hugh and his weekly trips to London. The procedure was plodding and yet alarming at the same time, like a visit to the dentist. At length the man addressed her.

'Would you describe yourself as a fascist?'

'I see myself as nothing more sinister than a traditionalist. I believe in putting the British interest before all else, it's as simple as that. Having lived abroad for a number of years I came to be involved with British Union in a roundabout sort of way, through . . . through neighbours in Sussex, where we had settled. I certainly am a follower of Sir Oswald Mosley. I believe he talks a good deal of sense. I believe that we'd never have got into this war if he'd been in charge. But if you are asking whether I am an admirer of Hitler, the answer is no. We have our own brand of politics here, we don't need his.'

This was the longest answer she had given and she felt her face reddening.

'And who were these neighbours of yours?'

Phyllis did not want to incriminate Nina and Eric, although their names and activities were surely known to the authorities. She cast about in her mind.

'There was a fellow called Gordon-Canning. We met him at various parties and so on.'

'And anyone else?'

'No one who comes to mind, no. Not that I can recall.'

'Are you able to shed light on the question of why your husband was in possession of a firearm?'

'No, I'm afraid not. He fought in the last war, as I expect you are aware. Perhaps he kept it from then.'

She thought she detected the trace of a smirk on the face of the older woman with spectacles, who had not spoken throughout. Phyllis dimly recalled Hugh having told her that the Leader had asked a number of senior people to keep a gun, in case of emergency; but he had not said that he was among their number and it had sounded rather far-fetched, at the time. She had put it out of her mind until the day they were taken in. The woman who had asked most of the questions now spoke again.

'Thank you for appearing before us today. The Committee will reflect on what you have told us and let you know of our findings. Is there anything else you'd like to tell us, before we conclude?'

'Well, I know it hasn't got anything to do with anything, but I have three children and none of this is their fault and yet they're deprived of both their parents in war-time, passed from pillar to post . . .'

She was cut short. 'Thank you. We'll certainly bear the family circumstances in mind.'

And the four interlocutors stood to signal that the hearing was over.

Back in her cell, Phyllis wept. She hadn't realized how much she had invested in the tribunal, but now she understood that a part of her had almost dared to believe that she would be released on the spot. A little splinter of hope had worked its way into her. This had let her imagine that the tribunal would take one look at her and know – just know – that she posed no harm to anyone, let alone her country. She'd allowed herself to picture what it would be like, arriving home: letting herself into the house, the gleam of the parquet floor, the welcoming curve of the oak staircase. The quiet. The gate-legged table where the post was placed on a salver she and Hugh had had as a wedding present, so that whoever was going out next could take letters to the pillar-box. In this reverie, there was no Hugh. Even the children weren't there, or not yet. It was just her and the empty house.

Her friends on the block gave Phyllis her privacy. People often emerged from the tribunal in tears and they knew, after months in prison, that grief passed more quickly observed alone. A woman whose house had been hit during an air raid had howled for her dead husband and the other prisoners had huddled around her like dairy cattle. Afterwards she could barely look anyone in the eye for weeks. They had learned it was better to let people do their crying alone and then proffer some gesture of sympathy: a cup of tea if there was one, or a cigarette.

It was agony, waiting for the tribunal's decision. She didn't like to consider how the discovery of the gun on the day she and Hugh were taken in might have prejudiced her case. How could he have been so careless as to have concealed a dangerous weapon among the children's things? When she thought of it she felt a horrible cold sort of anger towards him. But surely they would see that she wasn't the sort of person who knew anything about guns? Hugh had never so much as mentioned it to her. It must have been a relic, from his war service. Why else would he be in possession of such a thing?

Now when she woke up in the winter mornings she prayed, and again before she went to sleep. One evening it dawned on her that praying in bed wasn't good enough: that only kneeling was acceptable to God. Otherwise, why would people kneel in church? After that she knelt at her bed to say her prayers. It was surprising and somehow reassuring how quickly her knees began to hurt. It occurred to her that the hurting might be a sort of short-cut to God's attention. Prayers might move faster through pain than through comfort, like electricity moving through fuse-wire but not through wood. If only she had paid attention to the sermons in church! Surely she had heard that suffering created a kind of Communion? She couldn't quite remember. But if Christ had died in agony for her sake, then the least she could do was put up with sore knees. Welcome them, even.

The tribunal's decision came through on December 16th. Phyllis was to remain in custody. She was not given any reason why she must stay in prison, nor given an indication as to how long the term might be. A handful of the others received the same news at the same time. They sat forlornly at the long table, smoking, too dejected to cry. Someone went to boil water for tea. Another had been sent a precious jar of honey, which she now fetched and with some solemnity put on the table in front of them, to sweeten the tea when it came. At length Phyllis went to her cell to write to her sisters and tell them the news and to ask them to make arrangements to collect the children from their schools and accommodate them over the holidays. She asked Patricia if she would be kind enough to have all three for Christmas itself – perhaps for Christmas Eve and Boxing Day, if at all possible – so that they could at least be together. She didn't feel she could request that her sister have them all for the duration, but it seemed only right that they be united for Christmas itself. The rest of the school holidays she would have to trust to them.

As Christmas neared there was a slight shift. Whether this was a matter of policy or simply a relenting from the prison staff, no one knew, but things became a little easier. Parcels were still opened and any perishables disbursed, but the rules governing letters slackened. No announcement was made, but the women gradually became aware that they were able to send out several letters a week, instead of the previous limit of two per prisoner. Better yet, the limit on how much post they were permitted to receive was relaxed. For Phyllis, as for the others, this made a tremendous difference. Now all the children could write, instead of taking it in turns; so could her sisters.

At the beginning of the third week in December a letter came. It was in a large manila envelope and felt lumpy, as if the sheets of paper inside were of different sizes or had been folded without care. Phyllis knew the writing at once, slightly larger than other people's and with extravagantly sweeping crossbars on the letter 't': it was from Jamie. She had last seen this handwriting after her father died, when he had sent a sweet note of condolence. This new letter had already been opened, as all post to the prisoners was. Generally the knowledge that her communications had been perused by someone else before she saw them tainted the pleasure of receiving them, but in this case she had an unfamiliar feeling of pure joy as she held the letter in her hands.

Her friendship with Jamie came from a simpler and happier time. Unfolding the paper, she saw at once that it was only partly covered in words, the short paragraphs being interspersed with ink drawings: the face of a cow, a fat crow weighing down a twiggy branch, a cluttered windowsill framing a view of the farmyard. The drawings were delightful, simple and vivid. There were the same swoops of ink as in his handwriting, as if he had drawn the pictures very rapidly. Jamie did not ask her any questions at all, nor make any reference to her imprisonment, as her usual correspondents did. He said that he had bumped into Nina one day when she had come to visit her mother and that she had mentioned that it might now be possible for Phyllis to receive letters from people outside the immediate family. Otherwise he wrote rather as a kind uncle might address a favourite niece, describing in a few words and pictures a typical morning at the farm: the milky vapour of the cows' breath in the cold morning air, the puddles frozen over in the yard and how the ice on them squeaked under his boots; coming in at mid-morning for a cup of tea and to read the paper. He didn't mention anyone else.

After she'd read it once, Phyllis tucked the letter back into its envelope and put it under a book on the little table in her cell. Several times that day and in the days that followed, she took it out and looked at it again. It was like finding a precious piece of jewellery somewhere humdrum like a sewing box. When she answered she told Jamie how sorry she was that she could not draw, but that if she could she would depict for him the haughty face, pinched with disapproval, of her next-door neighbour. Then she would enclose the likeness of some of the women who had been kind to her, so that he could see something of the company she kept.

'. . . but perhaps it is for the best that I am no artist, for none of us are looking at our finest and no one would thank me for depicting them as they presently appear. If I confide that certain of my friends are in sore need of the services of the hairdresser, the dressmaker and even the laundry you will perhaps have some idea. If we had been camping out on a Welsh hillside during a rainstorm we would hardly look worse. Please do write again if you are so inclined and it isn't too much trouble. I loved the drawings especially since I don't have much of a view from my quarters here. (You are very good at drawing, Jamie, I should have said so when you showed me some of your pictures last summer was it? But to see the pencil portraits you had done of me made me tongue-tied, because it was funny to think you'd looked so much at me.) Your letter gave me such a lot of happiness I can't tell you and it was wonderful to see glimpses of your life on the farm, as good as a trip to the cinema, or actually better than that because it was like a visit home.'

It was only after she'd written the letter and was looking it over before posting that she noticed she'd written the word 'home' and understood that she'd meant her childhood home, the Grange. Yet when she visited home in her imagination, it was in Sussex she imagined herself.

Christmas came. The women tried to bolster each other along, but it was a sad day. They sang carols to keep their spirits up and toasted the Leader with watery fruit cordial and wore paper hats they'd cut out and glued themselves, but there were few smiles. A particular friend of Phyllis's was June, an unmarried woman of about the same age who'd been a British Union organizer at St Albans. She was a spry little person with thick wavy hair, and musical. When they put on their entertainments she accompanied a fellow inmate who played the upright piano on the cornet, tapping her small foot energetically as she played. June's sister kept a smallholding in Kent and had sent her a tin of shortbread fingers, which she handed around at tea-time. Various of the women had received fruitcakes, too, but the shortbread was the greatest treat. The cakes were low on fruit and tasted bitter, as if they had attained their brown colour with the aid of Marmite, or gravy browning. But the shortcake was heavy with actual butter that they could taste. No one had seen so much as a scraping of butter since they'd entered the gates of Holloway: the pale stuff they spread – or smeared, really – on their bread was hardly even identifiable. On Christmas night June came along to Phyllis's cell with a couple of pieces of the shortbread, which she'd kept back for them, to accompany their bedtime drink. One of the wardresses had brought in extra milk for this and someone had procured a tin of cocoa powder. Half a bowl of sugar appeared from somewhere, as if magicked by a genie.

'Next year I'm going to roast a goose and a whole bag of potatoes, just for myself,' said June.

'Next year I'm going to give all three of my children new bicycles. And I'm going to buy myself a satin nightie, like those ones people wear in films,' said Phyllis.

'And a pair of slippers with ostrich feather trim and high heels, to go with it,' said June.

'Exactly! And, what are those dressing gowns called, a peignoir is it?'

'Or is that a fancy name for a pair of spectacles?'

'I'm not sure. Anyway, a satin dressing gown to go over the nightie. Ecru satin. Then I'm going to loll on a sofa eating grapes while everyone opens all their presents all around me.'

'And I'm going to play gramophone music at top volume while I feast on my enormous lunch. A nice bit of Tchaikovsky, for preference. The Dance of the Sugar Plum Fairy, do you know it? It's festive as anything, lots of triangles. And I shan't go for a walk afterwards. I shall just sit about, eating nuts.'

'It'll be splendid,' said Phyllis.

'Yes,' said June. 'It will.'

14. Isle of Man, June 1941

Phyllis couldn't see why they had to keep the blinds down all the way from London to Liverpool, but it was no good appealing to their police guard, who'd already made it clear that he was a stickler, even before the train pulled out. Orders were orders. The women had already attracted a good deal of attention on the platform, despite the earliness of the hour: people had gathered at the barrier to jeer. The sensations of being out of Holloway and on the platform of a busy terminus were so overwhelming that Phyllis hardly noticed. The blinds had to stay down because the prison party – there were over forty women and an escort for each carriage – did not wish to invite the attention of travellers further up the line, as they stopped at stations. Nor did they wish the women under custody to know where they were going. This was absurd, for they had overheard the porter telling the guard how long the journey to Liverpool would take. In any case their carriages would surely excite more curiosity, swathed in black, than the sight of a handful of rather bedraggled-looking women in darned stockings, one or two of them in mothy furs.

It was fuggy in the carriage. A smell of staleness seemed to linger in the moquette, of cigarette ash and unwashed bodies. There was the underlying smell, too, of acrid coal dust; presumably because they were right at the front of the train, up by the engine. It always struck Phyllis as peculiar that a smell caused by burning could be so redolent of cold. A dead coal fire was exactly that: cold and dead. It was for this reason that she had always preferred log fires to coal, despite Hugh's insistence that wood fires gave off very much less heat. Then too, the smell of wood smoke reminded her of childhood; of long winter afternoons at the Grange with her sisters, toasting chestnuts. The tips of their fingers had blackened and stung, from trying to prise the hot shells off. Now that she thought of it, it occurred to Phyllis that none of them had cared very much for the chestnuts: they tasted of the glue on postage stamps and had a disagreeable, woolly texture. And yet the girls had loved the ritual of the wide flat chestnut pan with its long handle and the terrific popping sound as the shells split in the heat.

Phyllis was glad that she and June were sitting together. If they weren't permitted to look out of the window they could at least keep one another company.

'One could write a terrifically stirring piece of music based on the sound of a train,' said June.

'But wouldn't it just be a din?' asked Phyllis. 'They make such a racket.'

'That's just what I mean! One could incorporate an entire percussion section, make it start off rather slowly and then go faster and faster; and then bring in horns for the brakes and engine-squeaks and strings to represent the gathering momentum. I think it would be great fun.'

'You are daft, sometimes,' said Phyllis.

'I shan't deny it,' said June. 'But I manage to keep myself amused.'

With the other women in their carriage they played I Spy for a few rounds, but soon ran out of things to see. The guard who was travelling with them refused to join in, but turned the pages of his newspaper, licking his thick thumb each time in order to separate them. By and by they fell silent, each of them considering what this move would signify. There had been rumours of deportation. It was said that other prisoners being held under Regulation 18B had been taken to the docks at Liverpool and despatched to Canada, or even the further-flung colonies. There was talk of camps on the Isle of Man. Just the day before they had heard of some of the men being kept in abandoned housing at Huyton, on the outskirts of Liverpool: one of the women had received a letter from her husband, who was being held there. He complained of broken pipes, rats, makeshift roofing of corrugated iron which failed to keep the rain out. Some of the women wondered if they were being taken to join the men there. At least it was the summer, now, so there wouldn't be the relentless cold to endure.

For Phyllis the journey was wrenching: each mile took her further from home and from her children. Dreadful as Holloway had been, it had at least become familiar. Even though she was confined, knowing that the great city of London was swirling outside the gates gave some reassurance. Letters had arrived, from her sisters, from the children, from Hugh and from Greville, who was still exerting himself on her behalf but whose reassurances became more empty with each week that passed. Since Christmas Jamie had sent a letter every week, all of them illustrated with his own drawings. He never folded the paper in the same way, so the envelopes bulged as if they might burst and spill, like a paper twist packed too full with sherbet. He drew the pump in the farmyard, hung with icicles in the February freeze. As the weeks moved on he depicted the coming of spring: snowdrops under the old apple trees in the walled orchard where his parents had kept their beehives; the bright leaves of the quickthorn; cow-parsley and herb robert on the verges. More than anything, Jamie's missives gave Phyllis comfort and hope. How would his letters ever find her, now?

At length the train arrived and the women were taken to a waiting bus which conveyed them to the docks. They stood about on the wind-blown concrete concourse for what seemed like hours, in abject confusion. Even cheery little June struggled to maintain her composure. Phyllis felt her heart racing and she repeated a silent prayer, over and over, in her head.

'Please God, don't let it be Canada. Please don't take me so far from Edwin and Frances and Julia. I promise I'll be good and not ask for anything else.'

Then a porter came for their cases and they were led to a vessel, on the side of which the words 'Isle of Man Steam Packet Company' were painted. Phyllis felt the strength go out of her legs from relief and had to cling on to the handrail as she came aboard. She had only a very vague idea as to where the Isle of Man actually was – somewhere between Liverpool and Ireland, she thought – but at least it was within the isles of Britain, not too impossibly far away. Her greatest fear throughout her incarceration had been some accident befalling one of the children: a broken leg, say, or complications from measles. Not that she would have been able to do anything to help from within the prison, but at least there'd be some comfort in knowing that she was not too far away.

The same police guard who had travelled with them from London suddenly reappeared and walked them swiftly up several flights of narrow metal staircases to a series of small cabins, where they were to spend their passage. They were instructed not to roam the decks, but to stay put.

'Hullo, Officer? Sir? My friend's feeling rather giddy,' June said to the guard. 'Is there any chance, do you suppose, that she could have a cup of tea?'

To the surprise of all in their little party, he seemed to soften, now they were on board the boat. 'I'll go down and ask the steward to bring a tray presently,' he said. 'And I daresay a sweet biscuit wouldn't go amiss. We've a way to go. A little sugar wards off sea-sickness, I believe.'

One or two of the others fell asleep, rocked by the motion of the sea-swell and worn out from the exertion and uncertainty of their day. Phyllis tried to look out from the porthole, but saw only spray and roiling grey water, for miles and miles. She'd envisaged a passage no longer than that to the Isle of Wight, but the journey took very much longer, four hours or more. It was early evening by the time she felt the boat slow and judder as it made to enter the harbour at Douglas. There was a long delay while the other passengers disembarked. At last their turn came and they stepped off the gangway. Straight away a newspaper-man came forward and began to take pictures, until one of the police guards saw him and shooed him away. After that he turned his attention to their piled-up luggage. The next day the paper carried photographs of their cases alongside an article insisting that they had made their transit in the lap of luxury, accompanied by trunks full of expensive clothes.

At the entrance to the harbour a small group of islanders had gathered to gawp and now some of them called out jibes at the women. One or two had cameras and flagrantly took pictures, as if Phyllis and her companions were living curios in a travelling circus. At length they were led away from the dock and trudged uphill through the town before coming to a small but elaborate Victorian red-brick building: the railway station. The group were ushered through the ticket office and out on to the platform beyond. Phyllis almost laughed when she saw the waiting train. It was like a toy railway, standing only a few feet tall and with little carriages upholstered in rich red plush, like seats at an opera house.

'Where's the Seven Dwarves, then?' called out one of the women.

Everyone laughed. Terrible though it was to find themselves prisoners on an island miles from anywhere and with no knowing what their living quarters might turn out to be, a feeling of lightness became palpable among them. The absurdity of the dinky train somehow brought out an unexpected gaiety, as if they were after all holidaymakers.

They were not required to draw down the blinds for this leg of their journey, since the train had been requisitioned for the purpose of transporting them to the other side of the island and would make no stops along the way. The women in Phyllis's carriage – there were four of them, besides herself – agreed that it would be refreshing to have the windows open, for all that the cooler air before dusk was drawing in. Phyllis sat in a corner seat, drinking in the sights and smells of the countryside which unfolded ever so slowly outside. The pace was no quicker than the trot of a plump pony and with a similarly rolling motion. To begin with the track was hemmed in and gave no sight of sky. As they pulled out of Douglas there were banks of hills to either side, which with a pang reminded her of the Sussex Downs. The train went through the deep shade of a wood. A rocky siding sprouted lush fronds of bracken, dotted with tall occasional fox-gloves, before giving way to woods again. Phyllis caught a glint of a low waterfall giving on to a clear brown stream below. She could make out the white undersides of blackberry leaves and the compact white flowers where the berries would come, flut-tering from the motion of the passing train. The cool smell of wild garlic wafted from the carpet of white flowers beneath the trees. As they passed through a short tunnel, steam obscured the outlook altogether.

Then suddenly, and it seemed to Phyllis miraculously, there were long views: two-thirds of the window contained an expanse of blue, blue sky and below it were green pastures dot-ted with whitewashed farmhouses; and beyond the fields were glimpses of the sea. Everything looked bright and fresh and new. There was honeysuckle and fuchsia in the hedgerows and long low mossy walls of stone enclosed the neat fields. The train edged closer to the coast, then further inland, but the sea was rarely out of sight. In a small field of coarse reedy grass she saw thirty or more plump white geese standing stock-still, looking indignant. There were sheep and cows. At a level crossing she saw a Jack Russell sitting on the lap of an old man on a tractor, its ears cocked. There were rooks making their way home to their nests in high elms. Apprehensive as she was, sad as she was, Phyllis nevertheless experienced deep in her chest a lurch of something very like rapture: the world was really so very green, so extraordinarily blue. A little flicker of hope, no bigger than a pilot light, sprang to life within her.

She wished the train would go on for ever, chugging merrily through the woods and farms. But at length it stopped in a great billow of steam and she and her companions alighted. Phyllis found she had pins and needles in one foot. They lingered on the platform, waiting for the bus to take them to the next place. Their fragile gaiety was fading with the light.

'Don't just stand there, you lot! Chop, chop! They've kept some hot food for you, but you'll need to hurry it up.'

The speaker was a youngish woman in an unidentifiable uniform. She cradled a wooden clipboard in one arm and her skirt was too tight. She at once reminded Phyllis of her sister Nina. The women trooped the short way after her along a narrow shopping street, turning left and then right and then left again until they came to a church hall. Here their names were read off from a list on the woman's clipboard. Each was allocated her billet. They still had no idea how much further they had to go, nor what kind of accommodation awaited them at the camp.

Several of the women – June among them, to her chagrin and Phyllis's, for they had hoped to be put together – were led off on foot by a rather grumpy older woman. Their new guard told those who remained to follow her and led them out on to the pavement.

'There's a short-cut to the back of the hall, you'll find it for yourselves once you get your bearings. But we're going along the promenade now. Only takes a couple of ticks longer and it'll give you a better sense of the place and where your lodgings are.'

They found themselves on a wide crescent of stucco-fronted hotels which stood behind a broad street, following the curve of the beach beyond. The tide was out and little fishing boats lay on the strand. A light shone from above a long building to the left of the bay and was reflected on the wet sand below, hazy and yellow, like a late-summer moon. There was a low sea wall running along the edge of the beach, faced by a row of cottages. Out on the headland to the right of the bay Phyllis could just discern some sort of tower. It wasn't a town of any size: bigger than Bosham, but very much smaller than Bognor or Little-hampton. Despite being called a port, it was more of a resort: all the buildings they passed seemed to be boarding-houses or small hotels. They made their way uphill for only a few minutes, until they came to a small lane of just five or six Edwardian villas.

The first was double-fronted, with decorative barge-board details and a tiny balcony above the front door. A pair of bay windows on the ground floor flanked the door.

'This is you,' said the woman who reminded Phyllis of Nina. She checked the names on her list.

'Mrs Forrester, Mrs Bingham, Miss Parkinson and Miss Thomas: you're in number three. I'll just show you in, introduce you, if you lot wouldn't mind hanging on out here for a moment.'

'It's Mrs Thomas, actually,' said Margaret Thomas with a small self-righteous sniff. She wasn't Phyllis's most favourite fel-low prisoner. She very much hoped she would not be obliged to share a room with Margaret, who suffered from her sinuses, which meant that she was forever complaining of headaches and sniffling into her handkerchief. Rowena Bingham would be the best room-mate among the group: she was quiet and purposeful. She had worked at London HQ, organizing the speakers' training courses. There were rumours of an affair with a married man.

To their great surprise, they were introduced not to another guard in uniform but to a civilian woman, a Mrs Powell, who seemed to be the perfectly ordinary proprietor of what was under normal circumstances a bed and breakfast establishment. She did not seem especially pleased to see her new guests – there were no smiles – but nor was she markedly hostile. She took them up the stairs to the bedrooms on the first floor, of which there were three: two larger rooms at the front, each with a pair of beds and a smaller single room at the back, next to the bathroom.

'You can sort out your sleeping arrangements to suit your-selves,' said Mrs Powell. 'There's a meal waiting for you downstairs – if you'd come down sooner rather than later I should appreciate it.'

'You should have the single room, Margaret,' said Phyllis. 'Then if you get one of your sore heads you can rest undisturbed.'

'I don't know whether I'll be able to get to sleep if you lot are in and out of the bathroom at all hours, pulling the chain,' she said.

'Tell you what, we'll agree not to pull the chain after ten o'clock: how does that sound?' said one of the others.

Phyllis and Rowena's eyes met.

'Well, I'm sure we'll be able to sort something out, between us,' said Phyllis. As she spoke she turned into the bigger of the front bedrooms and put her case down next to the bed furthest from the door. There was a washbasin, two high beds with dam-ask pink eiderdowns, a rug. 'I'm going in here, anyway. We can unpack later. I'm starving.'

'I'll join you,' said Rowena.

★

It was the best night's sleep Phyllis had had since she'd been picked up from home by the policemen, over a year before. She could scarcely believe the feeling of actual bedsprings beneath her, yielding when she turned, and the delicious weight of the eiderdown and blanket on top. Her feet were not cold and there was no ache in the small of her back. Best of all, there was fresh air on her face. At Holloway it had not been possible to open the tiny windows. Here, she and Rowena had moved in unison to open the tall sash window as soon as they'd come up after supper. When Phyllis woke it was to an unfamiliar and slightly guilty sensation which it took her some minutes to identify as optimism. She realized that she was looking forward to the day ahead. Standing, she looked out across a sloping meadow of long grass down to the houses of Port Erin, which were clustered around the bay and scattered up the green fields that rose to the far side of the beach.

The sky seemed immense. Birds were chitting in the hedge which separated the narrow front garden from the lane. And here she was, in a room; an actual room, with a sprigged paper on the walls and a looking-glass and a polished chest of drawers. She looked down at her bare feet, taking in the nobbles of her toes and the gaps between them and the feeling of the tufted wool rug on the soles of her feet. She couldn't remember the last time she had been aware of her own feet – of any part of herself, really – other than to register how cold she was, or how hungry. It was as if she had been discarnated by imprisonment.

After breakfast the bossy young woman in the tight uniform appeared. She explained the camp to them: they were free to roam the lower part of the town and a certain distance along the path which led out to the north of the bay, as far as the cedar trees at the end of the lawn by the tea-room. The limits of the camp would be evident: fences and barbed wire. They must not engage in any activity which sought to advance their beliefs, nor were they allowed to enter into discussion about politics and the war with any member of the public or fellow internee. There were a great many other internees in the town, mostly German women, as well as Austrians. They were absolutely forbidden to discuss their ideological beliefs with the enemy aliens; nor were they to solicit the views or backgrounds of these fellow internees. They must remember at all times that they were here as guests of their Manx hosts and behave with courtesy. It was with their hosts in mind that the decision had been made that they should not be allocated work, apart from a laundry rota in which each of them would do her stint twice weekly.

This was in order to preserve the jobs of the local people. They were free to form societies for their own occupation and self-improvement: to practise calisthenics, for example, or art classes. They were also at liberty to join such classes as already existed in the town, of which there were many.

'Will we be allowed to attend church services?' one of the women asked.

The answer was yes. They were permitted to use any premises and/or establishment which was open to the public, including churches and chapels, library, shops, banks and post office, the dance-hall and tea-rooms. All goods and services must be paid for in full in advance: anyone attempting to persuade a shopkeeper into opening an account would have her privileges revoked.

'May we go to the hairdresser's?' asked Rowena.

At this the young woman smirked. 'You can try. However, I think it only fair to warn you that there is just the one hairdresser in the town and the lady in question has a son in the army.'

'And why should that pertain?' asked Rowena. Phyllis noticed that they were all beginning to speak like officials.

'I believe the lady has fairly strong views about your . . . your political affiliations. That is to say, she has said in no uncertain terms that she won't serve any of you. But if you wish to discover whether she is bluffing, you are at liberty to find out for yourselves. Perhaps I should tell you that one or two other shopkeepers have expressed similar sentiments. There is a feeling that your politics mark you out as traitors. To look on the bright side, though, there was some anti-German feeling when the enemy aliens first arrived here, but things soon smoothed over. Many of the shops began selling things the aliens had made, as a matter of fact: embroidered gloves and collars, carved figures, bits of drawn-thread work, that sort of thing. I daresay it will be the same for all of you, in due course. As I say, civility is the order of the day at all times, irrespective. Any other questions? I should add that you will see me every morning, so if you think of things you need to know I'll be coming up at the same time tomorrow.'

Phyllis asked about letters. Was there a limit as to how many letters they might write and who should they give letters to, for vetting and posting? Should they give their actual address for return post, or was there some central camp to which their correspondents should address their letters?

The young woman explained. Just as she was leaving, Margaret Thomas piped up.

'I don't suppose we're allowed on to the beach, are we?' she asked. 'Only I should love to feel the sand under my feet.'

The young woman laughed. 'Of course you can go to the beach. You can paddle all you like, but bathing is only allowed from the northern edge of the beach, away from the boats. It's rather rocky. There's also a sea-water bath, but you may not have spotted it from here, you can't see it because it's tucked in, under the cliff. It's actually the biggest sea-water pool in Britain. I don't imagine you've come with bathing things?' Here she smiled. 'I believe there are costumes and towels for hire at the baths. Otherwise Curphey's sells costumes, it's just down the hill from here on the right. Next to Collinson's, the big café with the dome.'

Phyllis could not believe their luck. If it weren't for the danger of swimming too soon after a meal, she would have plunged straight into the waves. As it was she had to wait out the requisite hour before she could go in. One of the others proposed a stroll out to the tea-room along the headland, and she went upstairs to fetch her purse. When she had left Holloway she had been handed her things, her handbag and the light gabardine coat she had brought with her and a small felt hat. These had been taken away on her arrival and she had never thought to see them again. Pinned to the lapel of the coat was a brooch her daughters had given her, in the shape of an old-fashioned galleon in full sail. Its cut steel glittered darkly, as if it were made from tarnished little diamonds. Phyllis had been delighted to see it again, remembering how excited Julia and Frances had been when they handed her the little box. Her old familiar bag was lined in soft suede the colour of face-powder, with a little side pocket edged with leather which held a mirror. Her lipstick had all but dried up, but her purse and hankie and comb were intact. Folded alongside them was a piece of paper on which she had written a list. Phyllis felt a jolt of sadness at the sight of it, for it seemed to her now that the woman who had written the list was an innocent who had no notion of what was about to happen to her.

Dark tan shoe polish
Order extra name-tapes
Baking soda
Envelopes – good paper for letters + tradesmen's
Return fish-kettle to P.

It seemed almost like something from a museum, the list, some ancient papyrus or fragment of scroll; an object from an altogether different age. It illustrated how ordinary her life used to be: the list could have been anyone's. But her pensive mood cleared when she opened her purse. For there was a five-pound note folded small and two ten-shilling ones, as well as a good handful of change: great riches. She recalled that Hugh had given her the notes in some haste, when it was evident that they were being taken away from their house. It was emergency money, in case she had needed a taxi or even an hotel after what they had both assumed would be an hour or so of questioning. He was normally cautious: Phyllis generally carried only a few shillings, while Hugh dealt with cheques and money orders and settled their monthly accounts. Now she would be able to buy herself a bathing dress and some new stockings and under-things. A bottle of lavender water, perhaps. She could send little presents to the children, if anything larger than letters were per-mitted: the sweets they liked – a stick of rock each, if she could still obtain them – and some small fancy goods. It gave her some little happiness to imagine making up the parcels, one for each child. But the feeling was bittersweet and didn't last. The reality of her new situation was that Phyllis was very much further away from her children than she had been in London. Lovely though it was to be free to wander the little streets and walk on to the sand, miles and miles and miles of water separated her now from everyone she most loved.

Phyllis, 1979

I'm not sure how I found out that it was Nina.

It did seem odd that Eric hadn't been taken into custody, he was so much more closely involved than I was, or even Hugh. He wasn't just a local organizer, he actually wrote a lot of the leaflets and things that were put out from HQ. Come to think of it, he was really rather good at writing, very persuasive. He managed to cajole a lot of the top people into coming to speak at meetings down in Sussex. He was very capable at a great many things, considering he was essentially a glorified mechanic. But I suppose we all underestimated him, because he ended up owning that string of garages all along the south coast: he did very well for himself and his family. Played golf with other local businessmen, sherry with magistrates, that sort of thing. Rotarians. And, to be fair, he was very good to poor Hugh after the war. Well, I suppose he felt guilty. I suppose it was what you might call an attempt at some sort of reparation. But we didn't know that at the time, we thought he was just being kind.

So I did wonder why they hadn't rounded him up, but there wasn't much logic to it, who they took in and who escaped their notice. One chap was arrested after returning from his sixth cross-Channel trip to rescue soldiers from Dunkirk. So much for our lot being traitors! Some of the people they detained were such small fry it scarcely seemed worthy of Her Majesty's Pleasure to keep them under lock and key. Little clerks, girls who'd made the tea. Mosley's actual secretary, Miss Monk, never got taken in, although she knew all his secrets; same thing with his mother, old Lady Mosley. She was a fearful dragon. They went to fetch one young woman District Leader, but she was away on her honeymoon at the time and they never went back for her. That's how ill-thought-out it all was.

The irony was, of course, that prison made me believe in the cause even more firmly than I had before. A so-called free country that would lock up patriotic folk, simply because they dissented from the prevailing view of the Government: how could I have any faith in our rulers after that? In the Isle of Man various charitable organizations came and busied themselves on behalf of the enemy aliens. Bishop Bell came and wrote a report, and some well-known Quaker character, and people from important-sounding councils for this and that. To be fair, they far out-numbered us: there were a good four thousand of these foreign women and children at Port Erin, with just forty-three of our lot. After Italy joined the war, some Italian women and women with Italian husbands turned up too. For the people who owned the boarding-houses it was like the best holiday season they'd ever had: every bed in the town was taken. The do-gooders wanted to make sure they had enough to eat and were being kept nicely. They bothered about them, but of course there were no such charitable efforts on our behalf, when we were carted off there. What they didn't like was the idea that the ordinary foreign nationals were being cooped up in the same camps as active Nazis from Germany and Austria who'd somehow got caught up in the same net and been brought over to the Isle. Some bright spark thought of introducing a de-nazification pro-gramme over there, in the island camps. The idea being that the National Socialists would be cured of their beliefs by the time they came out. They never put any such programme into practice, of course.

As I say, no one came to ensure that we were kept under humane con-ditions. British Union set up an Aid Fund for the victims of 18B and their families, people who were suffering hardship. But the charities and churches and politicians, they didn't bother about us, although we were British nationals. The idea was that we had it lucky, being out of the danger of the bombing raids and living in boarding-houses generally used by paying customers. But we hadn't broken the law. They only outlawed British Union in the same year as they brought our detention order, so technically we'd done nothing wrong. And it galled that these foreigners had people looking out for them while we had no one.

★

Even though I felt such dreadful guilt about the death of my poor friend, I still knew that it was terribly unfair that I should have been kept as a political prisoner for all that time. A third of my little boy's life, it was. I mean, as I say, I hadn't done anything: hadn't committed any crime. It was against Magna Carta, to lock us up like that. All I'd done was to believe that there was one man who could prevent war and bring Britain back to greatness through strong ties with our Empire and the hard graft of our own workers. A Greater Britain, that's what the Leader named it. You have to recall that what is now called the First World War was considered by my generation to have been the war to end all wars. We didn't want to see our men and boys mown down again, especially not for a quarrel that wasn't our quarrel.

We had a dear cousin who'd been killed and our own father had been wounded: we simply couldn't stand by and do nothing while another generation was felled.

Being locked up and then sent to the Isle of Man with no trial and no recourse to justice actually made me see what a dreadful system we were living under, and how much better it might have been under British Union, with Sir Oswald at the national helm. I don't regret my politics, I don't see why I should. I think history has proved us right. Look at the state of the country, now! Endless power cuts, grave-diggers on strike so that bodies lie unburied, no one collecting the rubbish so there are rats in the streets . . . it's a disgrace. People freezing to death in their own homes because the electric's been switched off. Socialist infiltrators picketing outside our hospitals and fire stations. All these foreigners taking over our little shops and whatnot. We had to let them in, you see, because of the break-up of all our colonies, our Empire. They'd been under our protection, we couldn't just abandon them. Mind you, one can't understand what they're saying, half the time. We used to be a great nation, a great Empire, and now look at us. Sir Oswald would never have let things come to this. I'll be honest: so far as I'm concerned, he walked on water. I think the world of him, still.

★

In any case. To get back to Nina and how I found out. I think it must have been through one of the chaps I met at the annual reunions. I expect you've heard that a few of us, loyal to the cause, go to a pub in the East End every November to celebrate the Leader's birthday. November 16th, it is. Sir Oswald always joins us, comes over specially from his home in France. A driver collects him from Victoria. There is such a bond, such loyalty, you see. That's what people never mention, when they do the Movement down. They think we were just a bunch of Nazis, but it wasn't like that at all. If they knew their history they'd understand that the Corporate State we were proposing was closer to what Mussolini had achieved in Italy than to the Germans.

I met a fellow at one of the early reunions after the war who had been a friend of the policeman in Chichester who'd tipped off the authorities about Hugh and myself; and it was he who told me that this same officer had been pally with Eric and my sister. Very friendly, they were.

Apparently he'd gone round and warned them that the powers that be were looking to round some of us up, but he said that if they gave him some names he'd see what he could do to keep them out of it. Well, you must remember that Nina was expecting a baby by then: of course she wasn't going to volunteer herself. Not that she could've known what was coming. To be fair to her, no one would ever have guessed that they'd keep us locked up for all that time. I expect she just thought they'd come and search our house and ask us some questions, perhaps take us in overnight or for a day or two. She couldn't have known I'd be taken away for all that time. Even after I was released I was still under a restriction order, which went on for a good few months after the war ended.

I've forgiven her, by now, more or less. Perhaps rather less than more, if I'm going to be really honest. It's funny, isn't it, that I was just saying what tremendous loyalty there was among us all and yet my own sister turned us in. But you see I find it hard to blame her completely, because she simply could not have had any idea what would happen to us, not then. And after all, it's not as if our involvement in the cause was a secret: lots of people knew that Hugh and I were active in the Party. If it hadn't been Nina, it could just as well have been someone else. Some busy-body from outside the Party may have made the call. More than Nina I blame the situation we found ourselves in; the war itself, the politicians who allowed it to happen. At the time it was widely felt among us that the Labour Party had made locking us up a condition of their joining the Coalition. The timing was certainly right: we were taken in in May 1940, same month as Churchill's Coalition government was formed. After the war, Aneurin Bevan claimed that the Labour Party had forced Churchill to imprison Sir Oswald. You may judge for yourself.

Sometimes I do feel that prison is what did for poor Hugh. He was so much older than me, I think his health was affected. Whereas I had yet to turn forty, by the time we got out. Felt ancient at the time, but now I realize I was still a fairly young woman.

We do keep in touch, Nina and I: at Christmas, birthdays. I usually send her a picture postcard from my holiday. No. The person I find it so much harder to forgive is my other sister, Patricia.

15. Isle of Man, summer and autumn 1941

It took several weeks before Phyllis found out that Hugh, too, was on the island. The men had been moved with the same secrecy as their female counterparts, so his letter telling her that he'd been relocated to Peveril camp was much delayed by having to be forwarded via Holloway. She learned that Peveril was situated up the west coast at the harbour town of Peel, an hour or so away from Port Erin. It was a relief that he hadn't been held at the notoriously awful camp outside Liverpool, where it was said that many of the men were suffering from serious ill health due to the punishing conditions. Privately, though, she felt a tight little knot of unease. The German and Austrian women were permitted to see their husbands once a month, when they were bussed into Port Erin from their camps elsewhere on the island. They were allowed to stroll about the town, arm in arm, quite freely. There were quite a few small children with their mothers in the foreign women's camp: it was touching to see their little faces, tight with pride, when their fathers lifted them up on to their shoulders and carried them down to the beach or along the esplanade.

Nothing of the kind had so far been proposed in their own case, but it seemed to Phyllis that the serenity of their little group would surely be ruffled if the men were admitted. These women had borne the privations of imprisonment together, with each other's help: the men would unsettle them, undo their routines and companionship. Such thoughts she kept to herself, for it would not have been popular with the rest. The other married women in the camp were up in arms when they discovered that the so-called enemy aliens were allowed to see their husbands while they, British women, were not. There was talk of getting up a petition, as well as writing individual letters of appeal.

Before such considerations arose there were several weeks of glorious weather that summer. It was impossible not to feel some sense of gaiety from the sheer relief of being out of prison, of breathing the sea air and sleeping on an actual sprung bed; of morning walks along the headland and apparently limitless quantities of milk and butter, and even cream. Because local farmers were hardly able to export their produce to the mainland, there was a local glut. Eggs were plentiful, too. When Phyllis took Rowena and June to a tea-room they had all three been so astonished to be served a cream tea – even if the red jam tasted suspiciously like beetroot and the scones were rather dry – as to be reduced to total silence. The best of it was being free to go outside. In the ground opposite her lodgings the buddleia came into flower and in the warm afternoons the bramble leaves gave off a delicious smell. To be able to sit on the tussocky grass with the hot air on her bare shins and the sunlight against her eyelids, the brightness creating whirling bursts of colour within her closed eyes: Phyllis could scarcely believe that such sensations were possible. Nevertheless the longing for family and home remained as sharp as ever. The absence of any release date to look forward to was never less hard to endure.

Time had dragged terribly, in Holloway, but here there was a seemingly endless round of things to keep them occupied. The British Council, the Society of Friends and the local Welfare Officers had between them furnished the reading room with a variety of books, although a lot of them seemed to be educational books rather than the stories which Phyllis preferred. And you had to hand it to them, the Jewish German and

Austrian internees were extraordinarily resourceful. They had among themselves arranged a constant programme of lectures and practical classes, everything from flute-playing to wood-carving. There were talks and lessons every day: European history, literature, mythology, pedagogy, dietetics, science. Visiting lecturers came each week to talk on everything from archaeology to philosophy. Most of the lectures were given by speakers, highly distinguished in their fields, who were interned on other parts of the island. In addition there were language classes in French, Italian, Spanish and even Greek. Those German-speakers who were less than fluent took English classes. All of this was quite apart from the Friday concerts and Wednesday recitals, the choral singing, dramatics, eurythmics, drawing, clay-modelling and music and movement classes. It was as if the sleepy little fishing port had unwittingly become a thriving university. With all the classes and talks and music being put on, it was like another Heidelberg. Most of it was too intellectual for her, but Phyllis joined a glove-making class, although she had to give up after the second lesson: she just didn't seem to have the knack. Instead she learned to crochet on a Monday afternoon and signed up for the French conversation class on Thursday mornings. Using her French vocabulary again reminded her of the happy times she had spent with Sarita. Those lessons with Monsieur Hubert seemed to have taken place in another lifetime: these were not nearly so much fun, but it was better to be occupied than to spend all her time brooding. June joined several musical groups and volunteered to give piano lessons to some of the children, only to discover that music teachers were in greater supply than pupils. Rowena was to take dressmaking and elementary Spanish.

The word was that the handful of captured German National Socialists did not involve themselves in these activities, preferring to keep their distance. Phyllis heard from her landlady that there had been some fear, when the enemy aliens had first arrived, of an eruption of hostility between the two groups. The National Socialists were put accordingly into a couple of boarding-houses some little way to the south of the town; while the vast majority of Germans and Austrians, the Jewish women and their children, were housed close to the promenade. Many of them, with their husbands and young families, had been living and working in London and other cities, refugees from their homelands. By May 1940 it was thought that the risk of German invasion was high and many of them were interned, for fear of fifth columnists. They were bewildered to find themselves captives on this speck of an island, miles from anywhere. It was clear that they posed no threat to national security: they were hardly likely to stir up pro-Nazi feeling, having themselves fled from the regime.

During the first week or two there had been notional efforts to keep Phyllis and her friends apart from the foreign nationals, lest arguments broke out. At British Union meetings Phyllis had of course heard of the dangers posed to English concerns by international Jewry. Several of the better-known speakers were vociferous about it all: in order to prevent them from prating, the Leader had proclaimed that only ten minutes in every hour-long speech could be dedicated to the growing economic threat posed by Jewish interests. It was all very complicated. International forces, business ownership imperilling British livelihoods, secret economic alliances formed in order to increase political leverage: such talk came up regularly. Be that as it may, Phyllis and her fellow internees agreed that they had no quarrel with the German and Austrian women, where individuals were concerned. They were all victims alike, here. Some of them had turned their backs, when the Holloway contingent walked into Collinson's; but on the whole they were accepted with fairly good grace.

The town's hairdresser remained their strongest opposer, refusing outright to allow them into her premises. To begin with there had been frank stares from various other shopkeepers, and more than once there was a hostile silence from island customers, a scraping back of chairs. Sometimes people called after them in the streets: traitors! They had been instructed to maintain their composure and civility in the case of such provocation, but sometimes it was very trying. Out on an errand one afternoon, one of the older women had been taunted by a group of Manx women and had shouted back: 'My husband fought for this country in the Great War. What's yours ever done – catch mackerel?'

But over the weeks relations appeared to thaw on all sides. The Germans and Austrians who ran the classes were kind, and Phyllis especially liked the older woman who taught the crochet group. Sometimes it seemed to her that the world would be a better and more peaceable place if men were kept out of things altogether.

Phyllis could not say that she was happy, and the unreliability and limitations of the post made her permanently anxious about her children. At Holloway rules surrounding letters had eventually been relaxed, so that there was no quota in place; all post coming in and going out was still subject to scrutiny and occasional censorship, but there wasn't a limit on letters. Here on the island the women had the run of the town, or most of it, and a great deal of freedom to do as they pleased. Yet they were suddenly confined to two letters a week, sent and received. Also, post seemed to take for ever to arrive. It was common for letters to come as much as a month or more after posting, which was worrying for those women who had children. It meant they fretted terribly if a child complained of some ailment or woe. The delay also weakened the bond of communication, the sense of being part of each other's daily lives. It wasn't much use to a child if he or she wrote to say that a favourite pet had died, only to receive a consoling reply some eight or nine weeks later: by then they would have put aside their grief and very likely installed a jaunty successor in the rabbit hutch or guinea pig cage.

Phyllis had to ask her sisters to write alternately every third week, so that her limit wasn't used up. She saw no reason to tell them that she wanted to leave the way clear for the long letters full of drawings which she still received from Jamie once a fortnight, but left them to assume that the children's post was her priority. The fact was that Jamie's letters brought her a great deal of comfort and she savoured each for many days. The drawings were so vivid and the things they depicted so delightfully familiar: the farmyard, the stooping old trees in the orchard, even the now dilapidated fruit cages at the Grange, where he had done a series of sketches. The net above the raspberry bushes sagged like a dew-weighed cobweb and was full of holes; in the letter he told her that blackbirds feasted openly on the fruit and barely troubled to fly off when he sat sketching.

Jamie's letters were like missives from the distant past, from the safety of home and her own childhood; whereas her sisters' were rather stiff, Patricia's especially. She supposed she must be difficult to write to. Presumably they didn't want to make her feel left out by describing high days and holidays, nor worry her by recounting their troubles. Any discussion of politics and the war was forbidden. Patricia's letters tended to go on at great length about the nuisance of rationing and ongoing arrangements about fetching and depositing the children from and at their schools. Nina's were cheerier and mostly revolved around the new baby's winning ways. 'It was priceless!' was a recurring phrase. Every so often she got a letter from Greville, assuring her that he continued to lobby for her release.

One of the younger German women at the crochet class was

an artistic type. She was in the boarding-houses where the Jewish women lodged, not one of the Nazi women who roomed at the southern edge of the town. Anna had long hair like a schoolgirl's and there was something slightly theatrical in her gestures, as if when she was a little girl she had been complimented in a ballet class and she'd taken it very much to heart. She always carried a small drawing book around with her and a little tin with charcoal and a few pencils. Anna was in the habit of stopping whatever she was doing on a whim and opening the tin: she was to be seen on the esplanade or at the outdoor café along the headland, sketching fiercely. She was already very adroit at crochet work and only came to class as company for the woman who ran it, who was one of her housemates. More than once Anna had been known to put down a lacy collar halfway through the lesson and instead start on a pencil portrait of one of the women in the class. It occurred to Phyllis that she might be willing to part with two or three drawings. In this way she could send something novel to the children and to Jamie.

Anna was delighted to find a customer. The foreign women were mostly pretty hard up, having left behind everything they owned when they came away to the safety of England. Apparently some of them had been obliged to leave in such a hurry that they had travelled with only the clothes they stood up in. It was fortunate that they seemed to be so adroit at handicrafts and art: several of them made a little money from providing local shops with items that they had made: felt animals, knitted and crocheted goods, embroidered needle cases, gloves and carved napkin rings. From Anna's sketchbook Phyllis chose a view of the harbour for Julia, a little scene of fishing boats for Edwin and a lovely drawing of a pair of finches for Frances. She asked if Anna would draw something else for her, something especially: a view from the esplanade up the town to the north, showing the front of the house where she was lodging, with the pasture in front and the curve of the bay below. She had this in mind for Jamie, so that he could see where she was. It made Phyllis feel that she was still a real person if someone she cared for could picture what her life looked like; otherwise she sometimes felt as though she was in a sort of limbo, neither quite a ghost nor fully of this world. She packed the drawings very carefully, sandwiched between corrugated paper. She sent the packets off to Jamie and Edwin first, and those to the two girls the week after.

Visits from the men's camp began as the summer gave way to autumn. A coach brought them and took them away at the end of the day: they were not permitted to enter the women's lodging-houses, but there were tea-dances, and they were free to walk about in the town and to visit the outdoor swimming bath, the cliff-walk tea-rooms and the beach. The women whose husbands were on the Isle had signed various petitions asking to be interned in married quarters: they believed they were in with a good chance of success, since the word was that the Prime Minister himself was in favour of couples being housed together. This was rumoured to be because the Leader's health – in former times so vigorous – had been sorely damaged by prison food and the lack of fresh air and exercise. Many of the women now included him in their nightly prayers. It was rumoured that he would soon be reunited with his wife, in prison, where it was hoped he would regain his health. The last thing the powers that be wanted was a martyr on their hands.

Phyllis felt much fonder of Hugh than she had feared she might. Being apart for so long, she had formed a picture of him in her mind that was not quite true to the reality. Yes, he was rather stiff and formal; yes, he liked nothing more than to be right, or better still proved right. But when he stepped off the bus from Peveril the warmth of his smile when he caught her eye touched her unexpectedly. He took her arm and they kissed, briefly, the roughness of his cheek against hers unfamiliar to her now. Here was someone who was absolutely on her side. And later, when he got back on the same bus at the end of the day, there was something touching about his retreating form, about the short hair at the back of his head and his upright carriage, as if he were a prep school boy trying to be good, trying to be brave.

'You'll never guess which individual is residing in the hotel next to mine,' Hugh said, after they had had lunch in the dowdy little pub near the railway station.

'One of the speakers from Chichester days?'

'No. That young fellow, Freddy.'

Phyllis remembered him all too clearly, the good-looking youth who had caused the embarrassment with their daughter Julia.

'Freddy as in Freddy from the summer camps? The son of Little Jim, you mean?'

'Well, I don't know who his father is, but yes. It seems he got involved in some trouble over in the East End, smashing people's shop windows, that sort of thing.'

'You remember Little Jim, he did the catering? Nice chap. Whistled a lot. It was his grandson who was such chums with Edwin. Has Freddy acknowledged you?'

'He's been perfectly civil. Hasn't actually acknowledged that we've met before; well, I suppose we hardly have. I don't think we ever exchanged any words on the few occasions I came to camp. Why would one've?'

Here he paused. 'Just between us, I think he could have had the good grace to at least look a bit, I don't know; not shifty exactly, but something at least approaching that. But there's been no sign of anything of the kind; much less an apology. A lot of water has flowed under the bridge, I daresay . . .'

'Well, yes. It's not uppermost in his mind, p'raps.'

'No. I don't expect it would be. I'd pretty much forgotten about it myself, to tell you the truth, until I caught sight of him at Peel.'

'Of course.'

On Hugh's second visit, Phyllis brought out her letters for him to read. The children did write to him, but not so often as they did their mother: that was understandable. And being an only child he had no brothers or sisters with whom to correspond. Most of his letters had been to MPs and tribunal people, lobbying for his and Phyllis's release, as well as for the other detainees. He'd had letters from her, but rather little else in the way of personal post; she felt rather sorry for him. It would amuse him, she thought, to see her letters. Frances in particular had something of a way with words; she'd picked up phrases from all those books she read, perhaps. Only the drawings and accompanying notes from Jamie she left in her bedroom drawer. Hugh had never shown very much interest in Jamie.

In early November word came that Phyllis was to be moved from Port Erin to married quarters at the island's capital, Douglas. Many of the enemy aliens had already been released by then and had gone back to the mainland to resume life with their families. Gradually, Port Erin had emptied. Her artist friend, Anna, had gone in September. Before she went she had made Phyllis a present of a drawing: a girl diving from the higher of the two boards into the town's sea-water pool. Now that their numbers were so sparse the classes dwindled: there was still music and movement and art, but the other lectures and lessons had stopped when the Germans and Austrians went, as had the weekly concerts and choir. There were informal recitals, mostly on the boudoir grand piano in the semi-circular ballroom at Collinson's, but there was an end-of-term feeling about them.

Phyllis was sorry to be leaving the little town. She had grown fond of her daily walk out to the café at Bradda Glen, overlooking the bay, and of the view from her bedroom window. On clear days it was possible to discern the distant hulk of the Mountains of Mourne to the west: people in the town used to say that if you could see Ireland it was about to rain and when you couldn't it was because it was already raining. But Phyllis didn't mind the frequent showers. The rain was what made the hills to either side of the bay so very green. It rinsed the sky, leaving drops all along the fence to the front of her lodging-house which were luminous in the glancing evening light after a downpour.

She would be sorry, too, to be parted from Rowena and June. Rowena was to be sent back to the mainland, but there was no job for her now in London: so she was to go and stay with her mother, in the Chilterns. She thought she would look for work in nearby Wycombe, which she hoped would be safe from the bombing raids. June, who having been a District Leader was more senior than Rowena, was to remain at Port Erin. Still no one was any the wiser as to how long they would be kept away from home.

The married quarters at Douglas were very much less comfortable than the boarding-house in Port Erin had been. They were housed in two tall Victorian buildings at the top of the town. There was a smell of cauliflower and stale mothballs and the landlady had bad hips, which made her ill-tempered. She complained about the many stairs she was obliged to go up and down every day: she planned to move to a bungalow once the war was over. Phyllis offered to help her by emptying the upstairs grates and carrying the buckets of ashes down; Hugh volunteered to bring fresh coal back up: but she was not to be appeased. She spoke accusingly, as if it was the fault of her tenants that there was a war on. Resentment hung over her like the unpleasant odours which lingered over the landings of her house.

If you stood on tip-toe you could see pasture in the distance from the room Phyllis and Hugh shared on the second floor, but there was no sea view. When some errand took her into the town – she was permitted to walk down to the centre, twice a week, as long as she signed out and then in again in the book that was kept on the hall table for that purpose – she walked along the wide esplanade, enjoying the cold salt air and the call of the gulls. But Douglas faced due east. It made Phyllis feel more cut off from home than ever, that you couldn't see the coast of mainland England from here, even though you knew it was there, far away across the expanse of grey sky and water. And Phyllis found it difficult to get to sleep, now that she had become accustomed to nights alone in a narrow bed. Without all the activities the Germans had put on at Port Erin, the days dragged.

But Hugh was kind, which was an unexpected comfort. Not since the days of their courtship had he been so attentive, so considerate. She saw a gentler side of him. When a letter came from Edwin, she handed it to him to read first. After a few moments she glanced across the breakfast table and noticed he'd gone pale. At once she felt her insides gripped with fear.

'What is it? Is something the matter?'

'No, no: he seems to be getting on quite well. Went to your sister Patricia for his long exeat.'

'Oh. But is everything all right? You looked . . . concerned, just now.'

'No indeed. Read for yourself.'

Phyllis took the letter, which was written on two sheets of paper; a rare treat from Edwin, whose correspondence generally read as if he was struggling to fill even one side of a page. The children had been taught, as Phyllis had in her own childhood, that thank-you letters must go over the page in order to count. If you didn't go over the page you didn't seem grateful enough. Perhaps with this in mind, Edwin and Julia always managed a line or two on the reverse of their first pages, before signing off. Frances's letters, by contrast, were sometimes three pages long, full of snippets about her time at school and of the sayings and doings of her friends and what matron said when she caught them larking about after lights out.

As Hugh had said, Edwin reported that he'd been to Rose Green for long exeat. While he was there the most tremendous thing had happened: Uncle Greville had given him his very own gun! It was called a 20-bore and it had belonged to Uncle Greville himself, when he was a boy. Then Uncle Greville had taken him out into the fields with his own gun which was a bigger gun and they'd had a go at some rabbits and he jolly nearly got one and Uncle Greville had got a pigeon and had taken a shot at a squirrel but missed. Edwin didn't mind that he hadn't shot anything and Uncle Greville said it was a skill he'd learn in time and he wasn't to take it to heart as it was his first time. Almost as much fun as shooting the gun was cleaning it and taking it apart: there was oil in a tin with a nozzle, made especially for guns, and a long stick with a rag tied to the end that you put down the barrel to get out any traces of shot. The gun came in its very own case which was made of old leather, with straps. It was the greatest fun and next time he went to stay with Aunt Patricia they were going to go out again and then one day, if he got good enough, Uncle Greville would take him on an actual shoot, with beaters and dogs and everything!

When Phyllis had finished the letter she looked at Hugh. She thought she understood what he was feeling: pleasure for the boy, but some little needle of sorrow that it was with another man that he had fired his first shot.

'It's awfully hard, being so far from the children. It's a funny thing, but sometimes their letters make it worse, not better,' she said, folding Edwin's letter back into its envelope.

Hugh managed a half-hearted smile. 'Yes,' he said. 'You're very wise.'

She knew herself how keenly she hoped to hear that the children were all right; but there had been occasions – more than one – when she had felt her tears coming to her eyes as she read that they'd been to some matinée as an end-of-holiday treat, or even just that they'd had fun at the coconut shy at a village fête. She would so have liked to have been with them, then; to have seen their faces, heard their laughter.

16. Sussex, autumn 1943

It was late September when Phyllis at last came home. She and Hugh had been sent together back to Holloway first. It was wretched to be back within the walls of the prison after the relative freedom of the Isle of Man: the smells, the confinement, the petty rules were all oppressive. Yet these weeks had been bearable because she knew, now, that their release was imminent. The children barely troubled to write any more, since their mother would so shortly be freed.

Patricia and Greville, and Nina and their younger child, Bobby – who Phyllis had never seen and therefore thought of as a perpetual baby, although he was now a toddler with chunky little legs encased in flannel shorts and not a babe in arms – came to greet them, bringing Julia and Frances and Edwin, who had been given special permission to leave their schools for the day. Only Antonia was at school, while Nina's older boy, George, was with Eric's mother. The adults had agreed it would be better for the children if they congregated at a London hotel rather than at the prison gate. In any event, there might have been press photographers outside Holloway. Patricia suggested a place near Russell Square, a large red-brick establishment with acres of claret-coloured carpet. Phyllis noticed the shock on their faces as they caught their first sight of her, before they'd had a chance to recompose their features. Only Greville registered no change of expression, but she had not forgotten how he too had blanched when he'd been to see her in prison, all that time ago. It was true that both she and Hugh were thinner, but so were the others. It was her almost-white hair that shocked them, she supposed. The children hesitated in front of their parents before stepping forward to be embraced.

'You poor darlings!' said Patricia, to break the ice. 'You must be gasping for a cup of tea, let's order straight away, don't you think?'

'You're looking very spruce,' Phyllis said to Patricia.

'Say hello to your auntie and uncle, Bobby,' prompted Nina. The child scowled and mumbled, ducking his face into his mother's skirt.

They all laughed. 'Well, I don't suppose I blame you, never having set eyes on us before,' said Hugh.

'So unnecessary to bring the child,' Patricia hissed into Phyllis's ear. A waiter showed them to a window table.

'Come and sit by me,' said Phyllis. Frances slid across the window seat and took her place by her mother, followed by Julia. Phyllis patted the tub-chair to her other side. 'Edwin, will you sit here?' she asked. The children's hovering made her feel quite shy.

'Splendid. That's the stuff,' said Greville to no one in particular.

Little Bobby would not sit in a chair of his own, but stood by his mother, making curious mewing noises to indicate that he wanted to sit on her knee. Patricia glowered. She had never made any secret of the fact that she found small children tiresome: that's what nannies were for. Nina picked him up and kissed the top of his head.

'Edbin,' he said, pointing at his cousin.

'Yes, it's Edwin, he's your favourite, isn't he?' said Nina.

'Edbin,' said the boy, this time with some determination. He shuffled crabwise towards Edwin and then stood with his arms lifted, wanting to be picked up.

Patricia raised an eyebrow in Phyllis's direction.

The absurd little pantomime of her eldest sister's disapproval riled Phyllis. Could she never resist an opportunity to do Nina down?

'Have you been to London since the raids?' she addressed her own children. 'Had you seen the craters before, and the rubble everywhere? It's awfully dramatic.'

'We could see the wallpaper, still, in some of the buildings, and the fireplaces: one on top of another, in the same place on each floor,' said Frances.

'Except there weren't any floors,' said Edwin.

'You don't realize how tall some of the houses are, until you see them without their sides,' ventured Julia.

'One had its staircase going the whole way up. The whole way up to nothing. There wasn't any roof,' said Edwin.

'When you see the wallpaper and sometimes the curtains, too – with flowers on them, or stripes – still flapping at the bombed-out windows, you can imagine the people who chose those patterns and that stuff; imagine how they must have thought there'd be nothing so safe as the homes they were making. It's sad, really,' said Frances.

'Well, yes. I hadn't thought of it quite in that way,' said Phyllis. 'I mean, I thought it was a pity, of course. But I hadn't thought about the people choosing the things.'

'I wouldn't like to go with bare feet. You could get horrible splinters, from all the broken glass,' said Edwin.

'I don't imagine the mothers let their children out without shoes,' said Greville.

'Shoes,' said little Bobby, delightedly, proffering his own pudgy foot in its small brown Start-Rite. Where the leather crossed the top of his sock in the shape of the letter 'T', his foot bulged slightly, like rising dough.

'You've got your very own shoes, haven't you, Bob?' said his mother.

'God knows what it's all going to cost, to rebuild,' said Hugh.

'Heaven knows,' echoed Patricia. 'Where will it all end?'

'The people all have to find somewhere to lodge,' said Nina. 'I wonder where on earth they all go. They can't all have obliging relations in the country, after all.'

'Well, no,' said Phyllis.

The waiter brought a tray with tea and a jug of scalding hot water, as well as a plate of rather mingy crumpets. They'd been left toasting for too long, so that their edges were sharp.

'What one'd give for a slice of Madeira cake. Just a sliver,' sighed Patricia.

'We've got plenty of jams and things, you'll find in the larder when you get home,' said Nina. 'We spent the first exeat picking blackberries, didn't we, girls? It gobbles up the sugar, of course, but at least it makes it go further. And we did a batch of apple chutney. That's more economical. Vinegar's not on the ration.'

'Wherever did you learn to do all this?' asked Patricia.

'Needs must,' shrugged Nina. 'There's a war on – in case you haven't noticed.'

'So kind of you. Thank you, Nina,' said Phyllis.

All the talk – all the personalities – was giving her a headache. It was absolutely wonderful to see the children, but she rather wished they'd gone straight home rather than trying to battle through pleasantries in this hotel. She'd have preferred it if it had been only Hugh and herself and Julia and Frances and Edwin: they wouldn't have been so fidgety if they'd simply come home for the afternoon. Her sisters meant well, but it was wearisome having to manage their petty little digs at each other all the time. After tea they went in two taxis to Victoria. Patricia and Nina had arranged for Greville to take Edwin back to school, while the girls would travel independently; someone from the school was to collect them at the other end. Nina and little Bobby and Patricia and Phyllis and Hugh would take the Bognor train. Phyllis wished that she and Hugh were accompanying the children back to their schools, but everyone had assumed that they would be exhausted, after their ordeal: it was thought they'd simply want to get home, to rest. It was a wrench to be parted from the children, so soon.

On her first morning in Sussex there was a thick fog, but as soon as Phyllis was dressed she stepped out of her house and along the sandy lane away from the sea. Hugh stayed at the house, anxious to check that the property had been adequately maintained during their absence. Nina and Eric had moved back into their own house, which had been let to one of Eric's employees. Phyllis carried on walking, scarcely able to see where she was going, until she came to farmland and pasture. She climbed a gate into a field. It was so long since she had been free to wander at will in the countryside. To be alone outdoors, unobserved. There was a lightness, a sense of infinite possibility: she might walk on and on for ever. The low mist gave an air of unreality which made her feel as if she could disappear into the vapour and no one would ever miss her or notice she'd gone. It was an odd feeling, made odder by the poor visibility. Phyllis was not fey, not given to flights of fancy, but the solitude and the intimation of space, combined with the strange, hemmed-in atmosphere created by the fog, flooded her senses with images: suddenly everything reminded her of something else. Perhaps, too, it was an effect of her new-found liberty.

She noticed things more acutely than she ever had before. The stems of blackberries were a rich purple, as if the juice of the fruit was blood flowing along the arteries of each slender branch; the withered black fruits still clung on, encased in cobwebs, like tiny sticks of candy floss. A flock of small dark birds climbed and cascaded and climbed again in the mist above her, like motes of ash dancing in the smoke of a blaze. Along the field-verges silver droplets of water clung to the grass, so that the ground before her looked almost white, like a snail's trail. Here and there were patches of longer grass where huge beads of water, like so many glass necklaces, seemed to be strung along each blade. Suddenly, without thinking, Phyllis knelt on the wet ground and at once felt her clothes, the wool of her heavy skirt, absorb coolness and moisture; she could scarcely tell which was which.

She felt the heat in her shins diminish as the cloth, like a soaked bandage, began to cling to her skin. Not minding, she leant and put her face among the long grass. She felt something like thirst, some instinct which could scarcely be checked. The silky cold leaves and the drops of water were delicious against her cheeks, her eyelids. Her skin and her body willed her to lie down, to stay and lie quiet here in the deep dew. But her mind told her this was ridiculous; that she would catch cold, or drown in the leaves like someone bewitched. Yet it was as if the low mist and the wet grass were a strong river whose current was urging her in and down. Only by an effort of will did she stand and recompose herself.

Back at the house, Hugh was in a state of some agitation.

'Oh there you are, I was wondering where you'd got to. I've been going through the post that's accumulated and there seems to be some sort of anomaly about my naval pension,' he said. 'It wasn't paid while we were . . . while we were away. And it doesn't seem to've been reinstated. Frightful nuisance. I shall have to write to the Admiralty, get it sorted out.'

'I'm going to book an appointment at the hairdresser's before I do anything else. I'm sure there are all sorts of things crying out to be dealt with but they'll have to wait, just for today.'

'Let me know when you're going in, there are one or two things I need to do in Chichester. I take it you will be going into Chichester?'

'I'd thought so, yes. Nina suggested that we might meet for lunch, at the White Horse.'

Phyllis realized that for the first time in her life, she didn't have a pocket diary. She'd had no need for an engagement book during her incarceration; but now she would be able to make plans once again, to book appointments, to accept invitations. Would there be any invitations, though? After Sarita's death she and Hugh had rather fallen away from social life and now it was uncertain whether people would welcome a couple who had been imprisoned for what most people seemed to consider a kind of treason. She sighed. Perhaps it would not matter too much, if they were dropped by some of what Nina called the county. There was enough to do without the endless round of drinks and dinners: there was the house to get back to rights, the Christmas holidays to make arrangements for, her sisters. In prison she had become accustomed to a small life.

As it transpired, this was to be the least of her troubles. After protracted correspondence it emerged that Hugh's naval pension had been stopped as a result of his imprisonment. Since he had been neither tried nor convicted, Hugh fought this with some vigour. There seemed to be a vague acknowledgement that the situation was unusual, but not sufficient acknowledgement to alter the case. Hugh felt very wronged by the Service. It was not only a question of the money: there was a point of honour, here, that he felt was being breached. He had served his country in good conscience. He was guilty of no crime. To simply halt the pension to which he was entitled was surely wrong. He lobbied his MP and wrote letters to the high and mighty, but nothing came of it. Then the rubber company did not renew the offer of part-time employment they had made when Hugh and Phyllis had first returned to England. He received a small annuity from the company, in recognition of the long years he had worked for them, but it was not enough to cover the children's school fees, let alone to maintain the house and his and Phyllis's expenses besides. Further, it meant that he had nothing to do, nothing to take him out of the house. His weekly trips to London had given him a sense of purpose, but now his reduced world seemed to diminish him. Coming into the morning room one morning, Phyllis was shocked to see how small he looked, in the bright sunlight: almost wizened. He always dressed formally and with care, but she saw now that his neck looked wrinkled and too narrow for his collar and tie, like the neck of a tortoise.

The sensible thing to do was to take the girls out of their school. There was a perfectly good day school, St Bride's, not far away in Worthing: moving schools was so much less of a stigma for girls than for boys. In any case, Julia was coming to the end of her education. A course in Pitman's shorthand and typing was a possibility next summer, either by correspondence or in Chichester.

What would happen once Frances had completed her Higher School Certificate was a different matter. She was passionately interested in history and always had her nose in a book. Her reports already hinted that she would be a suitable candidate for university, but while Hugh was pleased to have produced a daughter with brains, he considered that what he called Girton Girls were rather a nuisance: it was quite possible to become too clever by half.

Edwin, though, was another case entirely. For a boy not to have been to public school would be a major impediment: Hugh was prepared to go to whatever lengths were needed in order to make sure that he did. Selling the house was an idea, although they could not expect to do well from it, with the war still on and the future uncertain. Hugh considered Littlehampton or

244

Worthing. Here they could pick up a fair-sized Victorian villa for very much less than the value of their own house, with its desirable private road, well-planned rooms and proximity to the beach, albeit still cut off by barbed wire. Phyllis's heart rather sank at the thought of Worthing, which had always struck her as a dreary sort of place. If there had been any question of her and Hugh finding their way back into county life, even in a modest way, taking up residence in what amounted to suburbia would put paid to it; but Edwin's future came first. In any event she had never cared for their house as much as Hugh always had, having overseen its construction with such attention.

It was at lunch one Sunday that Patricia and Greville put their proposal to them. Afterwards Phyllis felt sure that they had been invited in order to place them at the disadvantage of being guests, so that they would be caught on the back foot. It was her brother-in-law who spoke. While Phyllis and Hugh had been away, he said, they had become very fond of Edwin. It had been especially nice for Antonia, as an only child, to have the company. It made Rose Green come to life, having the little chap about the place: he was such a dear fellow. They were lucky enough to have a nice house with some land. They were fortunate to be in a position to help, where Edwin was concerned. He'd already spent the holidays with them, they'd grown used to one another; the boy seemed to enjoy some rough shooting: if his parents were to agree to their proposal, he fancied that he might take Edwin up to Scotland for some salmon fishing next year.

'It would be an informal arrangement, of course. Not an actual, legal adoption or anything,' said Patricia, once her husband had finished. 'He'd still spend part of the holidays with you, of course, especially while Frances is at home.'

'I'm sorry, I don't quite follow,' said Hugh. 'What is it that you're actually suggesting?'

There was a silence.

'They're saying they'll pay Edwin's school fees if we hand him over to them,' said Phyllis. She could not look at her sister or at Greville. 'They're proposing that they buy our son.'

'That's hardly fair,' said Greville. 'The boy's been with us all the time you were away; with, may I say, precious little thanks from you. He's got used to being here. We've grown extremely fond of him.'

'He's not yours,' said Phyllis.

'Don't be ridiculous, darling,' said Patricia. 'No one's pretending for a minute that he is ours. We're simply trying to help.'

Phyllis was startled by the noise which came out of her mouth at this. It wasn't quite a sob, nor a howl of indignation, but something between the two. At length she spoke.

'Help? Is that what you call it?'

'I hardly think your tone is called for,' said Greville.

'Don't be so pompous, Greville. Just for once,' said Phyllis.

'Pill, really!' her sister remonstrated.

Phyllis looked across at Hugh, hoping that he would say the definitive thing, the thing that would make this dreadful proposal evaporate. But he simply sat, immobile, with his hands folded on the table in front of him. Phyllis felt a sort of curdled fury at the way he sat with his back so straight, the knot of his tie just so; at his hair tidily brushed back with the Bay Rum pomade he bought at some grand barber's in London. Even the clean neatness of his nails made her feel poisoned with her own anger. He was like a shop dummy: useless, utterly useless.

'It's very good of you, I'm sure,' said Phyllis, standing up. 'But we must really be going now. Hugh?'

'Well, p'raps you'll think over what we've discussed. You may feel rather differently on reflection,' said Greville. 'I don't believe you've had time to consider the matter yet, have you, Hugh?'

'Yes,' said Hugh. 'No.'

Phyllis knew that she had to get out of the house before another word came out of her mouth. She felt that if she tried to say anything else a stream of liquid venom might spill out of her. The sense of it – rising, hot like lava – was so overwhelming that she actually held one hand over her lips, to keep it in.

'That's right,' said Patricia. 'Sleep on it, why don't you: see how you feel in the morning. We're only trying to help, surely you can see that?'

Phyllis recognized the tone of her sister's voice. It was the same tone of false brightness that she used to address their mother: a special conciliatory voice for the mentally deficient. Patricia came around the table and put her hand in the small of her sister's back. Her touch was so light that Phyllis could not tell whether she was being ushered out of the dining room, or comforted. Perhaps it was both.

The one thing to look forward to before the children came home for Christmas was the reunion in early December, billed as the 18B Social and Dance. Here at least Phyllis and Hugh could be guaranteed a warm welcome. As among those who had been detained for the greatest length of time, they found themselves lauded, now, by other followers. Old friends from local meetings clasped their hands with real warmth when they met, and a special dinner in Bognor Regis, always among the most active branches, had been given in their honour. Hugh had been asked to write about his time in detention.

Phyllis planned to go up to London the day before the dance. She told Hugh that she was meeting up with Rowena and June, neither of whom she'd had a chance to see since their release. Both of them were coming to town for the reunion. They were staying in Bloomsbury, while Phyllis was at a small private hotel in Pimlico, to be near Victoria station. It was true that she was to lunch with her friends and they'd rather thought they might go together to Dickins & Jones afterwards: Phyllis needed to buy a refill for her powder compact and some new gloves and June wanted to find a hat and Rowena had nothing to wear to the dance. She was deliberately vague as to when she was to see her women friends, not that Hugh pressed her on such things. In fact she had altogether another plan for the evening. She had invited Jamie to dine with her.

It wasn't that there was any need for secrecy. She had known Jamie all her life, after all. But she had been so very grateful for the letters and drawings he'd sent her while she was in prison. Everyone else was so stiff and formal on paper, but Jamie – who was sometimes awkward and tongue-tied, in person – brought such animation, such a sense of life to the page. There had been times when, feeling especially lonely, she had gone to the back of the drawer where she kept her night-things and got out all of his letters and gone through them again, one by one, savouring the glimpses of the landscape of her childhood which they depicted. More than anything else, Jamie's letters had made her feel that the invisible cord which connected her to her old life was not after all entirely broken. Sitting against her wooden bedhead on the Isle of Man with his letters laid out on the counterpane before her, she was no longer simply a prisoner. She was someone with a past, a kind and decent place that she came from: she was not only someone in disgrace. Jamie had given her this and with it had come a glimmer of hope that she might one day be restored. She felt she owed him a great debt of gratitude and that it was right that she should thank him, face to face.

They met at the restaurant. The place had red plush seats and tablecloths as stiff as invitations and smelled faintly of methylated spirit and brandy and cigars. It was a speciality of the establishment to wheel a silent trolley across the thick carpet and flambé certain dishes in little copper pans at each table, steak with a heavy sauce, or crêpes Suzette. Jamie had got there first and stood as she was shown to their table, unfolding from his chair like an accordion. He was so familiar, so dear, that Phyllis began to smile even before they'd said hello. He looked very young in his white shirt, even though he was the same age as herself: perhaps it was because his skin was brown from living so much outdoors; or it might have been that she was so used to looking across a table at Hugh, who was so much older. To Phyllis it was not only that Jamie looked youthful; he seemed almost to shine, like a figure in a church window caught in the light. She found that she was so glad to see him that words failed. For the first few minutes they simply sat, beaming at each other. When they began to speak the words tumbled out of them in no particular order. Yes, he was still at the farm and had managed to keep on the dairy cows, or most of the herd. He had moved the milking parlour into a new building at the far side of the old yard and had brought in a full-time cow-man so that he could spend more hours in the art studio he'd made in the old byre, closer to the house. Three land girls – they weren't girls at all, but older women with tight perms and each as tough as an old boot – had come to help. They were rather garrulous. The three had become something of a fixture at the Plough & Harrow, did she remember it, the public house about a mile and a half away, at the crossroads? He hadn't known women could put back pints of beer in such quantities, nor use such dreadful language: they swore like stevedores, all three of them. Now he was preparing work for an exhibition at a nice gallery in Cork Street. Small landscape paintings, mostly, one or two portraits as well as half a dozen little figures in clay. Phyllis talked about what a shock it had been, to find London so altered, bomb craters and broken windows everywhere and rubble. She told him that they were thinking of moving house in the new year, perhaps to a nearby seaside town. She did not give the reason because she did not want him to pity her any more. She wanted to be gay and light. She told him a silly story about trying on hats with her friends this afternoon. He made her tell him all about all the children and then about her sisters. She said Nina was as bossy as ever and Patricia just as condescending as she had been when they'd played at being knights and ladies, all those years ago.

She had never paid the bill in a restaurant before. Jamie was most reluctant to let her pay; for all that he was an artist now, he still had certain standards. She'd paid in cafés at lunches, having Welsh rarebit with a sister or friend, but certainly not in a proper restaurant and at night – and she felt rather daring now. It was the first time, also, that she had had dinner alone with a man other than her husband.

'Shall I see you into a taxi?' Jamie asked. They were standing on the pavement, Phyllis pulling on the new green gloves she'd bought earlier. They were made of glossy leather, like holly leaves. She thought they looked fetching, with her camel-hair coat and autumn-coloured silk scarf. The night was clear yet mild, so she did not button her coat but knotted the belt loosely.

'D'you know, I think I'll walk. I'm only staying a few minutes away.'

'I'll stroll with you,' he said, falling into step beside her. It was nice of him, to adapt to her pace: being so tall, she imagined he'd prefer to stride out. Hugh always walked just a fraction in front of her, so that she had to struggle to keep up.

'It was so good of you, to write me all those lovely letters while I was . . . while I was away. I can't tell you what a difference they made. I've been wanting to thank you.' All of a sudden she felt very shy.

'Oh no, there's no need. You'd have done the same for me,' he said.

Phyllis pondered this as they walked. With a prick of conscience she realized that she wasn't at all sure that she would have done the same. She might have written once or twice, but she'd never have kept it up, she didn't think. She simply wouldn't have known what to say to someone who was in prison.

They had reached her hotel. Somehow Jamie was standing now in front of her. He hadn't yet stooped down to peck her cheek in parting, but she detected a preliminary movement of his shoulders and neck which heralded their bidding each other goodbye. Without thought or intention she responded. Before she knew it she had taken a step closer to him and taken his bare hand in both her gloved ones and was pulling him towards her, pulling his hand inside her open coat. She felt at that moment as if everything was pulling. At the same moment she raised her face up towards his, but he was so tall that her mouth only reached to his neck. She could smell his skin, a clean smell like freshly ironed linen. His neck was smooth and warm.

'Come up with me,' she said.

'Phyllis, I can't.'

'You can, Jamie. It's all right, Hugh'll never know.' It was inconceivable that he meant it: Jamie, who always did what she wanted him to. He didn't step back, and although he had somehow retracted his hand he had also bent down, so that the sides of their two faces were now touching, so that she felt the warmth of his cheek against hers.

'I've been dreaming about you kissing me for years and years, ever since that time when we were together, with the horses. Do you remember? I've dreamed about us spending a night together. I thought we'd never have the chance, but here we are. Haven't you thought about it, too? About me?'

When he spoke his mouth was still against her hair.

'Of course I have. I did. It isn't that. It's that I've met some-one, you see. I couldn't now, well, I wouldn't want to . . .'

Phyllis took an abrupt step backwards.

'But why didn't you tell me?' she said. She felt a disappoint-ment that made her want to wail, as if it was very much older and sharper than this present one; as if it had been waiting for decades to reveal itself.

'Well, you know that I've always cared for you very much; very much indeed. And somehow I had an inkling that you might have felt a bit the same, or at least that you did some of the time. Not always. Anyway, I didn't want to hurt your feelings. I thought we see each other so seldom that you didn't really need to know.'

'Who is she, though?' said Phyllis. It didn't make any differ-ence who she was, Phyllis understood that. Yet an irrational part of her thought she could use the woman's name as a kind of ammunition, to persuade him he'd made a mistake. If he heard the name coming from her mouth, he would surely change his mind.

'No one you know, she's not from here. England, I mean. Her name's Natasha. She's got relations in London whom she came to at the beginning of the war. She's a potter, makes bowls and plates with birds on. I met her at the gallery. She's been living at the farm with me.'

'Oh, Jamie. I feel so stupid now.'

'You really don't need to. You mustn't feel anything bad. I've forgotten already. It was nothing.'

'It's only that you're so very dear to me.'

'I know. As are you to me.'

Somehow they had each stepped back so that two feet of London air now stood between them. Phyllis felt that she might weep from the pity of it if she lingered for so much as another moment. She turned and stepped towards the pillars which flanked the hotel's entrance. The paint on the nearer column was coming away in big flakes, revealing an earlier coat in a slightly different, paler colour. It reminded her of the bark of the tall plane trees in the parks.

'You will keep in touch, won't you?' Jamie called after her.

But Phyllis could not answer and she didn't turn around.

Phyllis, 1979

I have to admit, things were pretty sticky after Hugh died. There'd been some capital — he'd had shares in the rubber company at one point — but Lord alone knows what happened to it; he may've sold out in order to pay for the building work when we moved to Littlehampton. His pension had been stopped some time before, you see. He'd made Greville his executor, which was normal in those days: people from our background thought money was men's business. Widows were just meant to grieve quietly and get some responsible male to manage the banks and bills. Although it was me, of course, who had to live with the consequences.

After the war, when the motor trade was on the up, Eric asked Hugh to come back and help out at the garage again. Well, I say the garage but of course there were several, by then. A chain of them. Not on the fore-court, he wasn't reduced to oily overalls. He helped in the office. Paperwork. It was good of Eric, he could see after we'd moved out of the house Hugh built that the light had gone out of my poor husband; and to be honest it was a relief to get him out for a few hours and to have a little extra money. Well, I say it was good of him but he owed us a lot, really. I don't doubt that he and Nina were spared prison because of having turned us in; but I didn't know that at the time. Didn't find out till years later and by then I was living up here and hardly saw my sister anyhow. They did well for themselves, those two, in any case: had their boys and their flourishing business and a big house adjoining a golf course. Eric had always aspired to playing golf, he was that sort of man.

Hugh was on his way home from the garage when he died. They said it was a stroke. The police thought he must have pulled over because he felt it coming on. It's meant to start with a feeling of tightness, isn't it; or is that a heart attack? *A travelling salesman stopped in the same lay-by to consult his map — we never knew how much later he pulled in, how long poor Hugh had been there; not that it makes any difference. He spotted the car and Hugh slumped in it. He went to a house up the road to telephone for an ambulance, even though he could see it would be too late. At the time I wished I'd asked the officer for the man's name, so I could have thanked him. Don't know what I wanted to thank him for; noticing, I suppose. Anyway.*

Whether there really was no money left or whether Greville decided it would be an opportune moment to reimburse himself for some of Edwin's school fees, I can't say. You may form your own opinion. Edwin was spending half his holidays with Patricia by that time, although he still came home for Christmas itself and for Easter. But I'd lost him by then, I knew that. I think the combination of our having been away while he was at prep school and then the financial difficulties and selling the house and going to so much less nice a place; a place where he didn't have any childhood associations — and of course his sisters not being at home so much any more, that was another thing — it all snowballed, until he actually felt more at home at Rose Green with my sister and Greville. I managed to limp along in Littlehampton for a year or two, in the house we'd moved to after the war. I took in paying guests during the school term-times to help pay the bills. To be fair, the old Party members were very good: they recommended me to people, so I generally had all three bedrooms rented out. The children's bedrooms, as they'd originally been. After Edwin had taken his School Certificate — he must have been sixteen by then — I felt there was nothing to keep me in Sussex any more, so when I heard about Lady Prendergast I made the move up here.

She was the mother of one of the stalwarts from the old days. Most of Sir Oswald's rich and titled supporters had fallen by the wayside by then, but Billy Prendergast was loyal to the end and I used to see him at the Leader's birthday every year. As a matter of fact he and I got to know each other rather well, if you know what I mean. Nothing serious; he was a married man. Just a night here and there. At one of our get-togethers, Billy told me his mother was looking for a lady's companion. You may hardly know what that is, but in those days grand old ladies often had a companion, who was meant to come from a decent background so that she'd know the ropes: how to be a useful fourth at bridge, how to write letters, that sort of thing. You were more senior than a maid – you didn't have to do any cleaning or ironing – but quite a lot more of a dogsbody than any friend would've been prepared to be. It wouldn't have suited everybody because you were at the person's beck and call, constantly nipping to fetch a rug for their knees, or their knitting. I didn't mind it at all. Lady Prendergast – she never told me to call her Chloe, so I never did – lived in a big old house near Sheffield, the sort of place that had a vast brass gong outside the dining room to summon people to dinner and an umbrella stand made out of an elephant's foot. Her husband had been something or other in India, but she'd been a widow for some time before I knew her.

I kept on the house in Littlehampton to begin with, got some tenants for it and split the income between Julia and Frances, who were both grown up by then, although neither of them were yet married. I hardly needed any money for myself – my living expenses were negligible since my employer paid all the grocer's and household bills. I mostly saved what I was paid. I hoped to get up enough to be able to give Edwin a little, once he left school after his Higher School Certificate. The pity of it was that Edwin had been put into the same situation as Hugh had been, in his boyhood: a father who died, a widowed mother, not enough money. Having to rely on relations to help out. I planned to sell the house once Edwin left school and give him a good bit of the capital so he'd have something to start him off. In due course he got my portion of money from the sale of the Grange, too, so with the lion's share of the proceeds from the sale of Littlehampton as well, he had enough to house himself. I used what was left to get this little flat. It suits me. Quiet, and I like the view across the hills. You get a beautiful light over there, sometimes, in the evenings. I go to the library on the bus, get my books for the week. Alistair MacLean, he's good. Len Deighton I like. I have my ciggies and I watch Crown Court on the telly in the afternoons. Write a few letters. There are still a few bods from 18B days that I keep up with. I had a couple of particular girl-friends in prison and they come up and visit once a year or so, or I go down to them.

I don't see my sisters. And I don't miss them, that's what's so odd. When we lived overseas I missed them like anything, but you get used to anything in the end and now they barely cross my mind. Talking about the past like this makes me think more about them than I have for years. Hypocrites, that's what they are. I'll give you an example. Some years ago Patricia and Greville stopped referring to the Leader as Tom and started calling him Mosley; that's if he was mentioned at all. Back in the old days they used to love calling him Tom because it meant they were his social equals, part of his inner circle: none of the rank and file ever called him that then, it was always Sir Oswald or the Leader. But afterwards they went on as if they'd never met him, much less entertained him as a guest in their house: 'We knew him a little, socially, yes. But we were never members. We've always been Conservatives, really.' That sort of thing.

I think in their heart of hearts Nina and Eric still believed, but they kept their traps shut. Eric didn't want his former affiliation to put the kibosh on his business aspirations. They both wanted to get on in the world and they knew it was divisive. A lot of people disapproved. Even people who'd been our friends thought we were a disgrace, because of the views we held. So much for a free country! You may have the freedom to express your views, but they'll still damn you for them. She comes across as straightfor-ward, but she's a sneaky one, Nina. I'm still angry, of course. But anger takes up a lot of energy and what's the point, now? What happened hap-pened; there's no undoing it now. It was a terrible thing to do to your own sister. And Patricia's was a betrayal which struck at the very heart of me: she tried to take away my child. And she succeeded, more or less. We were never as close again as we had been when he was a little boy.

★

I didn't tell them things, my sisters. They thought they knew all about me, but I always kept things back from them. They didn't know a thing about Jamie. They didn't know about the Leader's birthday reunions, every year. Certainly not about Billy Prendergast. He wasn't the last, either: there was another fellow later, but I won't go into that now. What I'm saying is, I had secrets of my own, and I kept other people's. People tended to tell me things; I think they thought I was a safe bet, not because they were interested in me, but because they were so interested in themselves. That's how it is, you see. Some people consider themselves to be the stars of life, and they relegate everyone else to the shadows at the back of the dress circle.

It's difficult, with the children. Well, I say children, but they're all in their late middle-age now. It isn't how I hoped it would be: I don't see as much of them as I'd like. I think the girls felt unfairly treated because I put their brother's education before theirs and set him up with a bit of capital. Instead of being grateful for the bit of extra help I gave them when they were starting out, they resented me when I sold the property and the income they'd had came to an end. I did what I thought was right: I stand by it. And they're ashamed of it all, the political views we had; which I suppose means really that they're ashamed of me. Frances in particular has never spoken one word with me about it. But then that's Frances. In a way she's the most like me, although she's much more capable than I ever was; but she keeps herself to herself. She became a solicitor, so I don't imagine it would have been good for her professional reputation if it had come out that her parents had both been jailbirds. Her husband's a bit of a Bolshie.

Julia's more vocal in her criticism. She came up here once a few years back and had a terrific go at me about it all, said it had ruined her life, having to live with the shame, et cetera, et cetera. She accused me of having tried to brainwash them, by taking her and Frances and Edwin to the summer camp. Of course I told her it was nothing of the kind: I hardly knew anything about it myself, at the time: it was just a way of keeping them entertained for the summer. She said it was wicked to have dressed them up in the uniforms, like dolls. There's no reasoning with Julia. By then her second husband had left her, so I reckon she was looking for something to blame the failure of her marriage on. She's one of those people who can't take responsibility for their own lives, I'm afraid. She's always looking for something to make her feel better – last time we spoke it was unpasteurized milk or some such nonsense. Faddish. I don't like to speak ill of any of my children, but I do feel she's rather immature. Doesn't stick at anything. She wears these dreadful clothes, skirts made of cheesecloth, beads; well, they might look all right on a woman half her age. Edwin's the most straightforward. Luckily his wife is very nice, so that makes things easier. I'd like to see more of them, but of course I live all the way up here and they're southerners. Between them they've produced six children, but I don't see a great deal of them either. The young aren't interested in us old folk. Edwin's middle one I'm especially fond of.

I generally have lunch with Antonia in November when I go down to London for the get-together. I expect she's told you. She's a nice girl, good sense of humour, she turned out well. Done very well for herself, too. She and Edwin are still very close, more like brother and sister, really, than cousins. Well, of course he spent so much time with her, growing up. She has him shooting, that sort of thing. She's like her father, easy-going, but cleverer than she lets on.

I go back to the Isle of Man, to Port Erin, for a week every summer. Funny, isn't it? You'd think I'd never want to set foot there again, but it's a lovely place, so unspoilt. It's like England was, before the war. One year I saw that there was a talk about the archaeological sites on the island and I thought I recognized the name of the speaker, so I went along. It was little Dr Bersu – much older now of course – who'd been interned as an enemy alien during the war. I remembered listening to a talk of his when I was first there. He and his wife had begun making a record of all the ancient sites when they were interned. With the approval of the authorities, of course. They volunteered to stay on after the war to finish the job. Actually they were lucky to've got someone so distinguished on the island. He'd catalogued every single antiquity and site, over time. It took me back, listening to him.

We all have our crosses to bear, our own personal sorrows. Mine is that the people who should be dearest to me, my own children, my sisters, consider me a bad woman. The grandchildren have been taught to be wary. I think I'm a disgrace, to them, really. After the war when the newsreel film was shown of what had gone on in Germany and Poland, those places, the horrors . . . It all got tangled up in their minds, as if we'd stood for such barbarism. I just wish they could have heard Sir Oswald speak: then they'd have known. He is an honourable man. He'd never have stood by and allowed such things to happen on British soil.

I think that was the big thing for my children.

With my sisters I can honestly say it was more that I stopped being in the same social class. After we were released from prison we were effectively social pariahs, and then to cap it all it became apparent that we hadn't any money. Hugh's naval pension was never restored. So of course my older sister didn't want anything much more to do with us. The irony was that my younger sister got caught up in snobbery of her own. She thought the sun shone out of your rear end if you were what she and Eric called a business professional. An accountant or surveyor or local auctioneer: that sort of thing. Well, I wasn't a business professional: I was the paid companion of an old lady from up north. Nina aspired to people who ran their own businesses and worked very hard to build them up, as Eric had. And of course Patricia aspired to mix with people who were so rich or landed that they didn't work at all.

After the war ended Hugh and I were in a kind of exile, even though we were living back in Sussex. We were in exile from our family and from the class that we were born into, the world we'd known and inhabited. And then I became an exile on my own. It was easier not to live close to the family. I am an exile from my own past, my own people. They're all ashamed of me, if they think of me at all. I am someone who is a nuisance to have to send a card to, twice a year.

That is what I have to live with, every day.

If you were to ask me who the significant people in my life had been, do you know what I'd say? It may surprise you. I'd say Jamie and Sarita, even though I only knew Sarita for such a short time, really. But my sense of guilt about her death has never left me; I still feel that I was in some measure responsible; although by now I acknowledge that there was probably nothing I could have done. And I haven't seen Jamie since just after the war, although we do exchange cards at Christmas. He married and had a family; his wife became rather famous as a potter. Much better known than him, as a matter of fact. People collect her things. They're a bit rustic for my taste, look like hardened porridge. Anyway, to come back to them: it doesn't make any difference, the fact that I can't see Sarita and I don't see Jamie. When I think about them now from all this distance, the memory of them is like a kindly dream. A dream of a more innocent and carefree time in my life. The reason these two both matter, still, to me is that I think I can honestly say that they were the only people in my life who ever saw the good in me. Who believed I was a good person. No one else ever looked for the good in me, and so no one else ever found it. But they did.

A note on sources

I drew on papers held in the Special Collections at the University of Sheffield Library and the Manx National Heritage Library at the Manx Museum, Douglas. The librarians at each were unfailingly generous and helpful.

Mr Jeff Wallder answered all my questions with kindness and courtesy.

I consulted a great many books while researching this novel, but there are three in particular without which it could not have been written:

Booker, J. A., *Blackshirts on Sea: A Pictorial History of the Mosley Summer Camps 1933–1938*, Brockingday Publications, 1999.

Gottlieb, Julie V., *Feminine Fascism: Women in Britain's Fascist Movement*, I. B. Tauris, 2003.

Pugh, Martin, *Hurrah for the Blackshirts!: Fascists and Fascism in Britain Between the Wars*, Pimlico, 2006.